Mabon

THE CLANDESTINE CHRONICLES

Book 1

KELLIE M DAVIES

First Published in Australia by Aurora House
www.aurorahouse.com.au

This edition published 2018
Copyright © Kellie M Davies 2018
Inside Illustration copyright Kellie M Davies 2018
Typesetting: bookformatting@gmail.com
Cover design: Simon Critchell

The right of Kellie M Davies to be identified as the author and illustrator of this work has been asserted in accordance with the Copyright, Designs and Patents Act 1988.

ISBN number: 978-0-6481851-6-1 (paperback)

All rights reserved. No part of this publication may be reproduced, stored in a retrieval system, or transmitted, in any form or by any means without the prior written permission of the publisher, nor be otherwise circulated in any form of binding or cover other than that in which it is published and without a similar condition being imposed on the subsequent purchaser.

This is a work of fiction. Names, characters, businesses, places, events, locales, and incidents are either the products of the author's imagination or used in a fictitious manner. Any resemblance to actual persons, living or dead, or actual events is purely coincidental. Latin translations may differ.

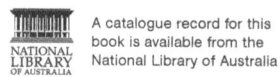

A catalogue record for this book is available from the National Library of Australia

Distributed by:

Ingram Content:
https://www.ingramcontent.com/
Australia: phone +613 9765 4800 | email lsiaustralia@ingramcontent.com
Milton Keynes UK: phone +44 (0)845 121 4567 | email enquiries@ingramcontent.com
La Vergne, TN USA: phone 1-800-509-4156 | email inquiry@lightningsource.com

Gardners UK:
https://www.gardners.com/
   phone +44 (0)1323 521555 | email: sales@gardners.com

Bertrams UK:
https://www.bertrams.com/BertWeb/index.jsp
   phone +44 (0)1603 648400 | email sales@bertrams.com

To my mother Margaret.
Although mine often did ...
your belief in me has never wavered.

> "At this day, it is indifferent to say in the English tongue,
> 'she is a witch' or 'she is a wise-woman'".
>
> Reginald Scot
> (1538-1599)

WHEEL OF THE YEAR

The annual cycle of solstices, equinoxes and agricultural festivals that have been observed by past and modern witches.

MABON

The celebrated second harvest of the agricultural calendar often couples with the Autumn Equinox – the sun's crossing of the celestial equator, giving indicative seasons to the Northern and Southern Hemispheres.

Day and night are equal, and Mabon brings a time for balance and mindfulness as we give thanks for what we have received during the harvest. We honor the change of season. As the warmth of Summer drains, we prepare ourselves for the dark and cold of the Winter months ahead.

Derived from Welsh mythology, Mabon was the name of a Celtic hero/God. Contemporary witchcraft adopted the title 'Mabon' in the 1970s under Wiccan leader Aiden Kelly for its ancient sound rather than who it stood for.

Late.

I wasn't a rule-breaker, but today brought with it a fog that stuck around; a gluey force field I couldn't escape. I handed a tardy slip to Mr Woodward and swung into my seat. Eyes on my art book below, I was well aware of the skull-drilling I was receiving from the other students.

What would have made this morning flow?

Perhaps if my father hadn't died today, sixteen years ago. Or it wasn't my birthday! Or if everyone wasn't looking at me!

Why is Lucy late? What's happened? Is she OK? Why is she wearing that skirt with those shoes? I wonder if she has the English notes on Bronte. I knew random questions would be filtering through their heads. Odd questions were something I was used to, but for the moment the answer was simple: my father had died on the day I was born. I never knew him and it stung, and today proved no different. I woke with a smile that quickly faded, recognizing a day that would be long and confronting. Today was a big deal. I would receive the answer to an age-old calling that had tested my family for generations.

"For Lucy's benefit, who can tell me what we are doing today?" He was an art teacher, but Mr Woodward was way snooty, not your usual grunge-inflicted, hippy throw back. "Miss Daniels?"

The girl sitting next to me smiled. "Finishing these color contrasts," she answered. Her smile turned into an exaggerated clown face the second Mr Woodward's back was turned and the class hummed with muffled giggles.

"Something funny?" he asked.

"No, Mr Woodward," she braved. She turned to me muttering in a sing-song tone, "Lucy's late, Lucy's never late!"

My eyes narrowed.

Liberty Daniels knew I was vulnerable. My embarrassment from attention, from anybody, was crippling. I couldn't walk alone through a graveyard without flushing bright pink. Strangely, making me squirm was one of my bestie's favorite pranks. Some best friend!

She winked and turned back to her sketch.

I flipped through my book, settling on a half-finished attempt at the ancient Northern Pin Oak tree that sat opposite the art room window. I hadn't put the effort in on this sketch, my mind always preoccupied in the days before my birthday.

This morning, with the light dappling across its jagged scarlet leaves, the oak looked magnificent. Once again, the onset of Fall had whispered for the production of its finest show, and the tree shimmered as leaves began their annual

Mabon

shed. Winter sat on the stoop awaiting its grand entrance.

A bright swirl of color drew my eye.

An oak leaf, far from home, spun lower and lower, in tighter and tighter choreographed circles. It leveled at the open classroom window and zipped directly toward me, fluttering back and forth until it landed with precision atop a stack of books close by. Thankfully this weirdness had gone unnoticed. I reached over and poked at the leaf before picking it up. A faint tinkling of bells began, sounding distant, but with the well-honed clarity of chiming crystal. I scanned the room. Nothing appeared out of place.

"Can I help you, Miss DeBane?" The gruff voice came from somewhere behind me and the swivel of heads and seats caused my immediate flush.

"No … no, Mr Woodward. Just trying to get a better look," I said. Not what I was doing at all – an oak leaf had flitted through my window like some stringless puppet – what?

"Yes, a definite color discrepancy there, wouldn't you say Miss DeBane?" I straightened in my seat as he arrived at my desk. "A stroke of brilliance, bringing your subject matter to class." His long elegant fingers charred with colorful smudges released the leaf from my grip and dropped it above my picture. Mr Woodward's heels clicked as he walked away.

I eyed the leaf, covering my work as if guarding a national secret.

Mr Woodward had left a great deal of blue chalk smeared across the glossy red surface of the leaf and I struggled to wipe it off with my skirt when I felt eyes penetrating the top of my head.

"Yes, Lib?" I ventured.

"What are you doing?"

"What does it look like I'm doing?" I flung the leaf, still tainted blue, into my pencil case and plonked down onto my elbows to stare at her.

"Er … okay," she drawled. "So what's your deal?"

"Don't you remember what today is? Any light globes going off?"

"Well, it is your birthday …" Liberty lurched forward, grabbing my arm. "Sorry Lou, forgot all about your Dad."

I knocked my art book to the floor. Even hearing the word hurt.

"Not good today Lib," I said.

"OK, so do you want to come over after school? For Mom's dried apple pie?" she asked, not missing a beat.

My hesitation prompted a further gush.

"Ruben's breaking that bay colt for Dad. You know the one you like, with the white socks? Sales are in two weeks …"

Watching Liberty's eldest brother, Ruben, working with horses was a sight.

"I don't know Libs. I'm so behind with this drawing and I need to get a start on the bio assignment, you know, the cycles one?"

I'd already chosen my subject, but Liberty didn't need to know that. "C'mon, I know how much you love Mom's pie and it's fresh, from this morning," Liberty sang.

"Ah … Lou, just for a little while … thank God it's Friday and all that crap. Can't you do your school stuff tomorrow?"

"What and trash my weekend? I don't know Libs." I cocked my head to the side. Ella Daniels was one hell of a cook. Her dried apple pie was like a sun drenched holiday

Mabon

in my mouth, all cinnamon spice and fluffy crusted. But I didn't relish giving up a Saturday for school work. On the other hand, an afternoon at the Danielses and I could cross paths with 'him'.

Liberty tugged at my sleeve for an answer. "OK, since you're playing hard ball – you have to let me do something for your birthday."

"I'll come eat pie and watch Ruben then." I sighed, defeated by Liberty's portrayal of a puppy, all big eyes and floppy demeanor. "Conditions," I said. "No nasty birthday surprises today at lunch. No singing, no tricks – in fact, no mention of it at all. Agreed?"

"You're all fun, you are," she said.

As we left the safety of the art room and entered the hallway chaos, Liberty sulked away. I watched as her head bobbed and weaved through the throng – just what did she have in store for me?

Sweet sixteen! Well not so sweet for me. Turning another year older was fine, in fact I couldn't wait until I knew how to navigate through this life … *in this body*. My problem was being the center of attention on a day when I'd rather not be, so keeping my birthday quiet was my primary aim. The balance between two major yet polar events in my life, almost cancelled one another out, and left me feeling exposed.

The feathered skim of fingertips across my shoulder blades snapped me out of my thoughts. "Jeez Mathilda, don't do that."

"Oops!" My sister's dreamy tone warbled as she steadied me by the shoulders, "Bit jumpy today, Lou?"

"Weren't you?"

"Nope." Mathilda leaned toward me – acoustically the hallways were brilliant, but cavernous. "A little excited maybe."

It made me smile. Mat's enthusiasm was infectious, lifting even the most tragically depressed from a 'black hole'. Between her and Liberty, I had little chance for self-indulgent thoughts, no matter what the universe threw at me.

"Can't seem to get past thinking about him today," I said. "How do you do it?"

Mat's steady gaze fell to the ground. "Well, it's not my birthday today, so that helps a little. I can't imagine how hard today is for you Lou, but think how Dad would feel if he knew you were moping around, not enjoying your day. He'd be like, crushed, don't you think?"

"I guess so," I said. "It doesn't seem to be getting any easier though."

Mat tilted my face up to look into her eyes. "It will Lucy, believe me, someday it will."

I shook my head, clearing the fog that had settled in. "Where's Abi?" I asked, scanning the hallway for my sister's mirror image.

"Relax, the honor student is after extra cred. She's meeting me at lunch. You want to join?"

"Thanks but Lib and I are checking out charter companies for the Euterpe concert in Missoula," I said. "You guys still in?"

Some football random lifted Mathilda up over his shoulder. "Yes," she said, waving and giggling as she was carried away.

Mabon

Suddenly, in the midst of a throng of chattering teens, I felt alone. Had it not been for the over-zealous waving from the end of the hallway, I don't think my smile would have returned. Liberty.

It had never mattered to me but Liberty was a good head taller than most in our grade, myself included. Her choice of attire verged on retro 'Matrix' come 'Montana Sky' – black military boots, cargos and a tight shirt for school; jeans and checks and a wide brim for home. At times she looked like she didn't have a dime to spare. Owning one of the most productive agricultural plots in the state, the Danielses bred and sold commercial livestock. They worked the land and, at the moment, business was good.

Liberty was the youngest of five children. The rest were all boys, and her brothers were a major influence on her work ethic and her 'look' – she was often mistaken for one of them. You'd think being 'pretty good' in the looks department and 'pretty fly' in the allowance department would be a dream – not for Liberty. She was the real deal, a loner, and for some reason she had chosen me to befriend two years earlier and we'd been tight ever since.

All in all, Liberty was charmingly odd. She repelled commerciality like a cat in a bathtub. Anything that was tanned, blonde and in any way girlie was on the outs with Liberty, which always made me wonder about her deal with my twin sisters, Mathilda and Abigail. They were just that – I put it down to a 'sisters' thing as Liberty hadn't experienced this before we'd arrived in Creston and my sisters adored her. Later that afternoon as I walked across the parking lot, a lyrical shout-out caught me off guard.

"Hey, hey birthday girl!"

The all too familiar heat began to rise through my body, rushing to my cheeks. Liberty was with my sisters, who were flanked by their friends, Zoe and Adele – all four boyfriends in tow. Around school, these seniors were a formidable group, and here they stood in front of me, every ounce of their attention undivided.

Abi glided over – you could hardly call what she did walking. She took my hand and spun me around, I grappled with my backpack trying to keep my balance.

"Hey guys, what do you think of our baby sis on her big day?"

What happened to not billboarding my birthday?

"Bad day, hey kid?" Mat's boyfriend, Frankie, stepped forward and pinched my cheek – a gesture he seemed to adopt just for me, not so intimidating. Frankie was sweet, a real nice guy rolled up in an attractive package of good looks and intelligence. I winced, which seemed to answer his question so he extended his hand and pulled me closer, under his protective wing.

"And on a lighter note," Mat said, reaching into her boyfriend's jacket pocket, "We got you something."

"You didn't think we'd forgotten, did you?" Abi gestured to Mat's hand as she produced a small cube wrapped with a gold gossamer ribbon.

Frankie tapped at his pocket, genuinely stumped. "Where did that come from?" he quizzed no one in particular.

I took the box skeptically. To be honest, I was expecting something from them, later tonight at our family dinner. But not here, not now.

As I gave it the once-over I heard the faint tinkling of chimes again, just as I had in art class. "Can you hear that?"

"Hear what?" the twins said in unison.

"Oh nothing," I replied. The notion seemed too stupid to repeat to sane people.

"Soooo, are you opening that?" Abi said impatiently. "Sorry," she muttered after Mat shot her a disapproving look. "It's just that we have, well, cheer practice now!"

"So we kinda have to cut it short." Mat placed her hand over mine.

The bells chimed again as if the wind had suddenly blown them to life. I ignored them. Maybe I was hearing things. "What is it?" I asked.

"Open the box," said Zoe, "and we'll all know."

I slipped a finger under the ribbon and lifted the lid of the small white box. "What the … ?"

"Hey Lou, that looks like the leaf you were playing with this morning. It's even got chalk on it." Liberty's shoulder clunked against mine.

"Yes … but how did you guys …" Realizing that now wasn't the best time to discuss my family's little secret, I studied my gift. There, lying on a soft cushion of white silk, was a silver spiky leaf, a tiny tarnished charm tainted with a blue smudge. It was an exact replica of my art class enigma.

The chimes started again, gaining momentum and volume. I felt dizzy. Someone caught my arm.

It was Liberty.

"You OK?" she said, her eyes scanning my face.

"Fine." I feigned a chuckle, fanning the white box in her direction. "They got me good this time."

Both girls looked elated, clearly the reaction they'd wanted, and they sauntered off triumphant. "To practice," called Mat over one shoulder as she flipped her bag to Frankie.

"Go easy babe," he coughed, catching it in the chest. "Happy birthday kiddo." He tousled my hair before heading after his girlfriend.

"Later. Go Braves!" Abi sent me an intense look as the entourage headed off toward the playing fields a couple of blocks over.

I could hear Dion asking why a leaf in a box was such a big deal. Abi's evasive response made him laugh, "You and your magic tricks."

Liberty's contorted face matched my confusion as we walked to her bus. "Man, your sisters can be total trippers at times. I mean, what was that all about?"

"Oh, you know." Well they were trippers at times. "Sisters can be a bit weird. You should be glad you only have brothers." I capped the box, tucking it safely inside my bag, for later discussion.

"Yeah right, like you'd love living with four older brothers."

I didn't like the idea. *Although …*

Turning, she caught me by the arm. "One of them, maybe?"

I grinned. My face was an open book for her to read.

"Maybe," I conceded. It was my birthday.

"Mom, I'm home."

"Mom?"

"Mat?"

"Abi?"

"Anyone here?"

No reply. The tiniest of chills rippled through my body. The chills I was used to. However, being alone in our new house gave me the creeps. My horror movie fetish was taking over my imagination.

It was great though – the house. The only downfall was having to share a bathroom with the twins, and I'm not joking, they were always in there.

Mrs Daniels had driven me home after an uneventful afternoon at their farm. Ruben was in fine form and the foals were cheeky – but there had been no sign of the real reason I was there. *He* didn't seem to be around much these days.

I kind of wished I'd said yes to Mrs Daniels as I heard her Mercedes roar away from the curb, but it was too late to take her up on the offer of waiting while I opened up the house.

I shivered, but wasn't cold.

"Where is everyone?" I muttered into the darkness, locking the front door behind me.

OK, so it was my birthday and maybe I had practically demanded that there be no recognition of the event, but had my family really skipped out on me?

Not hung around for dinner?

No vanilla cake with rose petal icing?

A single candle on top?

Nothing?

Oh.

There was a soft creak of floorboards to my right. I froze.

Even with the apparent full moon, the hall was pitch black. Where was everyone tonight? Why couldn't I remember? Was it because I'd been brooding about the duality of my stupid birthday?

I stuffed the house keys into my pocket, removed my jacket, then stumbled into the hall. "Klutz," I whispered, on hearing a smash. I prayed it wasn't my mother's heirloom vase.

I found the light and flicked the switch.

"SURPRISE!" Every voice in the room rang out in unison.

Blinded by the sight of balloons, confetti and the smiling faces of friends and neighbors, I stumbled backward. I tripped on the hall runner and fell into an awkward pile.

The laughing started with a familiar high-pitched peal.

With no time for embarrassment, I was scooped up from the floor by Teddy Langford, our neighbor, and a mammoth of a man. I tried to hide myself in the crook of Teddy's arm as he twirled me into the center of the room, my long skirt flapping around us.

Mabon

As the laughter began to fade into idle party chatter, she was there. I thought she'd be angry about the smashed vase, but she was laughing as well.

In her infinite wisdom, she had swapped out the heirloom with a plain terracotta pot she used to store house and car keys.

Coincidence?

No. Intuition was my mother's strong card.

"Happy birthday to you my darling youngest of three," she said reaching up to place fingertips on each side of my hot face. Her hands were cool and smelled of rose water. "Gotcha!" eyes wild with the thrill of her triumph.

Looking down at her from Teddy's arms, I sighed. "Mom. Why?"

"Teddy, pop her down here and we'll get this celebration started. Where's my broom?" she demanded, pointing to the pieces of terracotta on the floor. With a twirl of her hand she disappeared into the gathered crowd who were advancing with their well-wishes.

My face throbbed with fresh humiliation as I made my way around the party guests. Everyone was being that much nicer to the sheepish girl headlining as comic entertainment for the evening.

Most of our neighbors were here, and a few school friends. Mat and Abi, and their entourage all cackled like crazy about their afternoon trickery.

The laughs continued until I reached two of my mother's friends – her constant companions since our arrival in Creston, and as familiar as furniture.

"Oh, look at you growing up so quickly. I hardly recognize

you anymore," said Myrtle Tilderbran. Emotion stirred in her eyes as she took both of my hands in hers. "The only way I'll know it's you is by the thunderous beating of your beautiful heart, Little Soul."

'Little Soul' was the nickname my mother had given me. It wasn't used often, and especially not in front of my friends. I winced.

"Yes," agreed Violet Shawshank. "Or if you stop cooking me those wonderful butterscotch and chocolate chip cookies you know I love." Her eyes squinted together and the corners of her mouth curled up into a cheeky smile.

Unfortunately, Myrtle and Violet had lost their respective husbands a few years back, before we had arrived in Creston. As the story went, in a freak hunting accident, a renegade Bull elk had trampled the men to death. Afterwards, the grief was so intense that the only way the two women seemed able to function was in each other's company. They'd made it permanent with Myrtle moving into Violet's house. Theirs was a truly admirable friendship – they supported each other during a devastating period in their twilight years.

"Don't worry, I wasn't going to turn sixteen then vanish from the face of the earth." I laughed.

Myrtle and Violet winked at each other.

"We know, we know." Myrtle returned my hands, patting them for emphasis. "We are always close by if you need us."

"Awh, thank you." I paused. *Well, I guess they could possibly help me with my ancient history report due in a few weeks, if that's what they meant.*

Without warning a soft fabric pouch had been expertly delivered into my hand, reverse pick-pocket style. Stunned, I turned the bag over. It was royal-blue velvet, and embroidered with a silver thread, then closed off with a fine bow. Looking up to the two women, I was confronted by wide toothy grins. "What's this?" I said.

"Your bag of tricks," Myrtle said, amid odd looks and mumbles. A few others had gathered, giving in to curiosity.

"Okay," I said, jiggling the bag. "It's empty."

"It is?" Myrtle asked.

"Well then, let us be the first to add something." And with that, from some hidden pocket in her voluminous skirt, Violet produced a small ebony box.

"Inherited from someone close," Myrtle said.

I opened the box slowly, noticing that my mother had inched through the gathering to be at my side.

"Oh … thank you," I whispered. There was not much else I could say. I didn't really understand what I was looking at. "It's … a twig." My fingers shook as I lifted the hardened wood from its resting position.

Under the rumble of questioning mutters came a low howl.

In a clamor of slamming doors, a cool breeze spirited through the house, snaking in and out of the surprised party guests, billowing out clothes and messing up hairdos as it flurried around.

"Oh goodness." My mother exclaimed, "The way the winds rip down from the Swan somedays … well, it near scares the pants off me!"

She gave a hearty giggle and the rest of the crowd joined in, pealing off into groups of lively chatter, though many looked spooked by the mysterious wind blast. I glanced back down to the stick now cradled in my palm.

Coincidence?

Myrtle stepped closer. "Our friend had always insisted there was something odd about that little twig. Stirs up all manner of things." Winking as she spoke, Myrtle took the wood, box and pouch from my hands. "Best I give this to your mother for safe keeping. Don't fuss. You carry on with your party."

"OK," I said. *A twig! What was it for?* The rumination marched through my head, and converged with my birthday high, trampling it.

As Myrtle and Violet moved away from me, a distinct figure became visible.

Oh the cheek. I walked around the sofa toward the fireplace.

Seeing this as her opportunity, Erika Pendleton, a friend from school, bailed me up halfway to my target.

"So, happy birthday Lucy." Erika's heart was in the right place, but I had never met a bigger gossip. Somehow she'd managed to keep her mouth shut about the surprise all day, and since Erika and I sat together in English *and* Math, it would have been a grand operation.

"Oh hey," I said, eyeing my mark over her shoulder. "Thanks Erika. You could have let it slip you know, about the party."

"No way," she giggled. "I have a certain tight-lipped reputation to uphold. Oh, and I forgot to tell you what I heard about Ryan in fourth period yesterday. I'm so sure he likes me. I was walking to gym yesterday …" I wasn't listening. Again my eyes wandered over Erika's shoulder to the person I wanted most to talk with.

Liberty was leaning against the fireplace with a smirk on her face. Her aqua eyes drank in the atmosphere.

Mabon

How did she get here so quickly after I'd left her this afternoon? Oh ... so that's what Ella's drugstore detour was all about.

Liberty caught my eye, and made a revving gesture with her fists.

Motorbike?

Excellent, Ruben was here as well. I could thank him for his part in this afternoon's horse breaking charade too. Sneaky pair of Danielses.

Liberty paused, shook her head, and waggling her finger from side to side mouthed, 'Ruben'.

This one gesture made my heart react: *Thump ... th-th ... thump ... th-thump.*

I put my hand to my mouth, pressing three fingers to my lips. I gulped and scanned the room.

Liberty watched this little charade with a grin. She knew how I would react and, of course, decided that I needed to know about *his* presence at that precise unguarded moment.

"Thanks," I mouthed back to her.

She laughed that infectious high-pitched cackle.

I tugged at the neck of my t-shirt. Every fiber of the material was scratching at my skin. I tossed the idea of dashing up to my room and changing into something cooler and perhaps appealing, which I realized would only serve the purpose of making everyone wonder who I had changed for. Not one of my better ideas. I scanned the room for a second time.

"... then you'll never believe what happened ..." Erika was still talking. "Are. You. Listening. To. Me. Lucy?" she tapped the words out on my shoulder.

"Yes, sorry. I just thought of something. Go on," I searched.

I was beginning to think Liberty wasn't telling me the whole truth, this might have been another one of her pranks.

Would he have come tonight?

"... that's what Ryan actually said in the first place. Can you believe it?" Finishing up her one-sided conversation, Erika looked at me for a response.

"Really?" I reached out and touched her arm. "Look, I hope you don't mind, but I'm going to check in on Mom in the kitchen. No more surprises, you know!"

"Oh … sure … Lucy," Erika was looking over my shoulder, a bizarre doey smile on her face. Maybe she had stopped talking long enough to finally see that Ryan was here, at the party.

I was glad for the moment to escape so I could continue on my direct path to give a lecture.

I stepped backward into something solid and warm.

"Surprise," the deep voice whispered close to my ear. "Or is that one too many for today?" His warm breath tickled across the skin on my cheek.

Erika's sudden blank out made perfect sense.

Gil.

My chest rose and fell unevenly. My palms felt slick with perspiration.

Turn around, you idiot!

As I did, I came face-to-face with his chest, bound in a black t-shirt that strained to cover his well-defined form. I knew I had to look up into that face, into those luminous eyes, but I could feel the blood rush.

His hand was under my chin before I had the chance to react, lifting my face with his oil-tainted fingers. Obviously he'd been working on that rubbish pile he called an 'antique' that was stashed away in the farm garage. Must have himself a new part.

"Hey, can't I wish you a happy birthday too?"

I looked up into his face and was lost to those eyes – bottomless pools of jade flecked with yellow. I didn't want to keep staring, but it was impossible to look away. I tried to answer him, but all I could manage was a slightly audible gasp.

"I know these parties can be a little embarrassing." His lips were lifting and curling at the corners.

No.

If he smiled *that* smile, the one-sided, deviously handsome smile, not only would I faint but I would possibly explode from the rampaging blood rush.

Bam!

Positive that every single person in the room was staring at us, I stumbled backward a step, giving myself some space to recover from my heady stupor. His musky cologne filled every part of my being with each breath I indulged in it.

It wasn't fair to be in the presence of someone so intoxicating.

"Humiliating," I said, my hand unconsciously twirling a piece of hair. He stepped closer, cupping my shoulders in his broad bronzed hands, turning my knees to jelly.

"I've gotta bounce. Great party though."

"Okay, um, thanks for stopping by." I dropped the strand of hair as he ran his fingers from my jaw to my chin sending a fresh barrage of scarlet to my face and down my neck, making my entire body tingle.

"Mom's here, she'll take Lib home." He pointed to Ella who smirked when she saw us looking in her direction, no doubt a guilty admission to her part in the afternoon's 'cover-up'.

He leaned closer to me, taking my face in his hands, and kissed my forehead. His lips were warm and soft, but this felt a familiar kiss. From the outside it would have appeared a friendly gesture on a girl's birthday, nothing like the action that stoked the intense desire within.

Gil always stood that little bit too close to me; the comfortable way you do with a close friend or family member, and although I'd always wanted more, I was sure he thought our relationship was only platonic. I was family like his little sister – another Liberty.

"Grown up now, Lucinda." Gil's serious expression betrayed his tone, and the depth of his gaze hinted at something else, a sadness even. "See you soon?"

"Sure." My smile faded. *Please don't go.*

Almost a silent prayer, I didn't want to give up hope, though at the heart of it I knew my feelings for Gil were hopeless. He would never feel the same way about me and at times I wondered why I tortured myself by being in his presence. The truth was I couldn't resist. I was so attracted to him I could hardly bear it. It was a fine line of torture I trudged, intolerable to be near him, too excruciating to be away. I saw the splendor of his face every time I closed my eyes.

Gil was hot, that was fact, but it was his heart that I had fallen for. He was *that* guy, the one who opened doors, who listened, who had time and compassion for others. His style of intelligence was discreet, cloaked in a 'bad boy' exterior that really did nothing to hide the extent of his knowledge.

He was an *'intellectual rebel'*... as I often romanticized.

But ...

Gil was out of my league, *way out*. Besides, he was dating Elania Wordsworth. And had been for close on two years.

Lani, as she preferred, *was* in Gil's league. The perfect brunette with eyes the color of sunlit amber. She had an hourglass figure, and the most refined honey skin – almost as if she was tattooed in gold. Lani's flaw – she knew she was beautiful and at times that awareness made her mean.

That was until she met Gil. I couldn't blame her for this falter. Together they were the 'it' couple. Gil and Lani were both juniors at their schools, but where Lani projected future valedictorian, Gil was a gifted truant and consummate rogue. It was an odd pairing, especially for Lani's parents.

The Wordsworths were wealthy, living in one of the most identifiable waterfront properties on Bigfork Bay. They had moved there only a couple of months after my family's arrival in Creston. Lani's father was a highly respected heart surgeon who spent most of his time in New York and his birth place of London. Her mother was corporate in a leading medical research company based outside of Missoula.

Although she tended to drop mere threads of the story, Liberty had always commanded tight-lips when it came to the discussion of Lani's family. In spite of that fact, Lani was the apple of her parent's eyes – she never put a foot wrong (except for dating Gil). There had always seemed something missing when it came to Lani. I could never put my finger on it, but Liberty believed it was because Lani was adopted and had dropped hints about not fitting in. It was a snippet of information that I used in the face of Lani's commonly conceited demeanor, especially when it came to Gil. Lani didn't like interaction between Gil and I, and I often imagined this as jealousy. But Lani had nothing to be jealous of. Gil appeared to be charmed by everything she did.

A mirror-image of my feelings for him.

It was difficult, being in love with my best friend's brother. When Liberty had found out within weeks of my own epiphany, she didn't speak to me for a while. She slowly came around to an understanding and from that point was tolerant of my feelings for, and behavior around, Gil. She was never unconditionally sold on it though, but Liberty had enough respect for me to never straight out disclose my feelings. She simply played on the edge of my affection for Gil, poking me with her jibes. In the end, the balance was something I was content to accept. I could still spend time with Liberty and, if Gil was involved, it was okay with her.

"… and the signs, the signs … they're different this time, I tell you." A Dutch voice rose above a muffled whisper. There was a desperate edge to it.

"I've already told you, Christophe. There's nothing more I can do. It's just tea." The silence stayed awkwardly in the air. "You must believe me!"

Mr Vallen? But what could he want with Mom?

"I've lost two hundred already." It was an anxious plea from Mr Vallen. He wasn't fooling around, but he wasn't threatening either. There was a muffled thud from something being placed on the kitchen table.

"Dana … *please*. My family."

"Christophe." Dana's voice wavered.

I stiffened.

"I don't know what you want from me."

I stopped short of entry, alarmed. Christophe Vallen was beseeching my mother for help. But help of what kind?

Had we been found out again? *Oh no. I can't leave Gil and Lib. I don't want to move away from Creston.* I shuddered at the thought and stomped on the floor.

As I entered the room, Christophe, unshaken from his goal, pushed a small calico pouch across the kitchen table toward my mother. "Please," he muttered, turning and excusing himself from the room.

A whisp of a man, Christophe Vallen had migrated to America fifty years ago. He wasn't a 'talker', tending to keep to himself and his family, so his present behavior appeared completely out of character.

As he passed, our eyes met. His reflected rage, plain and clear. He was terrified.

I looked to my mother, searching her expression for some type of silent explanation, but found nothing. With Mr Vallen gone, she collapsed down to the table, her silky-blonde hair a perfect cushion for her relief.

"Mom, what the hell?" I stood opposite Dana with my hands resting stiffly on the kitchen table. No response. "Mom … Are we moving again?"

"No." It was a whisper breathed into her pillow of hair. "But we – I – have to be more careful in future."

I gestured toward the door after our neighbor. "What was that all about? Why more careful?"

"Mr. Vallen thinks we can help him," she sighed, quoting the word with her fingers. "Something terrible is happening to the sheep out on his farm."

"What?"

Dana kept glancing between the calico bag and the kitchen door. "Deaths – a lot of deaths," she sighed. "The strange thing is that no one seems to have any idea what's causing them."

Unexplainable stock deaths injected white-eyed fear into any rural township.

I stared at the calico bag. "What's in that?"

"Only one way to find out," she said, loosening the cream cord that bound the bag closed. "I'm making an educated guess it's dirt from Mr Vallen's farm."

The smell hit me instantly.

The putrid, metallic smell of blood and a recent killing.

My mother's lips moved, I heard nothing but the tinkling of distant bells, returning as they had in the school parking lot.

My sight went blank, replaced by an image of Christophe on bended knee. The soil in his hand turned red as it ran through his fingers and trickled down onto a sheep's skull resting on the ground beside him. Twisting his face toward me, the hollows of his eyes were vacuous, filled with an eerie lime glow. His mouth fell open, as if to speak, but no recognizable sound came out – just a long, low hum of sorts: the synchronizing resonance of a thousand voices drowning in the ever increasing swirl of ringing chimes. My hands flew to my head to block the sound as waves of nausea churned inside me.

Then, it stopped.

The cacophany of sounds and sights ... simply ... ceased.

"Lucy ... Lucy ... Can you hear me?"

Steeped in mental haze, I heard her calling to me. My mother had her arms around me, cushioning my head against her chest. I was now seated at the kitchen bench with no memory of how I had gotten there.

"What happened?" I managed, my mouth lazy like an anaesthetic was wearing off. I pushed away from my mother to stand, but my knees gave way and she caught me. "What's in that bag? I'm so ... so drained."

"I don't have the answers Lucy, but I think – "

"There was blood ... and Mr Vallen ... and a dead sheep with its head cut off ... and more blood." The words rushed from my mouth as the vivid images came flooding back.

"It was awful." I flopped back down onto my stool. Leaning my head on my hands, I came face-to-face with a piece of paper decorated with three simple scrawls.

From years of watching my family and their 'ways', I recognized the scrawls as letters from the Theban – an old magickal alphabet. I'd never been interested enough to know exactly which three letters I was looking at. The Theban was still used these days, but mostly for talismanic inscriptions.

Before I had a chance to ask, my mother blind-sided me, tapping her fingers on the bench. "Do you want to tell me what that was all about?"

"Well, would *you* mind telling me what *this* is about?" I retorted, gesturing to the paper as my hair fell over my eyes. I lazily pushed it back, drained of strength as my head slumped back down onto my hands.

"You should know what that's about," Dana implied, glaring. "You wrote it."

"I ... what?" Even in my stupor, I acknowledged that I hadn't studied the Theban. I had recognized the styling from my limited exposure to it, watching my sisters. So how was I able to write it? "I wrote this?"

"Yes, Lucy. You wrote it." Dana was firm.

"But I don't even know what I'm looking at. How could I have written it?" I shrugged.

My mother reached across the bench, slipping the note paper from under my nose.

"I'm telling you what I saw." She motioned toward the calico bag. "You had just opened that bag when you kinda went into a trance. You walked to the refrigerator, got down some note paper and a pencil, sat at the kitchen bench and scribbled those three letters, E.B.D in Theban."

She held the note with both hands outstretched to emphasize her point.

"I did?" What was being implied here? That I walked around unconscious and scribbled on tatty pieces of paper? I could barely move, still slumped with only the bench and my elbows holding me up. Each time I tried to straighten I felt I was fighting against a gluey force field.

"I don't remember any of it."

"Little Soul, I don't usually think this sort of thing is odd … but from you, it is." Moving around the bench in a floating motion, my mother pushed her soft hand to my forehead then returned a quizzical glare at the open calico bag.

"Hmmm … I wonder," she muttered, more to herself than to me.

"Guess I've had a big day, and that was weird." Rallying my strength I looked up at her. "E – B – D, hey?"

"You don't recall?" She pushed back my hair, her eyes urgently searched my face.

"N–n–no," I said. What was my mother trying to

pinpoint? "No, I don't, I just remember seeing dirt, it turned red and there was a sheep's head. Guess that's where death comes in." I pulled at my earlobes, twisting the black studs in them. "And then those damn bells. They're deafening."

"You're hearing bells?" My mother shifted. "What kind of bells? Lucinda, it's important."

"Chimes, you know, high and tinkling … like," I paused, tapping the bench, "like a wind chime or something. Why?"

"When did they start?" she demanded, slapping the table. I looked at my hands.

"I don't know," I mumbled. *Why was this so important? I was more intrigued with knowing the Theban alphabet somehow.* "At school, this morning."

"It sounds as if in synchronicity your chimes have begun with the phase of the full moon. Your father foretold it. We must start now." My mother's face contorted with the gravity of a situation lost on me. "Call your sisters."

"But Mom, start what? What do these letters mean? What was that about Dad?"

"I'm sorry Lucinda, I don't know what the letters mean and at the moment we have more important things to attend to. Please … your sisters!"

"Why, Mom? What more important things?" I threw my hands into the air.

"Lucinda! I think it's time."

I didn't argue with my mother's cryptic inference. I had lived with the knowledge this day would come, as had my mother and my sisters before me. Now an odd sense of fear surfaced – *my inheritance* was not going to skip me.

My family had moved from another town two years prior

Mabon

when a few residents had begun making accusations. They were correct, of course, but we couldn't stay another minute for fear the town would learn the truth for themselves. So one night we fled, under the dark blanket of the New Moon with the disguise of a necessary lifestyle change. My mother moved us to Creston, Montana, taking up a job at the local bookstore in the quaint nearby tourist town of Bigfork. My sisters and I transferred schools and we began our new life.

My family was meticulous in our craft, forever trying to stay 'hidden'. Unknown for our ways, often there were situations in which we could help. In fact, helping others transformed from being my mother's passion to being our livelihood.

My mother made tea.

But these weren't just any old teas, and they weren't just herbal teas.

Milled through our hereditary craft, Dana fused her knowledge and studies of eastern and western naturopathy and ancient herb lore to create mixtures with that little extra 'oomph'. That extra something no one could put their finger on – but it kept them coming back for more.

A tea with Dana seemed to lift the spirits of anyone who stopped by our house, and it didn't take long for the word to pass around. With complete and proven confidentiality my mother seemed to help, taking folk into our conservatory with a cup of tea, an open ear, and a compassionate disposition.

"Must be something in that tea of yours," they would often laugh.

Yet the phrase, said in jest, couldn't have been truer.

Wise-women have always been there to help mortals over the centuries with the philosophy of 'What they don't know, won't hurt them.'

'They' being the humans, and my family … not so much!

Although she continued working at the bookstore, starting up a business of her own was a 'no-brainer' as Dana received inquiries from out of town. From there it snowballed and 'Incidental Antidotes' became a full family operation. Everyone pitched in. Of late, my sisters had added a branch to Dana's business and began building their own following in mixed and perfumed potions billed as 'Nitty Gritty Elixirs'. Just as Dana had done, the twins had a secret added ingredient.

Magick.

It was never about making money. It was always about people – about their depth and complexity. We could add a little bit of magick to help soothe their cares, even if by a tiny amount – a mother wishing to be heard by her son, an employee wanting recognition, or a rider hoping for a stronger tie to their mount.

Seemingly small things.

Still, that was the way my mother and sisters could help. I, on the other hand, couldn't have helped if I tried. I was not gifted as they were. *Yet* … and there existed my internal battle.

It was possible to be missed – looked over in some inherent way. And I thought, perhaps even expected, I would be left a mere mortal with no magickal appellation or association, but from Dana's urgent tone, I knew I was wrong and the position I found myself in was terrifying.

Mabon

I wasn't sure I wanted inclusion – magick caused our continuous moves. It caused confusion and family fights; these we had learned to live with. But highest on my 'cons' list was it caused a dramatic change within oneself – and that's where I drew the line, where I wasn't sure that witchcraft was for me.

It was difficult for all of us, the secrecy and non-acceptance, and although my family appeared to take the entity 'witchcraft' within their stride, I was privy to what happened behind closed doors. There was no rest for our kind, no understanding, no real tolerance. It was a sobering thought that brought me back to the reality of our current situation.

On the eve of my Initiation, were we about to run again?

As I wandered out of the kitchen and into the hall my thoughts switched to the daunting task of dispersing my birthday party.

Abi and Mat appeared simultaneously from different directions. "Lucy, people are starting to wonder where you ran off to," Abi scolded.

"Is everything alright?" Mat asked. "You look a little pale. Did you see a ghost or something?"

Hmmm … yes, something or other.

"It's okay, I'm fine." Being easily caught out in a lie, especially by my sisters, I deftly changed the subject. "Mom wants to see you both in the kitchen."

"Lucy?" Abi rounded on me.

"Just go see Mom and she'll tell you everything." As quickly as the twins had materialized they disappeared.

As I resurfaced into the great room, the party numbers had dwindled. People had departed but left messages of 'thank you' and 'birthday wishes' with others to relay. The coffee table in the center of the room was strewn with gifts and I was humbled. I did not want to leave this secure little town. Of the multitudes of places we had lived, I truly felt this was home.

Sitting on the sofa, pulling at the curled ribbon stuck to one of the gifts, was Liberty. It was obvious she was disappointed so I shuffled through the remaining guests and plonked down next to her.

"Hey you," I punched her on the arm. "You little sneak. So that's why you were so interested in Ruben's horse breaking stunt this afternoon. All a ploy to keep me away from the house and preps, hey?"

No answer.

I pushed back into the sofa, waving my arm across the laden coffee table. "S'pose I'll have to open all of these soon. Don't know anyone who could help me do you?"

Liberty was silent, her eyes fixed to the ribbon she was pulling at.

"I know you liked my present best," she mumbled as the ribbon smacked back onto its gift box. "I saw the way you blushed when it surprised you, but then it left and went to stupid Lani's house."

Rrrriiipppppp.

The decorative ribbon was torn clear from its fixture, Liberty stuffed it back into the pile. "Sorry, just thought he might hang around longer. Lani had some emergency." She looked at me, forlorn. "Probably broke a nail."

We shoved each other into the sofa, spirits lifted with our laughter.

"You brought Gil, for me?" Of all the silly pretty trinkets she could have bought me with her ridiculous generosity, she paid nothing for the one I had wanted the most. And practically wrapped and delivered him herself, even if it had only been for a short, but delicious time. I grabbed Liberty in a bear hug, whispering, "You are the best."

A few seconds later she pushed me away. "Hey, this is meant to be a party."

"Actually Libs, I need your help with something." I faced up to the seriousness of my mother's request and my lack of skill when lying to Liberty. "Mom's just told me she's not feeling the best."

"Oh," she said, looking toward the kitchen. "Is everything okay?"

"Not sure. She said she hopes it's not that viral thing, but she's asked me to clear the house, just in case. Can you help?" I pretended to scan the room, knowing the veil of suspicion Liberty held me under, her eyes piercing. "Pretty great way to end my party, hey?"

My mother hadn't re-emerged from the kitchen and I knew she wouldn't. By now she would have begun her various preparations for this evening's event, my sisters roped in.

"Sure Lou, whatever you need." Expressionless, she nodded as she began to walk toward Erika.

"Lib." I grabbed at her hand. "Thank you."

She sighed as she walked away, this was far from over.

I sped from dwindling group to group explaining Mom's predicament. Everyone knew what I was talking about, it had practically been an epidemic in Bigfork and concern for my mother was rapidly replaced with fear for their own health as people filed out of the house at an astonishing rate.

Presto!

Party over – no magick necessary.

Standing on the front porch waving to the last of the guests, I was aware of an uncomfortable feeling in the pit of my stomach. I turned to see Christophe Vallen approach from the shadows.

"You know something Lucinda." It was a demand rather than a question, almost spattered through his teeth. His hand tightly gripped my arm. "What is it?"

"Mr Vallen," I gasped. "What are you talking about?" I shook his hand off.

"I know your family. I've known your kind in Holland." Christophe's face was within inches of my own. Was I imagining the red glow burning at the edge of his pupils?

"You *must* tell me." His whispered words soured into a low growl.

"Anything I can help with Christophe?"

Teddy.

As he maneuvered me around his daunting mass, Teddy 'helped' Christophe down the stairs and into his truck.

"Now you pass on my respects to Cassandra, won't you?" Teddy offered as Christophe muttered something in Dutch, clambering into his flat bed, his eyes never leaving mine, I was unable to break their ghostly hold.

Part 1

The haunting vocals of Stevie Nicks filled the darkened kitchen. Candlelight rhythmically lapped the walls, dancing on the cool breeze wafting through the back door, standing slightly ajar.

Dana hummed along with Stevie, emphasizing the last line completely out of tune. My mother has a cracking sense of humor. She always said there are times to be serious and times to be carefree, and the latter should outnumber the former by many a degree.

After sending home a well thanked but protective Teddy, I had returned to the kitchen to observe my mother and sisters busying themselves with the necessary preparations for the ritual that was soon to begin.

"Mom, what do I have to do tonight?" I said, stumbling over the question and into the kitchen bench. "Ouch!"

"Geez, you really didn't think this was going to happen to you!" Abi blurted out as she whisked away the herbal concoction she was mixing. It had started to froth and overflow onto the table.

"Don't let her get to you." As the levelheaded twin, Mat frequently extinguished Abi's spot fires. "Now, go shower. I've left the initiation robe hanging on the back of your bedroom door."

She grabbed my hand as I turned to leave. "I can't tell you what happens, it's different for everyone."

It didn't make me feel any better. Although I'd seen my family's magick at work, I had never participated (well, I couldn't participate) and a part of me didn't wish too.

There appeared to be a loss of innocence connected to this ritual, one I had witnessed firsthand in my sisters. Girls became women overnight, both mentally and physically. Necessity in its purest form had shaped the ritual in this way and once initiated, hereditary witches tended to immediately possess the confidence required to carry on the ancient secret.

My mother warbled with Stevie as I walked from the kitchen. She called out after me, "Not a shred of clothing under that robe, Lucinda."

Lucinda? Dana meant business.

I turned on my heel and stuck my head back around the door. "You're kidding, right?" Surely this had to be some demented little initiation hazing. *I had enough body confidence issues to cope with.*

"No, Lucy. *Dead* serious." Her hand halted in front of a laden spice rack.

"But why?"

"You are being presented tonight for the first time

Mabon

Lucinda, and you must be in a manner that's uninhibited. There are no 'ifs nor buts' concerning this ritual. This is the way it has been for centuries."

"I know how you feel Lucy." Abi had put down a large bushel of rosemary. "Here." Abi stretched her hand out, and walked me up the stairs. She lowered her voice to a whisper, "I was unsure too."

I found this hard to believe of self-assured Abigail, but the message came across clearly – Abi might have been afraid during her initiation. Her unyielding façade had kept the truth at bay.

"It's hard at your age, feeling the way you do, but you'll be fine Lucy."

As much as I appreciated her thoughts, it didn't resolve the 'nudity' issue.

"Ok, thanks Abi." As I turned into my bedroom Abi cleared her throat – a nervous doormouse picked at her nails, staring at me through the hair that had fallen across her face – the façade had cracked.

"Your initiation is something really different, Lucy. It's so special," she began. Her eyes twinkled and the corners of her pretty bow lips gently pulled into a subtle but genuine smile. "Our heritage is a mystical gift. So many others dream of being like us, we are lucky." Her message was crystal clear and I was grateful for her disclosure – Abi rarely let her guard down. "You should try to be thankful."

I plonked down on the edge of my bed, staring at the floor. "It's not that I'm ungrateful, it's that I don't really know what to be thankful for yet."

I looked up as she crossed my room, picking up a plush

teddy bear that held pride of place on my desk. I loved that thing. Gil had won it at the *Auction and County Fair* last year and absentmindedly given it to me. I guessed it was because Lani wasn't there and I was standing next to him at the time. I pictured his face and wondered what changes this initiation would bring for me in relation to Gil. And Liberty. And life, for that matter.

Abi tugged at the bear's fur then came back to sit next to me on the bed. "You'll soon know everything and more." If it was a statement that was meant to spook me, it worked. I retreated to my bay window, and gazed out into the night.

"I know it's special and all; I'm just embarrassed about the naked bit," I said, heat stung my cheeks and I stuck my face further into the shelter of the darkened window. "You guys are all perfect, and I'm just … well …" The tone was a giveaway for my emotions and I felt Abi's hand alight softly on my shoulder as she wrapped her long, fine arms about me, her chin wedged in the side of my neck.

"We all felt the humility of the moment, Lucy – that's one of this ritual's greatest gifts. And it's not like we are going to parade you around town in your birthday suit." Her chuckle shook against my neck. "I can guarantee you will surprise yourself. Besides, it's just us – your family – and it's not for long." She covered her mouth as she brought it to my ear, "But don't tell them I told you that part, OK?"

"OK." I smiled, feeling better for our little chat. Abi's demeanor was vastly different from her usual disposition. She spun me out of her tangled hold, laughing as she did.

"Glad to have helped, baby sis." The self-assured Abi was returning. She paused, primping her face in the tiny mirror that hung by my bedroom door. "See you downstairs. Oh, and hey, wash your hair in that pomegranate shampoo I left in the shower."

"Is there some kind of significance?" I pondered the cleansing properties of the simple pomegranate.

"No." Her reflection showed a cheeky smile that beamed at me from the mirror. "It just smells really nice." With a giggle and a toss of her golden hair, she trotted off down the stairs.

As I undressed I thought about what Abi had said, and agreed. I sniffed at the pomegranate wash. It smelt heavenly, so I lathered up, and somewhere in the euphoric mist of the shower I decided that if being a witch was my destined path then I would need to follow it with the best of intentions, nothing less. My sisters were levelheaded girls who had taken their inheritance in their lengthy strides – *why couldn't I? Why shouldn't I?*

Besides, it *was* true. I was lucky to receive this bestowed gift.

Witchcraft, to the modern world, had become a religion of sorts – a neo-pagan belief system – which often followed a tragic turn leading to its vilification. To my family, being a witch was a reality – sometimes a harsh one – that led to particular behaviors, isolation, ridicule, and sometimes *death*, as a result of its power.

We DeBane's hailed from strong lineage, as both my mother *and* father had magick woven through their lines. The females in the family passed on their hereditary witchcraft. It was rare to find a male with a magickal soul.

The craft had skipped a few generations in my father's

line, investing in his mother Arvilla, my grandmother, who had in turn passed it down to her son, Hugh. When my sisters had first displayed their 'talents', my mother had confessed her hardened suspicions that, if I was to follow, we as a family would be the first full-family of hereditary witches since the Benenati family based in Benevento, Italy in the 1400s. Even with my father's passing, this still presented us as unique within the witchcraft realm.

Lines of purity were not expected of witches as love operates in mysterious ways, and we were never expected to choose a partner under any other pretense. Usually, if a witch founded a soul-connection with a *mortal* mate, which was the common occurrence, inherent witchcraft would thread itself through the line, picking and choosing its enlightened carriers. In this way, the 'gene pool' as such, was never convoluted or contaminated. The craft always managed to continue on in its journey making another hereditary witch to carry on a treasured magickal history. It was at this point in my train of thought I realized I could hear the chiming of bells. My chimes had returned.

Finding the white robe behind my bedroom door, I pulled into the silk, double-knotted the waist sash with care as instructed, then stumbled down the stairs.

As I turned the corner into the dimmed kitchen, my anxiety had all but departed, replaced by excitement. There she appeared, celestial in a way that I had never seen my mother before. With blonde hair flowing, her radiant skin was draped in a jet black robe with white edging, its hem trailing the floorboards of the kitchen.

"Wow, Mom –"

Mabon

She placed a finger to her lips and led me to the cellar door. As she placed her hand on its plain wooden surface, a symbol began to appear. She brushed and blew at it as if removing dust and grit. Once fully revealed, she placed her hand to its center and the etched figure began to glow faintly.

I knew this symbol well. I had often vigorously questioned my mother about it, being the same one emblazed on the ring that adorned her right hand. Tarnished with age, the silver was molded into a flat elliptical disc, with a slight convex. At its center was a winged Tyet, embellished and branded into a terracotta carnelian stone representing the ancient Egyptian Goddess Isis, the deity of my mother's ancestry. If you liked that sort of thing, it was a smart choice as Isis was the goddess of goddesses, so the story went – the Goddess of motherhood, magick, fertility and so much more. She was a perfect fit for our kind's quest, but as with my hesitations regarding witchcraft, I was dubious with respect to the notion of a 'goddess'.

I stared hard at the glowing image thinking about the shallow position of my own beliefs, but as the icon grew from strength to strength Dana clasped her hand around mine. "Are you ready?" she said.

I shrugged, not knowing the answer. Deep in my stomach a tiny flutter began. The door swung open leading down a candlelit stairway.

Our 'wine cellar' was a purpose-built, circular room beneath the glass roofed conservatory. My mother adored her occasional glass of red, a passion she shared with Teddy, who had in fact, cut a circle in the floorboards of the conservatory, raised it on hinges, and with the help of a certain blend of tea, no questions. When the giant trapdoors were raised, they allowed the light of the moon's phases to flood fully into my family's service and the cellar below.

It was best for everyone that most rituals were celebrated here, away from prying eyes and too many answerless queries. We never were the type of family who would traipse off at midnight into the woods, scouting out some secret location that would more than likely be found by a hiker, who would later report some satanic worship. My family left that to fairy tales and the odd Hollywood blockbuster.

The stone was cold as we descended the stairs, but the room was not. I became aware of the alcoves lining the curved wall. Each held a squat white candle and a small vial of what I was told was frankincense – for the cleansing, purification and spiritual aspects of my initiation. The room was lit with hundreds of white pillar candles, many looked as if they were floating. I presumed this was a trick of the eye.

The wine cellar – original swept dirt floor, Mom's heirloom chaise lounge and side-table, her collection of wines aging row after row – had never looked the way it did tonight. Racks were now covered in rich burgundy draped velvet, excluding one, which had bottles, but I guessed they held something other than wine by the way my sisters scuttled back and forth from that particular rack – choosing a bottle then emptying a dash of its contents into a large caldron that sat dead center in the room. It frothed and bubbled as if being heated over a fire, but there was nothing underneath it, only the soft glow of moonlight pouring over it from the open roof above. I could see the moon was complete, but hidden behind a wisp of fairy-floss cloud, awaiting its unveiling.

"Self-heating caldron. Doubles as central heating." The twins, giggled. They looked at me with wide smiles, trying to contain a fizzing excitement that sparked back and forth between them. It was contagious. The tiny fluttering in the pit of my stomach escalated, dancing with the faint tinkling of chimes, underlying my excitement.

"Mom," I squeezed Dana's soft hand with unintentional vigor, causing her to flinch. "The chimes have started again."

"I thought they would." She dismissed my comment with a nod of her head, and led me to a chair. "Sit down here until we are ready for you." As she smiled, broad and gentle, she pulled me in for a warm hug. "This is an amazing event for you Little Soul." She combed my hair back from my face in a single move, as if it had been the mere shadows of her fingers in my hair. "All of my girls, touched by the craft." Her eyes began to mist. "Whoever thought we would be blessed so?"

And with that she yanked several hairs from my head.

"Yeow," I sulked rubbing at the inflicted site. "Necessary?"

"Sorry Lucinda. I don't think you would have given them to me if I had asked, now would you?" Dana quickly crossed the room to the caldron and threw the hairs in. Her lips moved in incantation.

"Probably not," I whispered under my breath. My head still stinging, I sat down to watch the proceedings. I had seen Abi and Mat work simple spells, usually in the chaos of their room, and I had seen my mother work more complex ones in our kitchen, but I hadn't seen any of the rituals that took place here. I wasn't interested. Maybe somewhere buried in my subconscious, I truly believed in what my family did but I didn't think this line would choose me, yet here I was swathed in a white robe, seated on the edge of my stool, awaiting my inheritance.

Kind of cool? *Very.*

My sisters, their concoction finished, stood close together chatting about their weekend plans. It was comical that they were discussing social plans dressed from head to toe in black hooded robes. I wondered what Dion and Frankie would say seeing their girlfriends like this.

"Girls, are you prepared to begin?" My mother added a few more ingredients to the caldron which turned the steam a shimmering shade of royal blue.

The twins stepped forward and filled two tiny decorative vials with the steam, double quick, and replaced them on the altar. The caldron was pushed into a large recess in the wall.

"Let us begin." As my mother spoke these words, the room flooded with the moon's luminosity. I almost jumped right out of my skin.

Gliding across the cellar floor, Dana stopped in front of the altar, a table covered with a pure-white cloth embroidered with more symbols. They were Theban, and with my fresh thirst for knowledge of our craft I knew studying this alphabet would be my first assignment. I was told the letters, embroidered in a shiny pewter thread, symbolized the Universe.

With her back to me, Dana unsheathed her athame; a three foot long sword that I'd never laid eyes on. With a splatter collection that illustrated the deliciously dangerous, I had somewhat of a fascination with death …. and blood … and knives. My sisters had spoken in whispers about this sword, it wasn't really something you brought up at a Sunday lunch.

Dana moved to the center of the moonlit circle. She held her athame out high at arm's length for presentation. I was mesmerized by an iridescent-silver light rippling from the filigree iron handle, along the swirling plumes of the blade, to the point then back again. Dana clasped the sword between both hands and a strange contentment crossed her features as it pulled her hands down until it rested, tip down, on the dirt floor. The dull thudding of my heart accelerated as my mother walked away from the sword. It balanced itself, upright.

All three witches took their places. Dana stood in the north quarter in front of the altar stretching her hands out for the twins to take in theirs. She pressed on their hands and they all smiled at each other. Abi winked in my direction and my pulse quickened.

The ritual, *my* initiation ritual, was about to begin.

Part 2

"All to center." Dana bowed.

I slid back into my seat, the flutter in my stomach now an increasing churn, as the chimes in my head changed pitch.

"Earth beneath our feet as our bodies above,
Air in our lungs as our thoughts abound,
Fire around flesh as true passions alight,
Water through veins as emotion takes flight."

For me it was simple enough, but bursting with new meaning. I processed the words. These were the four tangible elements Earth, Air, Fire and Water. Each denoted by a tall candle perched on a silver stand. Each candle was a different color, indicating a compass point. The fifth element was the Spirit itself.

The bells in my head were ringing, rattling around in my flooded gray matter. I tried to block them out but they grew louder. I baulked at the distraction.

Ignoring my reaction, Dana grasped the handle of her athame. She steadied her bare feet, grounding herself. In a swift herculean movement, she swung the sword above her head until its tip pointed directly at the full moon. There was a loud crack as a tendril of brilliant moonlight struck the sword.

I scuttled backward, heart racing, and crouched on the ground beside my up-ended chair. I tried to move again but fright had rendered my legs useless.

Standing in the moonlight, Dana unperturbed, began to cast the Circle. "I call for this Circle. Protect this place between places and time out of times." Her commanding words ricocheted around the room, which was now experiencing odd gusts of wind that teased the candle flames, making them appear to extinguish and re-ignite.

Beginning in the north quarter, represented by a glass jar filled to the brim with what appeared to be soil, Dana lowered the sword's tip. Light sparked as she trailed the sword in a semi arc, illuminating the ground as she went, leaving an eerie trail of blue flame in its wake.

"Come essence of Earth. Keeper of the North. Bring thy traits: stability, power and the physical. Hear me." Dana stopped, the sword's point hovered before the glass jar, which she stared at for a long moment, then continued her arc.

"Come essence of Air. Keeper of the East. Bring thy traits: knowledge, communication and thought. Hear me." Again she paused, her sword tip hung before her, her eyes intently focused on the second glass jar. Contained was the representation of air, a swirl of sparkles floated around the center of the jar.

Squinting my eyes helped me recognize what I was looking at – a teeny wind funnel, a glittering tornado under glass.

The twins 'shushed' my gasp, giggling between themselves. Dana was single minded, her focus solely on the rites, she moved her athame toward the southern compass point.

"Come essence of Fire. Keeper of the South. Bring thy traits: transformation, passion and glory. Hear me." A single flame danced as Dana spoke her words. No candle anchored it, just a stunning vermillion flame under glass, writhing to a silent drumbeat.

Blood rushed, tainting my cheeks and left my skin

tingling and slick with perspiration. It was the flame of passion that embodied a quiet wanting within me, Gil flashing before my eyes – his arms, and chest, and face, that beautiful face. *Why is it so hot in here?* I tore my eyes away from the flame. My body immediately cooled with relief. I wiped the sweat from my forehead, refocused my train of thought and followed Dana to her last point.

"Come essence of Water. Keeper of the West. Bring thy traits: purification, movement and emotion. Hear me."

Water trickled from an invisible source directly above the fourth and last glass jar. The bubbling sound, a muted background melody for this astonishing sight. The jar never filled, it simply emptied into nothingness.

I watched in disbelief as all four glass jars, carrying their differing elements within, lifted from the floor, inch by inch until they were at knee height. The glass jars remained perfectly still, perched before their quarter candles and standing proud on each element's behalf.

Dana continued, her sword tracing the circle to its completion at Earth, the trailing blue flame now extinguished leaving behind a full pentacle, etched into the dirt floor, undulating with a glowing liquid. My eyes flicked back and forth between my mother and the pentacle. In the meantime, the twins had silently walked around the edge of the circle and were in the process of re-seating me. My eyes remained hard on the pentacle, my brain busily analyzing.

The twins returned to their quarters. From my seated vantage, I noticed the liquid illuminating the pentacle was a metallic liquid silver, reminding me of Mercury from science class. I wanted to touch it, pool it into my palms and stir it with my fingertips.

Mabon

"Earth, Air, Fire and Water, you are with us now. Hallowed Be." In unison, the three witch's words harmonized, breaking my stare. I shuffled my bare feet back and forth on the dirt floor.

"Hallowed Be." Once more the twins repeated the blessing, although this time Mat motioned to me with her piercing blue eyes.

"Hallowed Be." A whisper emerged from my trembling lips. I cleared my throat and repeated, "Hallowed Be."

Dana smiled and my confidence rallied from nowhere. I wasn't really into ritualistic nonsense, but on the mixed wave of excitement and anticipation, something inside me was changing, like history had awakened within my veins.

"My blade is charged with the elements, may it aid to establish my will and intent." Swinging the sword above her head, my mother stood with her arms stretched out, athame in her right hand. She paused again, taking stock, grounding and re-centering herself. "Spirit, come to our Circle. Guide and guard us tonight, watch over these Rites. Hallowed Be."

Again the twins repeated the blessing, although, this time I needed no nudge, my voice rang out, as my body once more crept forward to the edge of my seat.

The Spirit had been called.

The room pitched with darkness.

Every candle extinguished and even the light of the full moon seemed to disappear. The air, thick with expectation, wedged tight in my throat. Time slowed, but my thoughts remained at their same rapid pace. As I waited for something to happen, the anticipation alone smothered my every query as they came swimming to the surface of my mind. The balance was barely manageable. Adrenaline pumped through my veins, urging me to push off from my chair, or strike out with my arms, or run.

Escape.

Faith had me believe that I would be fine, that the light would return with my family unharmed – that my life would remain mostly unchanged by this night. I had to believe that I would be the same person I had always been. I had to believe that Gil would still be in my life, whatever capacity; I didn't care as long as he was there and he was happy.

Hope.

A single minute speck of light drifted down from the conservatory roof. It floated and fluttered, dancing on a non-existent breeze. It reminded me of the journey my oak leaf had taken earlier today – now resting, nestled beside its silver replica in the white box at the bottom of my neglected school bag. The speck continued its path becoming brighter still the lower it fell, illuminating the room, until it touched down on the dirt floor.

Extinguished.

My chair began to shake, vibrations filled the air, candles fell, and bottles smashed. My hands clenched around the seat. I was ready for flight with my feet apart and stable on the ground.

As suddenly as all the light had been sucked from the cellar, it returned with blinding brilliance. I threw my hands up to my eyes. The chimes returned in accelerating magnitude, deafening. I was in agony – pain from sight and sound, crushing my skull with the intensity.

Then the pain was gone as before, dissipating instantly.

Mabon

Part 3

My name was being called out, that much I was aware of. I flinched at the touch of something on my arm, only to realize it was my mother trying to pry my hands from my face, repeating my name over and over in a whispered melodic manner. The blur of my vision refocused. I was still seated, although now cowering, with my head in my hands.

"You're alright Little Soul. The first time's confronting." Dana was standing above me, stroking my hair and face as she spoke.

I needed water, and pain killers. The confusion of chimes, sight impairing blackness and dark, dark thoughts, had left ringing pain in my head.

"I know this will be hard to comprehend, but you have been favored." Her voice sounded different, the words repeated themselves, echoing into silence. She took both of my hands, raising me from my seat, where we waited until I steadied myself. I shook my head, and found relief had blessed me, my chimes hushed. There was no pain, just clarity. I smiled, feeling as if I had woken from a rejuvenating sleep.

"Come with me." The echoing disappeared as Dana led me to a spot about two paces from the pentacle's edge. "You must wait here till I signal for you." I wobbled on the spot as she walked around to the altar to prepare. Abi and Mat silently materialized, one on either side, stabilizing my sway.

"Some simple instructions. You will be asked three questions. Answer as honestly as you can, from your heart." Abi was methodical. She pinched my cheek smiling, then cupped my shoulders and turned me to face Mat.

"This is important Lucy, it sets the tone of your journey." Mat's eyes began to cloud. Was there something she was holding back? It had me wondering if honesty had been an issue for her.

Or was it still?

I looked past the novel, entertaining facet of witchcraft, into the serious side that I had not given much, if any, consideration. Where would this journey take me? From my family? From Gil? From Liberty? The low, powerful slink of negativity entered, creeping, then settled into a darkened corner of my mind. What if being a witch didn't suit me? Could I change my mind *after* the initiation? Could I reverse the process and what would the price of this revision be? Questions rained fast, questions that I hadn't dare ask before. All the while I could feel a twinge, something dark and painful, and terrifying.

"After the final question, step into the Circle, but leave your robe behind," Mat continued.

The vision of my robe falling to the ground and pooling about my bare feet threw my heart into a state of panic. I had forgotten about having to 'nude up'. My gaze dropped down to my hands, scratching at a nonexistent itch, holding onto my last few seconds of dignity. I felt Mat's fingers lifting my chin, "Lucy, you'll be fine." Her smile was so warm. Although I loved both sisters dearly, Mat had always been there for me when I needed to talk, especially during my 'many questions' phase regarding our father. "Please, you must place your heart in trust Lucy. It's easy to lose the path at this point."

"What does that even mean Mat? I don't understand."

"Trust. You'll soon see."

Both twins returned to their quarters outside the pentacle. As my mother began the Initiation Rite, I stood motionless, afraid to move or speak after Mat's resounding remark.

It's easy to lose the path at this point.

I glanced across at Mat, she was staring straight ahead. My knees began to wobble, panic was on the rise. A soul-enhancing experience was about to happen, but I would have to pay a dear price for it.

What was I willing to pay?

I didn't know the answer to that, I had to put my faith in trust, and faith in *anything* was hard enough.

"Who stands tonight on the precipice – the Circle before – their past behind?" Dana's command broke my train of thought. Clearly the question had been aimed at me, but for a second I'd forgotten how to make sound.

"I do," I whispered. The bravado that had overwhelmed me not moments before had fled, taking every shred of my confidence with it. "Lucinda DeBane."

"Do you enter this circle with your heart in a true state of love and complete acceptance?" Stretching her hand toward me, Dana smiled and nodded for me to respond.

Just answer the questions as honestly as you can.

I glanced at Mat again, she returned my look mouthing the word 'honesty'.

"I don't know."

It had taken me a moment to break the sentence down, search through it for dual meanings, weigh up the consequences, and then word my honest answer. Sharp, quick images of my Mom and Dad, the twins, Lib and Gil, passed before my eyes. Before I felt it happen, a smile sneaked onto my face. "But yes, I think so." I felt light, happy with my answer and took a single step toward the moonlit circle.

My mother stood, her arms flung wide, athame aloft. I was to enter the circle between the North and East quarters, between Earth and Air – a nonexistent state. I pushed onward, my happy thoughts were stretched, but still held out. I straightened, preparing for the next question.

"Thy path may be smooth yet troubled, be ye prepared for thy role in full?" A gentle smile lifted the rosebuds of my mother's cheeks.

I knew I had the strength to go ahead, but still I deliberated, revising my answers. Time had no bearing here. It could have taken seconds to answer or hours, I was unsure.

Honesty. Mat's words echoed.

"No, I am not prepared." Pausing, I had to collate my thoughts. "But I come to this … Circle … empty. I am ready to learn."

I stole a quick look at Mat, who was staring intently at the pentacle and was immediately concerned. Doubt's dark clouds began to crowd over my head. Had I given the wrong answer? Was I supposed to answer 'yes' to everything even though I had been told to answer honestly? Were these trick questions?

I felt lightheaded. This time I didn't want to step forward, I just wanted to run. Panic bubbled from the depths as my pulse soared and my heart stucattoed in my chest. The room swirled.

'Believe in yourself.'

Mabon

Through the confusion that fogged around me, I faltered, surprised by the sound of a different voice inside my head. Its familiarity and strength put me at ease, and I wanted to believe this voice. *I wanted* to believe in myself, *I wanted* to believe my decisions were true and *I wanted*, most of all, to have the strength to take the next step forward in my journey.

The chimes tranquilly piped up, the churning inside my stomach stopped and I felt a warmth emanate around my body, caressing my fingertips and toes. Through my turbulent thoughts, Dana's smile had stayed, patiently waiting to continue.

"Suffer ye shall, for evil accompanies good as the balance prevails. Will thou stand tall for the trials ahead?"

Suffer?

What? My newly acquired protective blanket of confidence began to suffocate me. Here I stood on the abyss, staring out into its nothingness. What the hell was I doing? My answer to this, the last of my questions, would seal my fate, and I wasn't entirely convinced it was the path I wanted to follow. How could I choose between something I had always known and something I knew relatively nothing about?

I looked around the room.

The three witches standing before me were the only family I knew. They were three of the most beautiful, poised and self-assured women. Contentment appeared a friend to them all, and yet as my eyes lingered a moment too long on Mat, they uncovered an expression possibly lost on its bearer. My sister was preoccupied, her eyes told a tale far different to the other smiling faces in the room, a deep seeded conflict.

The realization hit me.

This *was* Mat's issue!

What was the reason for her last minute instruction, or was it a warning? Was it at this point, she had faltered, and if so, why?

Another quick glance at my sister clarified the issue. I watched in silence as a stray tear crept down Mat's cheek, leaping from her chin. As I tried to read Mat's face, my blood boiled with confusion. How was I meant to know the answer to any of this? I was only sixteen and this was a decision that would change my life.

I have to answer.

Clang, clang, clang.

My thoughts were callously ripped away by another bout of mind numbing chimes. This time they were menacing, intent on damage. I sank to the floor my hands clawing at my ears.

Please stop, please. Can't think.

There had to be a switch, some telepathic dial that would decrease their sound and shut them down, or mentally manage them.

Can't think.

Doubling over, my forehead hit the dirt floor. *Why isn't anyone helping me?* Had I been abandoned? The iridescent glow of the pentacle enticed, a mere hand's distance away.

'Touch it.'

Again the voice. It was breathy but powerful this time, softly commanding and something inside my head snapped

– touch the pentacle then everything would be all right. I didn't know why, I simply believed it. Releasing one hand from its grasp over my ear, I crept it forward, fingers leading. The pain was splitting through my skull.

'Touch it.'

Again the voice resounded.

'It will soothe your fire.'

Inching my fingers toward the pentacle's edge, my nails broke in the dirt and blood dotted my fingertips. I was almost there, one last push. It caught in my throat, but the scream poured from my mouth. My mind went numb – the agony beyond my threshold. Blackness descended across my eyes like a sudden heavy rain.

I was gone.

* * * * *

Hidden from the full moon, in the dark shadows of the tree line a distance from our house, a lone figure followed the beam of light that shot upward from our rooftop.

"Ahhh, the Interceptor has surfaced," she whispered, her lips curling into a knowing smile. "Finally."

V

His fingers trembled as he brushed them along my collarbone, followed teasingly by his lips. I was frozen with the fear of breaking his attention if I moved, and my euphoria would end. This also meant I wasn't breathing, so I sipped shallow breaths, hoping he wouldn't notice. Every now and again he produced a soft, deep chuckle that would vibrate against my skin. This game was unfair, he clearly knew how he affected me, but continued – relentless.

"Lucy," he murmured, tilting my head to one side as he pressed his lips to the hollow at the base of my throat.

"Lucy," he whispered again, as he kissed the side of my neck, trailing his lips along my skin. My shallow panting abandoned, my chest rose and fell, deepening with my breaths.

"Lucy." His lips slipped along my neck until they lingered beneath my earlobe. Now not touching me at all he repeated, "Lucy. Lucy. Lucy."

My skin had raised in goose flesh, my heart thumped out his name, and I floated around in a vortex of rapture with no means or will to escape. His breath was warm as it swirled across my skin in delicate rings. With intentions clear as he turned my face to his, I reached up and wove my fingers into his hair, entranced, wholly lost in his eyes.

"Gil" I sighed, on the brink of pleasure.

"Gil?" the voice questioned.

Only *that* voice didn't belong to Gil.

My eyes snapped open.

"Yuck!" Liberty straightened up. "Lucy that's gross. What the hell were you dreaming about?" She skulked across the room, slumping down into my desk chair. "I'm not Gil."

"I can see that, can't I?" I deflected, kind of angry. Not so much with Liberty, more circumstance, being prematurely ripped from the welcoming lips of Gil, even if it was a dream. "What are you doing here anyway? I thought you were going to that horse thing in Kalispell with Ruben."

"I did Lou ... yesterday. Remember?" Liberty looked more confused than I was. "Geez, no wonder you couldn't come to the phone."

I quickly calculated. Apparently today was Sunday, *right*, so I had in fact slept clear through Saturday.

Holy Crap! How did that happen? Why didn't anybody wake me? Or warn me, for that matter?

Liberty up-ended my pencil case and began doodling.

What else had I missed?

I needed a minute to compose myself, so I fluffed about the bed covers, pummeling my pillow with a little too much vigor.

"Nice job," Liberty said, leaning her elbow on my desk and raising her eyebrows as feathers shot out from the end of my beaten pillow.

"Oh, give it a rest Liberty, I was asleep." I thought she was still referring to my dream, she corrected me by flipping her middle finger. I tossed back the covers and swung my legs over the edge of the bed. There was a shared look of humility as we both burst out laughing, doubling over.

"Ouch!" I flinched, I was sore.

In an instant, my head was filled with hazy images. The full moon, an ancient athame glistening under its light. Four glass jars smashing, their contents spilling across the dirt floor of our cellar. Dana, arms aloft and black robe swirling. Brilliant white light mixed with blasting chimes. Thick vapor billowing from an upturned caldron. Pain. Mathilda and Abigail, their faces smiling and laughing. Shadows dancing across the brick walls. Flames. Agony. Flowing luminous silver liquid. Peace.

"Oh yeah," I muttered, checking my hands for shining silver remnants.

Had it all been some bizarre dream? There were too many aches to call Friday night's events anything close to a dream.

"It's okay," Liberty said as she picked up my prize teddy bear from the desk and threw it at me, hard. "I understand, but the guy's my brother right."

The bear landed on the bed next to me. I picked it up, fluffing the fur around its cute button nose, smiling to myself.

"Hey," Liberty said, swiveling around and around on my desk chair. "I see your Mom's alright."

"Yeah, not what she thought, just a migraine. Probably overloaded with excitement." It was a straight out lie, but it was the cover that my family had agreed on; that much I could remember. Partially true, easy to remember, kept clean to be retold. The way a 'tall tale' had to be told to be believed. "She hasn't had one so bad in ages."

"Well, your Mom said the phone has been ringing again today. She thought she'd spoken to practically everyone in town yesterday," Liberty reported matter-of-factly. She had stopped swiveling in one direction and was winding up to swing back the other way. "They say you should always spin in both directions, you know, some Kinesiology crap."

Ignoring her, I was still confused as to why I'd been left to sleep for so long.

I knew I had a lot to catch up on. Grilling the twins for information was a priority! There were too many gray areas from Friday night.

"Yes Lib." I jumped up, catching the back of the chair as it swung around in front of me, "and some people shouldn't spin at all."

She laughed as she fell from the chair and I tickled her sides – her Achilles' heel.

Within seconds, Liberty spat out, "Okay, okay."

Liberty pulled herself back onto the chair. "Well, it's ten o'clock, sleepy head. We better go before we have to give up altogether on the ride Lou." She began tapping her fingers on the desk before settling to examine the photographs on my cluttered shelves, lingering on her outright favorite: an artistic shot my mother had taken of my father just after their marriage.

"What, ten?" I faltered, "Oh shoot Lib. I'm so sorry, my birthday ride. I was supposed to be at yours hours ago." I had completely forgotten the trek into the mountains Liberty had organized for my birthday. Regaining my composure, I raced to my clothes hamper, located my favorite jeans and shimmied into them, buttoning up under my nightshirt. "Guess I over did it watching out for Mom Friday night."

"Yeah, guess you did," she said handing me a shirt from the floor. "But what kept you up last night? Oh wait, after this morning's effort, I don't really want to know." She doubled over laughing, repeating 'Gil, Gil' in the same tone that I imagined I had used in my sleep this morning.

I flushed red, which only furthered her amusement. "Okay, I guess I deserved that one," I said.

Dashing into the bathroom, I fought on my shirt then splashed cold water on my face. *Get it together*. I didn't want to disappoint Liberty any further so I decided to abandon my thoughts of the initiation and, hesitantly, Gil. Cancelling today to begin my interrogations was totally out of the question.

Ting ... ting ... ting.

"What the ... ?" I began, my chimes pleasantly pealing. I tripped over my own feet, double taking at my reflection in the bathroom mirror. I didn't look my usual 'plain' self. Well, I still looked exactly like me, but now distinctive.

What was it? I leaned in closer to the mirror, turning my head from side to side, then up and down. I couldn't put my finger on it. I looked like I had been tweaked, a subtle photoshop.

First to catch my attention were my eyes. Although they were the same unusual turquoise they'd always been, they now shone with a steeled quality. "Whoa!"

"Everything alright in there?" Liberty called from my room.

"Yep, fine," I lied, "Water's just a bit cold this morning."

I continued with my inspection, all the while aware of the melodic accompaniment inside my head.

Although the tiny burn scar above my left ear, acquired from my scuffle with a hot curling iron was still there, my skin looked clearer than it ever had before, as if I had just scrubbed the daylights out of it. *Drinking all that water must be paying off.* As I pulled a comb through my usually unruly hair, I couldn't help but notice how much more manageable it was this morning. I twisted my ponytail forward and examined it – definitely softer and smoother with a healthy shine. *Abi,* such a sneak for making me use that pomegranate wash. It probably did have a 'special' ingredient in it.

There was something else. I stepped backwards to take in more of my reflection, turning this way and that, then tugged at my shirt, distracted every now and again by the severity of my eyes.

My mirror image gave the appearance of a taller, leaner and more impressive girl than I was. Had the bathroom mirror been replaced? No, it was still me, but where before I had looked a little blurred around the edges, I took on a fresher, clearer dimension, a sharpness I'd never really seen before. Considering Liberty and I had been conversing for the past 15 minutes, and she hadn't commented on my appearance, maybe it wasn't that noticeable.

Or maybe I'm just seeing things!

I had a lot to contend with after Friday night so maybe, just maybe, I had overloaded and begun to hallucinate.

"That's it!" I resigned. Now, along with hearing things, I was also seeing things.

"I thought we were going?" Liberty said impatiently.

"Yep, just grabbing a few things to take." Entering my room, I dashed to my bedside table and shoved on a baseball cap and a pair of sunglasses before Liberty had a chance to look at me. I stuffed an extra set of clothes and a jacket into my backpack and fronted her, confident that I was adequately masked. Liberty glared at me.

"Lucy, are you– "

"Ready to go, absolutely," I said. "How did you get here anyhow?"

"Gil dropped me on his way to see Lani." She smiled, an unusual thing for her to do while speaking about Lani. Normally she screwed her face up when she mentioned Gil's girlfriend. "Funny, you must have known." She wrapped her arms around herself and muttered "Gil, Gil." Now I understood why she was smiling. *Cow.*

"Well lucky you got off my bed when you did!" I deflected, winking then punched her on the arm.

"Oh no, Lucy that's just plain nasty." She covered her ears singing *la, la, la*.

From the golden-grassy flats of the Daniels's cattle paddocks arose the northern mountains of the majestic Swan Range, like some mythical humped beast emerging from calm waters. The area had been Liberty's playground for her entire life. In fact, all of the Daniels children had been lost on this range at one time or another. They always found their way back home. The peaks were in their blood. Liberty's great, great grandparents led pack strings across the range, preparing to guide big-game hunters into the untamed mountainous areas.

Open season brought countless stories of prize fish, Bull elk and huge Grizzlies, told around the campfire on many a seasonal night when we'd camped out with Liberty's father, Cleaver Daniels. He was a king among story tellers, scaring Liberty and me to our wits ends. Our camp nights kept us forever retelling the tales, though we could never tell them the way Cleaver did.

Cleaver often needed a night under the stars to clear his head, ground himself, and re-awaken his appreciation for all that he had. The boys would usually go with their Dad. Some nights all of them went, and some nights Cleaver had just one companion by his fire. Often that single companion was Ruben, the eldest son, the one destined to take over the ranch.

The scene was a familiar one that day, when my mother ushered Liberty and I out of the Mustang at the stables for our ride, Ruben was lunging a large Appaloosa.

"Call me when you get back and someone will come pick you up, OK?" My mother craned her neck to see Ruben in action. "Would you look at that … amazing!" she added. The horse reared up as if on cue.

I shoved Liberty forward, "I'll see you later." With my mind in another place, I was scrambling to get to the stables and Gil, if he was about.

"Be careful today girls." Dana pulled the car into drive and began up the road to the house. Dana and Ella were good friends, always dropping in for a chat, although today Mrs Daniels had requested to see Mom.

As Mom and I only had a quick minute alone, she hadn't had a chance to fill me in on much, opting only to warn me that even though my new world was exciting, I had to go slowly, with much observation.

Slightly on edge at the thought, I walked through the enormous red barn to the open arena on the opposite side, spying our horses. I grinned to myself whenever I saw Liberty's huge brazen painted horse Zeke and my little trail pony Smokey lined up next to each other. Smokey couldn't have been more different if he'd been pink with purple spots. A good three hands shorter than Zeke, Smokey possessed

Mabon

none of his beauty. He was a sturdy, but scruffy old gray horse. I didn't care about his looks, he possessed the gentlest nature, just what a novice rider like me needed. He was 'my horse', not that he had been given to me, but he was kind of reserved for me, no one else rode him and I adored him. Liberty owned several horses but Zeke was her favorite. One eye was brown and the other translucent light blue, which made his appearance menacing. Nothing could have been further from the truth – Zeke was a big softie.

Riding was an innate skill for Liberty, teaching me to ride was not. It wasn't that I disliked horses, it just took me a while to get the hang of riding … and horses.

My first camp out night with the Daniels clan celebrated six months of riding lessons. It turned out to be a bit of a party with all of the family coming along, even Ella, who would normally leave such nights to her boys.

I fondly remembered this night as my first real introduction to Gil, and wow, had I been impressed. Fortunately the fire burned all night, masking my continuous blush. Unavoidable considering Gil spent most of the night sitting next to me.

Simply hanging out with Gil had been so easy from the start. We talked and laughed and even shared a few secrets. Well, Gil had. Liberty had asked him to 'play' for them. At first he had drifted over the question and continued talking, taking the conversation in another direction. The second time Liberty was more direct, saying that he was too embarrassed to play as there was a 'newbie' in camp. I think the comment had embarrassed me more than Gil. He simply jumped up, grabbed the guitar case from his saddle and messed up Liberty's hair as he passed. I on the other hand, was blushing so hard I had a face full of fire.

Gil played well, Flamenco – a Spanish style. That night, I was enchanted by a stunning piece, a soul-captivating serenade made all the more attractive by the man plucking the guitar strings, and those of the heart wedged deep within my chest. I watched every tiny inflection of his handsome features with such strong desire. The way his lip would curl up on one side as he encountered a difficult riff. The way he nodded his head in encouragement as the notes flowed effortlessly from his fingers. The slight adjustment he would make with his shoulders, his arms bringing the guitar neck closer to his face.

Every now and again Gil would close his eyes when the music reached certain notes, not only did this emphasize the piece he was playing, but it also delighted me to see him experiencing his passion.

I had fallen so deeply in that moment, I found it near impossible to tear my eyes away. I prayed I wasn't drooling or something unsightly. Thankfully, no one had noticed the little red-haired shy girl burning, in the midst of her first true feelings of profound love and desire – thick and greedy.

The atmosphere of the open sky, the fire and the captivating music made this a magical experience of a different kind for me. I was moved in two distinctly different directions, one of love and one of loss. I knew that my family would possibly have been similar if my father had lived, not in the musical way, but I thought that we too would have had such moments of unity.

We were both surprised to see Zeke and Smokey saddled

and ready for our outing, until Liberty piped up saying something about Ruben's apology for not being able to come with us.

I walked to Smokey's side, patting him gently on the neck as he swung his head around to snuffle at my pocket. He knew I always had sugar cubes. They were my security blanket and I felt in control as long as I could keep Smokey happy with little treats. He slobbered a cube from my hand and softly crunched it. My hand was drenched with thick gluey saliva. "Smokey, what's the deal?" I mumbled, wiping my hand down the front of my jeans.

"Oh good, I see you got my apology for missing today's ride hey?" Ruben rounded Smokey referring to the slobber. We shared a laugh as he eyed me over suspiciously. "You're not still getting over Friday night's party are you? Hiding behind those huge sunnies?" He moved around trying to see my eyes through the sides of my sunglasses.

"No, just sun protection," I answered – it was partially true.

"Well you'll need it today. Look, I've got to go." Ruben nudged me with his elbow. Aside from being a caring brother to Liberty, he was also a businessman. "The boys are having some trouble moving the calving heifers to paddock four."

"Do you need me to help?" Liberty asked.

"No, no. You girls go on. It's nothing that the boys and I can't handle," Ruben said, referring to his younger brothers Gil, Ethan and Aiden, as he tugged at the Appaloosa's halter, urging him to move forward. "You girls be safe up there today. How far are you going and when will you be back?" he called over his shoulder.

"You know already," Liberty shouted. "Back around five."

Ruben halted and swung around so quickly his horse reared up. "Whoa, sorry boy. Lib, isn't Gil going with you?"

All the blood drained from my face.

"No," she mumbled, "Lani."

"Oh, great. Some help he'll be today," Ruben returned.

Liberty, flipping to serious again, said, "Are you sure you don't need me?"

"We'll be fine. You guys just be careful up there," Ruben said, quickly adding, "Lib, you got your gun right?"

Liberty patted the rifle tucked behind her saddle and winked.

I rounded on Liberty as Ruben headed into the barn.

"Before you yell at me, I was trying to make up for your birthday." Her eyes dropped to the ground as she kicked at the dirt. "Look Lucy, I know I shouldn't be saying this cause you know how I don't like to get involved, but … well … I'm pretty sure Gil likes you."

"Huh? How come you've never told me this before?" I asked, floored.

"You've never asked me."

Her answer was right on. I had never asked her because I valued our friendship and knew that a relationship with Gil could overlap but never mix.

Liberty shook my arm. "Don't read too much into it, alright? I can't confirm anything. I just know Gil. He's different when he's around you. He's Gil, but when Lani turns up, he's weird, like he's at her beck and call."

In awed silence I stood, flummoxed by this new snippet

of information. Happy, elated even, but now totally confused and unsure of how to proceed.

"You're sure he's not here?" I asked.

"No Lou," Liberty shook my arm again. "Don't go getting all funny on me now."

All of a sudden I was in an enormous hurry to get out of there, buoyed along by the unnerving notion that Gil may walk around the corner of the barn at any given second.

I kicked up a gear. "OK Lib, let's go." I scrambled onto Smokey urging him into a trot before Liberty had even placed a boot in Zeke's stirrup.

"That's the spirit!" Liberty called out after me. "Hey, maybe you should wait up a minute though." Liberty's voice was lost on the wind as Smokey cantered toward the arena's side gate. "Lucy, you're going the wrong way."

"Luccccccccy."

VII

About an hour into our ride, Liberty began asking some weird questions, about fashion and girly stuff of all things.

"What's an 'up-do'?" she muttered, throwing a quick glance over her shoulder.

"A what?" I chuckled.

"I know you heard me. What is it?" Liberty's tone was harsh, the way it gets when she's startled or embarrassed. I defended myself from flying branches as we rode single file – the thought hit me that she may have been doing this on purpose.

"Why are you asking me this Lib?" I deflected another flying branch.

"Can't you answer the question?" She huffed, as another branch flew past me. I ducked just in time.

"Sure," I pulled Smokey to a stop, allowing a gap to form between us. "It's a hairstyle. You know, when girls with long hair have it styled up on their heads for an event, like Prom or something." I paused. "I don't think your hair could be put …" I gulped. I'd never known Liberty to comment about beauty related things, even with the social media push to be perfect. "Did someone ask you to the dance?"

"No, no … I'm just curious is all."

I knew this was a big, fat lie. "Liberty, it's me you're talking to. How cool!" I knew Liberty could clam up quickly, so I trod carefully. "I could do your hair if you wanted, that is if you don't want to go into town to have it done?"

"I saw a sign in town and just wanted to know what it was, that's all." She urged Zeke into a trot as we broke into an open meadow. "Let's go up to the right, cross the stream and come back down to the pond."

Liberty had clammed up, and I knew when to leave well enough alone.

Riding through this part of the forest was serene. The ranges were exceptional, and there was no better way to experience them than from the saddle of a plodding horse.

The past year and a half of riding had been uneventful for me. When it came to the scary wildlife this area had to offer, I'd been spared. Sure I had seen the odd bear or cat print in the snow during the last snowdrifts of the season, but I had never encountered the real thing and was happy about that fact. Liberty on the other hand, prayed for an encounter.

She was tough, she had to be with four older brothers. A fighter with the scars to prove the warrior she was, although these were not the scars from a backyard sibling brawl.

Liberty had been attacked.

She'd dismounted her horse and unknowingly cornered a 180 pound mountain lion. All the Daniels are trained to handle such situations, but the male lion was wounded and threatened. Liberty sustained considerable scarring to her legs and the back of her neck. Luckily she'd been out riding the ranges with Ruben that day. His quick thinking saved her life. Ruben had set rules to follow if we were riding in the mountains: always with a companion, and always with a rifle.

I couldn't carry a gun or shoot but Liberty competed. I imagined after the attack she saw that mountain lion in her Ruger's sight every time she looked through it.

There had been another reason for the guns and shooting practice.

A Grizzly.

Reported sightings of a large brown bear had been on the increase over the last two seasons in the lower ranges. This bear didn't seem to move back onto the highlands after winter. Somehow, it had evaded the ranger's removal tactics and had still managed to attack and fatally wound a hiker the previous summer season. The rangers ended up giving locals a free ticket to shoot it on sight.

The Daniels's cattle had been terrorized of late by something and there was no second guessing as to what the creature was. After seeing the aftermath of one attack personally, I understood why this type of bear was titled so. Dead cow parts had littered the paddock, with an unknown number of cows counted in the mess.

The financial effect these 'attacks' were having on the Danielses had begun to show when they were losing up to seven cows a week, sometimes in calf. Working with the rangers lately, Ruben had tried trapping and baiting through the lower ranges that backed onto the Daniels's property, to no avail.

The competition between the Daniels and the Grizzly was intense, and protecting a ten kilometer property line was nearly impossible, so Ruben would often move the cattle from paddock to paddock trying, in vain, to save them from this conniving beast.

The Swan Range would appear a place full of peril for two girls to be riding out alone, but on horseback, and with Liberty armed with her precious Ruger, I felt safe.

On most days during the summer months, Liberty and I would wander the ranges on horseback. It was difficult to decide where we would venture as both Liberty and I had our own 'special' spots.

Some days we would sketch and chat, some days were silent.

As it was my birthday present, I could have sworn blue that we would be heading to my all time favorite spot, above Lake Blaine, but Liberty had another idea in mind.

I was hungry by the time Liberty tugged Zeke to a sharp stop just ahead of me. Smokey pulled even, and the picturesque cove came into full view. A small rock overhang, polished smooth by the constant trickle of water flowing over it, served as a natural spout, pouring fresh mountain water into the crystal pond below. The pond shallowed onto a narrow black pebble beach. Its aqua waters eddied around larger chunks of rock that had broken away from the hillside above, smashing their way down the avalanche chute and ending their rumbling travels in the pond below.

"Wow Lib. I thought for sure you'd take me to Wildcat today." I slapped her on the arm. "How did this one escape us?"

"I didn't think this particular creek ran this far down from Lamoose. Ruben and I stumbled on it the other day," she replied.

After dismounting, Liberty and I walked the horses

through a short chute of bear grass at the end of its seasonal bloom. White flower heads waved faint sticky fragrance as we passed down to a clearing beside the pond.

The towel flopped backward as I tried in vain to wedge the end under the folds around my head. *Damn silky hair.* As I twirled the towel around my head for a second attempt, I noticed the scrutiny I was under. Liberty, who, after toweling off, was leaning against a nearby rock. "I don't know exactly what it is about you that's different, but something is," she said, tousling her hair with one hand.

"If you really must know, the twins got to me on Friday night while we were watching over Mom, part of my birthday present." Another lie.

After shedding my wet hat, clothes and sunglasses to dry, I could barely believe what I was seeing.

Tweaked.

My arms and legs appeared more muscular, and my skin had a fresh look, kinda shiny. I had been waiting for Liberty's questions, and brainstorming some answers during lunch. The best I could come up with, that at least fit some of the criteria, was that my sisters had given me a long awaited 'make-over'. "Besides, you know I've been trying to eat better, not so much crap," I continued.

"Why didn't you just say that? Your sisters have been dying to pin you down for a make-over forever. I just wish I'd been there to see it." Liberty giggled, relaxing back and closed her eyes.

The sun warmed our bodies after the chilly dip. We hadn't planned a swim but today was unseasonally hot, and we had joked around until I'd 'accidentally' pushed Liberty in, merely seconds before joining her – clothes and all.

"I didn't want to make a big deal out of it you know, but it's hard to get anything past you and Ruben," I said, shaking my head vigorously. "No," I winced, "it can't be."

"What's wrong?" Liberty asked, one eye open.

"No nothing, I just thought a wasp or something had caught in my hair," I said.

I was leveling up in lying. Was that a good thing?

Liberty returned to her former post.

Ting … ting … ting.

There they were again, a faint tinkling of chimes in my head, barely making sound, which was why I questioned myself. I had also begun to relate these chimes to incidents of magickal bearing, an alarm that told me I needed to be alert. I whipped my head around, scanning both directions. Nothing. Ringing softly, I wondered if they worked in some strange volume-equated-danger-intensity manner. I walked over to Liberty, continuing to examine our surrounds and began pulling on the extra jeans and t-shirt I had packed.

"Hey?" I hoped Liberty would be more open to this line of conversation now that we'd swum and eaten and chatted about other stuff. "Can I ask you a question without you flipping out?"

"Depends on what you're going to ask me, doesn't it?" She didn't move a muscle.

"That's not fair," I joked. "I share everything with you." I wrapped my arms about myself in a hug that she could only see from the back, moving my hands up and down as if being groped. "Clearly whether I like it or not!"

She giggled, pulling her extra clothes from her saddle bag. "Okay, okay. What do you want to know?"

"I want to know if it was Eddy Geiger who asked you to the Fall dance?" I spat out.

"What? No," Liberty began.

"Because I've been waiting for Ash Dresden to ask me," I said. Her mouth hung open. "We could double date, you know, them being best friends, and all," I concluded.

Liberty was silent as she finished dressing. I could tell she was displeased but Eddy was a great guy and they clearly liked each other; neither of them would make the first move.

"Well?" I glared at her. "Did he?"

"I was going to ask him," Liberty mumbled. I could have sworn there was a cheeky smile beginning to lift the corners of her mouth.

Zeke's abrupt snort alerted us to movement about fifty yards above, in the tree line. It was a massive brown bear and it hadn't seen us at that point, but it was standing on its back legs, sniffing at the air. It wouldn't take long before it caught sight of us.

I was petrified, tingling all over from a surge of adrenaline.

"On my say, run to Smokey and jump on quick," Liberty whispered. "Grizzly." Her face turned white. "My gun … it's on Zeke." My heart ripped through my ribcage and dove into my stomach. The horses were grazing a mere twenty yards or so away. Could we make the distance?

It's true on a track surface that a horse would easily outrun a bear, but here in the ranges where the ground was uneven and littered with outcropping rocks, it would be hard for the horse to keep its footing.

Mabon

Liberty turned back toward the bear, her hand squeezing mine. The bear was nosing around an area we had swum to, not half an hour ago. He was preoccupied with our scent.

"Go," she whispered.

I ran.

My heart and head pounded, and my legs willed the rock strewn ground to become even.

I ran.

My mind raced through the possible outcomes, highlighting the worst results. What if this Grizzly reached us before we reached the horses? What if the horses broke free? The bear would have us for sure, well me anyway, Liberty could run like lightning. Would I die quickly or would the bear simply play with me the way it had some of the Daniels's cattle, leaving me in agony from missing body parts?

'Stop it at once.'

The voice sounded furious and I was startled at first.

'Don't think, just run.'

We were close. The horses were visibly agitated, but hadn't moved. And although my lungs were at explosion point, I realized that Liberty hadn't passed me. I jumped for Smokey clambering into the saddle before whipping around to find Liberty. She scrambled up a rock next to Zeke and dove onto his back, searching her saddle as she landed.

There was no sign of the bear.

"He's still here somewhere," Liberty said as she de-holstered the 12 gauge. It was loaded. "What are you doing? Move!" she screamed at me, slapping Smokey hard on the hindquarters, forcing him into action.

An action that didn't last long.

As Smokey rounded the first tree and headed into the clearing, there was a loud thud as he was hit with force by the bear. It knocked him off balance but didn't knock him down, and by some ridiculous stroke of luck, it hadn't unseated me either.

The Grizzly had Smokey trapped, backed into a rocky corner; a granite coffin.

Its eyes as black as night, projected evil. It gnashed its razor sharp teeth together, and clawed at the air.

The bear lunged forward, swiping at Smokey. Smokey reared up, hooves pounding in defense.

I held fast. My chimes had returned at full volume, deafening me.

Another swipe, and Smokey jumped sideways. I lost my footing, swinging around on the saddle, and coming face-to-face with ripped flesh. The bear had made contact.

No. I scrambled around on the saddle gripping for my life when the growl that followed was particularly nasty. As the Grizzly slashed again, I looked deep into its eyes.

What's that?

My breath escaped me as it lunged forward for its final strike.

Liberty stood behind the bear, the 12 gauge tucked snuggly against her shoulder; her prize tagged in the focus.

Bang.

A single blast spun the bear sideways, crippling it long enough for Smokey to take off with everything his trail pony body could muster.

Bang.

Mabon

We whipped across the clearing as a second gunshot ripped the silence, echoing. Ten seconds later there was a third almighty CRACK, the loudest yet.

Liberty?

Intuition hinted that she was okay, but there was something different about that bear. I'd recognized something but couldn't put my finger on what. I had to go back, help Liberty, but Smokey had bolted and was approaching a rocky outcrop along the narrow ridge. He was bleeding and frantic. He jumped, clearing the outcrop and galloped onward. Nothing I did seemed to stop him. At best I could hold on and hope he would slow of his own accord. I didn't thinking falling at this speed would be painless. Winding in and out of trees, my face whipped by branches, over fallen logs, Smokey raced, and I couldn't do a thing but watch in fear as my recognition of the area grew dimmer.

Lost.

I was sure that Smokey could find his way home, so all I had to do was hold on. I tried speaking to him in hushed and comforting tones, gently pulling at the reins as I did so, but at first it seemed to make him go faster.

Shortly he began to falter, his legs not carrying him as they should, more like some clumsy dance. I eased back on the reins as he began to give me his head. We slowed, eventually stopping, his will and body broken.

"Smokey, it's okay boy," I lied, dismounting to check his wounds. Blood gushed, soaking his legs and mine from the huge gash in his flank. I wasn't sure what to do.

Hopelessly looking around for something or someone to help me, I remembered my cell. I had stashed it in my pocket after dressing at the pond. "Damn," I cried out, *no signal*. Murphy's Law. Smokey danced backward a few paces, snorting and threw up his head. "What is it?" I whispered, *please no more trouble*. His eyes darted around.

He jolted forward, ripping the reins from my hands. The force threw me backward through the brush. I slid and slid and slid.

VIII

"Lucy."

The familiar voice echoed through the brush line above me. Was I losing my grip on reality, as well as on the rocks I clung to? My fingers, numb from their grip, were beginning to show a faint-blue tinge as the hours rolled on. I wasn't sure how long I'd been stuck down the avalanche chute, and I wasn't sure how far I'd fallen. There was a rocky outcrop a few yards above me and a slither of one below, wide enough for me to stand and grip whatever I could.

"Hello?" I called out. I had to be sure I wasn't imagining this voice. *Gil's voice.*

"Where are you?"

"Here," I paused for a response, looking up the rise from where I had fallen. "I'm ... down here."

The bushes on the outcrop above rustled casting shards of rock and leaves down on top of me. "Below you, be careful!" I put my head down and clutched tighter as the debris fell.

"Are you hurt?" Gil was standing on top of the outcrop above. He didn't look thrown when he spotted me.

"Just a few scratches." My voice wavered, I was so tired.

"Lucy you have to listen to me." His voice was soothing, going against the grain of my predicament. "I'm going to throw down a rope." The rope's end slapped onto the rocks next to me. "Now, you'll have to tie it around your waist."

"You're kidding right?" It was more sigh than disbelief.

"Lucy, you can do this." Gil was unwavering in his command. I fumbled the rope around my waist, trying to jam the end under my arm.

"No, this won't work," I called out.

"Slow down and try again." His face was far calmer than my thoughts.

I took a breath in, readjusted my hands, then lost my footing on the narrow ledge below but scrambled for the rope, steadying myself.

I can't hold on.

Vertigo dimmed my vision. The rope slipped through my fingers. "Gil!"

"Lucy, Lucy." His voice soothed. "Stay with me."

I became aware that my hand was touching Gil's face. One muscular arm hugged tight around my listless body, and the other was snuggly coiled in rope. *How had he gotten to me so fast?*

Gil smiled, "I've got you. Up Jack."

We lurched upwards, scraping along the rock face a few yards. "C'mon boy, up Jackal." Gil's tone was firm, as more ground slid below us.

When we'd been pulled to the safety of a leveled spot, we lay clinging together, trying to catch our breath. It had the beginnings of a cold night, yet as I shivered all I could think about was what I had nearly achieved – Gil and I plunging down an avalanche chute to our deaths.

Idiot. "I'm so sorry." The tears began. "You could have been killed."

"So could you." Gil rolled up onto one elbow. "Did you honestly expect me to leave you out here?" His hand, covered in blood from the twists and turns of the rope, touched my cheek. "Libs would have been pissed if I couldn't find you."

I spattered a giggle through faint sobs, picturing Liberty's scowl. "Ouch". Gil's face broke into a wide beaming grin.

"Oh Liberty … is she okay?" I begged. It had been hours since I had seen her. The image of her blasting the bear with her 12 gauge flashed before my eyes. My breathing quickened.

"She's just fine, killed the bear. Pretty impressive, and Ruben's one hundred percent sure it was the Grizzly we were after," he said, placing his hands behind his head. "She searched for you for a while, but realized she needed help with evening coming on, so she got down to the Brook's and called home for help. Just about everyone is out here searching for you. I'd better text Ruben again." He sat up and searched through his pockets, finding his cell. "Sometimes the signal's a bit weak up here, let me check." He concentrated on his phone for a moment. "Trusty old phone. I'd better tell them we have to stay up here tonight. We're not stumbling down through the mountains in the dark." His fingers frenzied at the keyboard, sending off a text. "Damn, the signal is so weak."

"Oh my Mom. She'll be so worried." I lay rigid, too zapped to sit up.

"I'm sure Ruben's told your mom. Don't worry, they know you'll be safe up here with me." His thumbs were still busy on the key pad, trying again to send the message through.

Then it struck me – I would be staying up here, on the mountain, all night, *alone, with Gil.*

The breath sucked from my lungs.

"Now that Grizzly's dead, they won't be so concerned," Gil added. "Besides I've got Smith with me and Ruben knows that."

"Who's Smith?" I leant up on one elbow, I was curious, I hadn't realized there was someone with Gil, although heading out on a search without a partner could be asking for more trouble, especially with Ruben and his 'companion' rule.

"Only my trusty Smith and Wesson."

The Daniels and the Swan Range had many things to teach me about living under the Big Sky.

"It's a long way down. I couldn't see how far before," I said, realizing what could have happened if I'd fallen further. I touched Gil's arm, tears clouding my sight as a rush of emotion surged, brought on by my traumatic day. "I need to tell you something."

"What is it?" Gil had pulled himself into a seated position.

Could I unveil my feelings now?

"I …" Beginning to feel the familiar flush of blood to my face, I looked away, turning my face into my grazed hands.

No, this isn't the right time.

I couldn't be sure, but I had to face facts: we were recovering from a high stress situation and Gil had simply done what anyone would have in the same circumstance.

Mabon

Keep telling yourself that and he'll never know.

"Lucy, it's okay." Gil turned my face to his. "You can thank me later, maybe when I have to muck out Jackal's stable," he chuckled, springing to his feet. "Ouch, that hurts."

"Sure Gil," I laughed. "Mucking out Jackal's stable is worth a saved life." Relieved that I'd paused, the situation would have been so awkward if my confession of love had been rejected, however polite Gil may have been about it.

"Stay here a minute. I'll check on Jack." Gil pushed his way through the rough undergrowth that surrounded us.

Gil had found me … was it luck? I didn't know, luck seemed so random and Gil had found me … Gil, the person I would most like to spend a night under the stars with. I'm not sure I wanted to call it luck, fate seemed much more appropriate.

"Look, it's getting too dark and I don't think you're in any condition to ride further," he said, breaking back through bushes. "There's a clearing a little way down toward the river. We'll camp there tonight."

"Okay. So what can I do to help?" Shrugging his shoulders, Gil untied Jackal, readjusted the stirrups on the saddle, then patted it, gesturing for me to climb on. Smokey was my cute little trail pony, Gil's steed Jackal was a completely different beast. He was an enormous purebred American Quarter horse, jet black with a regality complex and a massive power packed rear end. Amazing to behold when given the respect to be ridden correctly, as only Gil could do, but a real handful when he wanted his own way. I found Jackal down-right scary.

Clearly sensing my hesitation, Jackal swung his enormous

head around and nudged at my pocket. I'd forgotten that I'd pocketed some sugar cubes for Smokey after re-dressing from our swim.

Smokey!

"Gil," I ventured as he boosted me onto Jackal's saddle, both of us stifling pained gasps from the effort. "Did Smokey make it home? He was hurt real bad and I didn't know what to do."

"I don't really know how to tell you this …" Gil began with a tone that made me straighten in my seat. "I found Smokey."

"Oh, thank goodness." I couldn't explain how relieved I was.

"Wait. I'm so … Lucy …." Gil stopped Jackal and placed his hand on my leg, gripping it slightly. "He's dead."

"What?" I fell forward onto Jackal's neck, burying my face into his thick mane. It must have been the wound, he'd lost so much blood, and I hadn't known what to do, how to stop the blood. Then he'd just fled. I clamped my eyes shut, but the images of my poor pony, dead, kept flooding my mind.

"It will be okay. I hate to say this, but it's much better this way. He would have been in pain, there was so much blood loss. It would've been quick." He rubbed at my leg, which only made me sob more. "I'll come back up," he continued, "with the boys and bury him here, where he loved to be."

I was crushed, the tears were flowing and I didn't care. I was a curse to the Daniels family. If I wasn't out killing one of their favorite horses, I was trying to throw one of their sons down an avalanche chute.

I would be banned for life, for sure.

IX

Gil sat motionless, the fire's light washing wave after golden wave across his chiseled face. His jade eyes sparkled. Knowing a direct ogle would embarrass him, every now and then I stole quick glances, each time adding something newly observed to the image that sat prominent in my mind.

The sharp curve of his jaw.

The high arch of his brow.

Those long lashes.

I felt sneaky, and my heart skipped with each glance, but I simply couldn't help myself. I'd experienced a slight physical change on the night of my initiation and this change seemed to have naturally flowed across into my emotions – heightening them. I felt more intensely for Gil than I'd ever thought possible. Although I adored him, I would never disclose my true feelings to him unless I was sure he felt something in return. And even though Liberty had confessed her inklings about Gil's feelings for me, rejection from this new height would only prove impossible to recover from.

We sat together, but not too close. Gil had fashioned a log stool for me, while he lay, sprawled across the blanket roll he normally kept attached to Jackal's saddle. Meanwhile, munching loudly on some grass, Jackal snorted, breaking our concentrated silence.

"Gil?" I started.

Bowled over by his direct gaze, I swallowed hard and continued, "Gil?"

"Yes Lucy." His eyes flicked back down to his cell, still trying to send the last message to Ruben.

I was thankful for the fire's light camouflaging my pink cheeks. "Well, I wanted to formally thank you, I mean, who knows when or if I would have been found if you hadn't have come along."

"I'm just glad I found you alive. This area is notorious for it. Don't you remember that guy in June last year who walked clear off Mt Aeneas?" He looked down appraising the damage to his hands as he spoke, turning them over individually. "You're lucky it was nothing worse than a few scratches."

Jackal snorted again, this time jerking his head up. Gil rose to settle his favored ride, cradling his head and speaking to him in hushed tones – something soothing in Spanish, Gil's second language. Jackal calmed down. Gil returned, this time finding a spot directly across the fire.

He sat, stretched back on a nearby rock, inviting. I'm sure it wasn't his intention to appear this way, but then again I found everything that Gil did seductive. He could pick a big wad of food out from his teeth and I would find it seductive. Gross, but seductive. I tried not to look at him straight on, yet was damned, finding the pull of his intense gaze far too hypnotic to ignore.

Mabon

"Lucy, what happened to you?" he asked.

"I thought I'd already told you." I fidgeted with a strand of hair, twirling it over and over in both hands as I spoke, diverting my eyes. "OK, Liberty and I were swimming at this new ..." A throaty grumble interrupted my speech.

"You *have* already told me that part," he interjected. "Let me rephrase. What has happened to *you*?" He gestured at me with his hand, waving it up and down.

"I don't understand." Another fat white lie. I knew exactly what he was referring to. From the second I'd heard his voice, I knew I'd have trouble. But after having the entire day, with most of it stuck half way down an avalanche chute, I'd had enough time to think, and knew for certain it wouldn't be easy to get 'the new me' past Gil's critical appraisal.

"You, well, you look different," he spat the statement out, tossing his cell from hand to hand.

Crap.

I had to stick to the same angle – it appeared to fool Liberty and Ruben. I didn't want the secrets, not with Gil, but the other side of the argument held fast to historic fact. *No one* could know about my family, ever, *period*! If I wanted to be near Gil it was clear I had to find a way to keep my secret from him.

"It's nothing. Kind of embarrassing actually." I looked down to my hands still madly twirling the strand of hair.

"Try me," he said, stretching his arms up behind his head.

I bit my lip before a lustful sigh could escape, the heat from the fire like a cold shower in comparison to what my body alone was generating. His arms rippled with firm, tight muscles, highlighted in the glowing embers. The snug navy crew neck sweater he wore showed every inch of his powerful build – long hours of hard manual labor on the farm had carved a rugged physique. Beneath the navy cotton, glinted the reflective surface of the tarnished silver chain that Gil always wore around his neck. I had seen it many times before knowing it had been a gift from Lani when they had started going out. I loathed that chain yet loved it at the same time. I longed to be it, lying flat against his collar bone, touching the smooth bare skin of his torso, sliding over each muscular ripple.

Shameless.

I had to regain control. I dropped the hair strand and slapped at my jeans, removing invisible dust. "Gil, I'd rather not, it's girl stuff," I stated.

"OK, I just wanted to know how you've come to … er … look this different in two days." His eyes met mine directly and I glanced away. I had to, I'd seen a different expression in those eyes. *Could it be possible? Could Liberty be right? Could Gil actually harbor feelings for me too?* I fidgeted again with the same strand of hair, biting my lip, trying to smolder the fire raging inside.

"What? Are you keeping tabs on me now?" I said returning his look, fire with fire.

"No," he deflected. "It's just on Friday you looked one way and, well, now you look *another.*"

Before I could stop myself, I had thrown my face into both hands, trying in vain to hide. It was all part of the show I had to refine. "Oh God, I could kill the twins. I knew it looked terrible." After a minute or so, with no response from Gil, I peered out through a gap in my fingers. He was still staring, clearly waiting for an explanation. Surrendering to his gaze, I dropped my hands away, shaking my head. "They kinda gave me a make-over of sorts."

"Really, they did, did they?" Gil's stare and my 'white lie' made a terrible mix. I was expecting him to retaliate at any second. "You know I could have sworn there was something else to it." His eyes traced a long line up my body, sending shivers down my spine and a fresh surge of blood to my reddened face. I mirrored Gil's movement, crossing my arms over, almost a signal of surrender – I was being driven crazy without so much as a touch.

"What do you mean?" I shook my head.

"I don't know, you're taller or something. More confident maybe." His appraisal skimmed the surface, but he could never know. "Maybe it's something from the inside coming out."

"OK." I shrugged, shaking my head. "No, it's the same old me."

He didn't look convinced. "Don't get me wrong, I think you've always looked good but, tonight, even under the scratches and stuff, you look kinda striking."

Whoa ... was he kidding? What was happening here?

I looked away off into the darkness to some imaginary point, searching for an explanation that I hoped could save me from myself. I stretched my legs out, roughly rubbing them. All of my blood had appeared to have left my extremities, looking for other more 'yearning' places to boil.

OK ... calm down ... then answer.

"Thanks Gil. The girls must have done an okay job then?" I gave him a thumbs-up and crossed my legs over as

I stared into the fire – my deliberate unwavering gaze taking tremendous effort to maintain.

"Sure." From the corner of my eye I could see Gil was not convinced. He changed track, looking back down at his cell, still attempting a message to Ruben. "Anyway, use my blanket roll when you want to sleep. I'll sit here and keep an eye out."

I stretched up, pretending to need sleep when I truly could have sat there entertaining myself with my view of Gil for hours on end. "Yeah, I'm pretty exhausted now that you mention it. Sleep would be good," I yawned, standing up, as wobbly as a new born foal, then limped around to Gil's blanket roll. Lying down on my side, facing the fire, I knew that every movement I made was being watched. "So you'll be right there?" I asked, aware of the crisp clear night, stars blinding.

There was a long pause. I pushed myself up onto one elbow. Gil seemed preoccupied. I wondered if I'd confused him with my lies. He stood, walked over and sat next to me, resting again on a nearby slab of rock.

"I'll be right here." He tucked a piece of my hair behind my ear. It wasn't a brotherly gesture. I felt my face flush as his fingers traced a short way along my jaw. Liberty could be right about Gil, he'd been saying the right things all evening, but the price for a wrong guess was too high. If there was ever going to be an action to further our relationship, it would have to be Gil's doing. I would rather have him as a friend, than not at all. "You might have to move over soon though … I'm getting pretty tired myself." He pulled his knees up and rested his taut arms around them, letting his head fall forward.

"OK," I choked out, shuffling over to the edge of the blanket roll.

How could I sleep now? Every muscle in my body stiffened in anticipation. "Night then," I muttered.

"Night." He sounded strained, it had been an obscenely long day for both of us.

I must have drifted off to sleep, even with the irregular thumping of my heart in eagerness for the delicious moment when Gil laid next to me. I didn't remember a time that I had felt so exhausted yet so content.

"Lucy, wake up." I shivered as I felt a hand trailing through my hair and across my shoulder. "Lucy?"

With a jolt I was awake.

What time is it?

It was still dark. Gil was lying beside me, his body was warm and pressed against mine, with his arm around my waist. My heart skipped. Maybe I had plunged down the chute, taking Gil with me, and this was ... *Ouch*.

No, this was really happening I deduced after pinching myself.

It was the way in which Gil was leaning his body into mine that was suggestive. His arm wasn't draped over my body, like out of kindness to keep me warm ... it was clenched to my waist, pulling me back, hard against him. He was leaning up on one elbow, his lips inches from my ear as his breath blew across my cheek.

"Lucy, wake up," he whispered again.

Was this the sign I had been waiting for?

I was still unsure. Deciding not to shy away, I rolled to

snuggle further into his protective arms. If ever there was going to be a moment, I wanted it to be now.

"I'm awake Gil," I said, gazing up at his tanned face and into those hypnotic eyes, searching my very soul. If my intuition was wrong he would simply push me away and hopefully make light of the situation.

But he didn't.

For a very long minute, he *didn't* move at all.

We were so close, our faces inches from each other, yet both blind to the vortex of howling wind that swirled around us. His eyes moved to my lips as his finger tips followed his gaze, tracing a tingling path from my temple across my cheek bone. I closed my eyes as his fingers continued along my jaw line then a small, but tantalizing way down my neck.

I'd wanted this moment for so long. I was at my physical end, such a height of pleasure, that I barely noticed the crashing din of chimes echoing in my head. But the movement was subtle, the slight adjustment of his body and I knew before the words had formed.

"*No*," Gil whispered.

Then, there was nothing.

Just the whistling wind, rushing past my devastation.

I didn't want to open my eyes. The fresh sting of humiliation clamped the lids together tightly. My fear realized, I rolled onto my side away from him. I felt his trembling hand grasp my shoulder, lightly shaking me, sadness tainted his tone. "Lucy, I'm sorry." He was hard to hear above the rustling of the leaves that eddied around. I covered my face against the debris.

How had I allowed myself into the exact situation I had

fought to stay away from for the last two years? Damn heart. I struggled with the tears – they, beyond any other reaction, would let him know how I truly felt. Not that I hadn't just set myself up to fail.

"Lucy … please?" His voice raised with the wind's pitch and an urgency foreign to Gil, but I didn't dare look in those eyes. What do I say now? What do I do? How can I face him when I had just shown how clearly ready I was for this? How obvious my feelings were – for complete and utter rejection.

The howling wind halted in an unnatural fashion, floating leaves and debris dropped instantly from the night air. Jackal threw his head up, stamping his hooves on the dirt and whinnied, causing Gil to spring to his feet to comfort the panicking beast, which in turn broke my indulgent self loathing, only to realize that bells were clanging at full volume inside my head.

I curled up into a ball on my side, hands cupped over my ears.

No … not now, in front of Gil.

He would think I was having some kind of mental break down, and perhaps I was. Desperate to appear sane and hide the irrational riot that raged in my head, I knelt, eyes shut and tried to concentrate.

An unfamiliar word formed subconsciously then spun around in my thoughts.

Satis, satis, satis …

Enough, enough, enough …

I was willing the noise to silence with a word I had never heard before let alone spoken, like I was throwing an egg at a tornado. I felt lost in my new world, not having a chance to discuss my acquired 'talents' with my mother or sisters.

There was fair indication that my chimes were related to magickal workings as I had previously considered. I clocked back through my memory as best I could, recalling their development.

The first chiming emergence had been the dancing oak leaf. The second, during my initiation ritual. The third was the Grizzly attack. All three sessions had been different, but in all three instances, the chimes had begun before magick had occurred.

Were they a magickal warning or a warning of magick?

Concentrate, my thoughts wandered to Gil. Had he noticed yet? I squinted sideways through the pain, to see Gil still checking over Jackal in the campfire light, and with his attention drawn elsewhere I closed my hands over my face. I needed my wits about me, needed to quiet the din crashing around in my head and focus on what was *possibly* about to happen.

Satis, satis, satis ... I chanted over and over, and soon this new word became a tune of types, a melody of relief, soothing my mind and soul. Clarity invaded, slowly at first then gained momentum spreading throughout the corners of my mind.

Satis, satis, satis ... I could feel, hear and see again.

"Lucy, what are you doing?" Gil had finished with Jackal and was staring at me with an odd expression. "Look, it doesn't matter. I need you to understand, what happened before – "

Jackal snorted, tossing his huge head in the air, ruffling his mane as an aggressive quiver shot along his body.

"What is it Jack?" Gil moved backward a few steps allowing the horse his head.

It was apparent that Jackal was aware of something we hadn't yet perceived.

It happened in a split second.

"Watch out!" I screamed, unheard as the ferocious wind recommenced its savage riot.

Jackal reared up, mane flying, his lips curled back over his teeth, the struggle of terror evident in his eyes. He spooked, crashing into Gil and knocked him down. Gil's limp body was dragged yards before the reins caught over a jutting piece of granite, viciously snapping. The sound cracked like a gun shot and the last I saw of Jackal was his four white fetlocks disappearing into the night at an impressive rate.

I raced to Gil, throwing myself on the ground as I reached his side. He was unconscious. I positioned my body in front of his face, protecting him from wind-swept debris as I checked his pulse.

He was still alive, but there was blood pouring from a gash at the back of his head. The blood was hot and sticky on my fingers. My stomach turned.

Stop the blood.

Thoughts dashed ahead as my hands tore through the cotton shirt I had knotted around my waist at the pond, ripping long stretches of fabric and tying them together. I bundled up a piece of the fabric then, by feel, located the lesion, pushing the cloth along its length, and coiled the remaining strips as tightly as I could around Gil's head.

Don't die ... please Gil, don't die.

I had received my warning, my chimes rang it out

loud and clear, only I had not known how to decipher its message, and the result was Gil lying in front of me with his head smashed open. How could I want this apparent *gift* of inherent witchcraft? I didn't know how to use it.

Suddenly I was alone again in the wild.

I leaned over Gil pulling his body toward me, hugging him close, sobbing softly. He felt cool, as if his body temperature had dropped. I had to move him back over to the fire where I could wrap him in his blanket roll. Gil was taller than me and heavier. Surprised by my own strength, lifting him up under the arms, I dragged him backward. By the time I had positioned him on the blanket roll, we were again under attack from the violent gale. The force of it began to whip wreckage around the campfire. The fire's flames leapt in different directions. The danger of the fire *alone* was enough of a threat in a windstorm. I pulled the blanket up over Gil's head protecting him from the dirt and dust I kicked around to extinguish the flames. I could barely see.

The wind whipped about my hair and clothing, strong and undeniable, causing me to stumble as I raced back to Gil. I pulled the blanket back from his face to faintly make out the slight movement of his lips. I placed an ear close to his mouth, desperate to hear what he was mumbling, over the shriek of the vile wind. Something about *'Jackal'*, then something like *'not the right time'*, then nothing as he slipped back into his comatose state.

A hissing sound began behind me, like a red hot pan being immersed in cold water. Even with the stars and waning moon, now veiled by the swirling dust, I couldn't pinpoint the sound's origin, without the fire it was too dark.

I huddled over Gil's body, protecting him as best I could. The hissing grew louder then missiled, whizzing over my head. A large tree branch collided with the ground on the opposite side of Gil, missing his arm by inches and spraying us with dirt. I spluttered and coughed at the rising dust, Gil turned his head, still mumbling. Abruptly, the hissing began again in front of me, across the smoldering fire.

A shot of adrenaline pulsed under my skin. I felt anxious, edgy, I had to move. I sat Gil up, resting his head on my shoulder, and tried to lift him to stand. I wasn't sure that it would do any good, but it was worth a try, we had to get to shelter, away from this demented wind.

A crack and a small burst of light sent another tree branch hurtling toward us. It smacked into the ground, shattering where Gil's head had been only seconds before. These were no random assaults. I tried lifting Gil again and found that getting him to stand wasn't too hard, he was cooperative even in his dazed state. *Now where?* I was as likely to walk us down an avalanche chute again, as I was to walk us to safety.

The hissing corkscrewed and echoed on the wind around us. It darted through the trees, ripping at their branches, scalping them of their leaves and whipping the debris around us – slashing at bare skin and tearing at our clothing.

Was the forest attacking us? The wind its associate? I doubted it. An odd feeling of intentional harm crept into my mind as the hissing began again somewhere off over my shoulder.

I had to do something and quickly.

'Ground yourself.'

The voice came quietly this time, instructing not

demanding, cutting through the thickening negativity generated by the surreal wind. Relief washed over me. I knew this voice and trusted its authority, happy to feel supported, have some sort of ally against whatever supernatural force I was dealing with here. Besides, as a witch, I could do something. I just wasn't sure what. Something now coursed through my blood that made me different. Something that had been passed down through my family members, generation through generation, placed before me to govern and protect and one day, willfully pass on. A supernatural legacy? I had to be able to defend myself and Gil, *didn't I?* A single thought entered my mind. *Protection.* This thought formed the plan. *Cast the Circle, call the Elements and ask for protection.* My thoughts shaped faster than I was able to comprehend them and as they converged, a plan rolled in.

'Earth, Air, Fire, Water.'

The voice again invaded my thoughts, stronger this time, as if watching the events unfold with no recourse other than these four collective words.

"Earth, Air, Fire, Water." The passion startled me as I began the chant, drilling absolution through my core.

"Earth, Air, Fire, Water," I spat through clenched teeth as my determination grew. I would not lie down for this supernatural victor, Gil *needed* me. Kneeling in the dirt beside Gil, my hands struck out above my head, stretching to the dark night sky. The actions felt automated, not of my own doing.

"I call this Circle, contain and protect it." My concentration centered allowing me to know what needed doing.

I was aware of Gil although he was not in my line of vision. I knew he was breathing again at an even rate and was relieved. I could almost sense him at this point; could almost tuck him into another corner of my mind, dealing with my present encounter, while watchful over my charge.

"I summon thee, essence of Earth. North. Hear me." Wavering slightly, my voice echoed out, the wind appearing to steal it out of the air and make off with it into the night. I could have sworn I felt the ground beneath tremble with my words.

"I summon thee, essence of Air. East. Hear me." I continued, my spirit beginning to rise, building my confidence for the task at hand as my voice boomed against the wall of wind building before me.

"I summon thee, essence of Fire. South. Hear me." The fire that had been smoldering only seconds before erupted into flame. A single fireball shot meters above my head and shattered into a thousand splinters of light with a roaring crack. Fingers of flame were tossed about on the wind. The dust rose in a whirling vortex, and I blinked as it stung my eyes. Mentally I checked on Gil, he was quiet now, motionless except for the rise and fall of his chest.

"I summon thee, essence of Water. West. Hear me," I continued, suddenly aware of the moisture staining my cheeks, black tears rolling from my eyes, splashing down into my waiting hands. I fanned them into the air with the last of my words.

"Spirit, I summon thee."

"I summon thee."

"I summon thee."

Bringing my hand down, I swung it low and clockwise, as a faint arc of flame followed in the ground, etching a full circle in the dirt around Gil and I. Picturing as best I could, the endless line, a circular barrier forming its protective bubble around us, I closed my eyes, needing no distraction at this point.

An iridescent blue line appeared out of the blackness. Mentally, I stretched it, pulling and shaping, psychologically forming a brilliant orb that encircled Gil and I, above and below ground. There could be no gap, no fracture. As I strengthened and smoothed its surface, I became aware of my hands, physically following my thought process, pulling and stretching in their motions.

The air had grown still and quiet.

Ever so slowly, I opened my eyes, fear bristling against my insides.

Before me, the surface shone as radiantly as a million stars, I blinked to adjust my eyes. It was real, an orb, transparent and fluid.

The skin of the bubble moved as if liquid in state. Mesmerized, I reached out to touch it, then snatched my hand away.

Beyond the protective surface of the bubble reigned chaos. The hiss had turned into a demonic screech as the wind pelted everything in its path at the orb. For a second my courage wavered faced with the impact of a rock the size of a small car. I forced myself to refocus and push on, continuing to mentally boost and strengthen my protective sphere. There appeared no right or wrong with my mental exercise. Witchcraft came with inherited verbal guidelines and history, loads of history, but no real instruction manual. I was working blind, but my process *was* working.

"Spirit," I began then paused, appreciating that even

though our dynamic may have changed, I would do anything to keep Gil safe. "Protect him."

I knew where I stood with Gil, and it was a gift, a gift of insight. Instead of being fraught with disappointment, I felt light, victorious with the fact. I would always wish it was different, but at least now, I knew. I loved Gil, in some strange and fathomless way, but now I could move on. We would never be anything more than friends from Gil's perspective, and I'd be okay.

An entire tree uprooted and flung itself at the orb. I felt the mental flinch as it hit, and in retaliation, returned to my psychological strengthening with gusto. The sphere spun and pulsed with radiant iridescent light – rallied resilience glowing.

The action outside our insulated bubble was intense and I watched in despair as the reignited fire spun and swirled dangerously close to the tree line of our small clearing. As the destruction continued, it became evident that the orb wasn't being included anymore. I noticed a particular pattern beginning to emerge.

From the center of the action, a faint lime light began to grow. It shifted and re-shaped, unraveling then reforming like light clouds in a gusty sky. It hovered a moment, slowly losing its transparency. Then a high-pitched screech, followed by an explosive whack and the eerie lime specter shot like a firecracker at the orb. Physically I felt the blow, falling forward onto Gil's chest, to which he softly murmured my name. I looked up to see a form floating outside the orb – an arm's distance from us.

"Praesidium," I breathed the Latin, another word that

may or may not have resulted from years of subliminal learning. "Protection, praesidium, praesidium," I repeated it over and over. Fear had sewn my eyelids tight.

I hugged Gil close to my body willing the orb to maximum strength. I was exhausted; from the day, from my intense feelings for Gil, from this supernatural battle only days into my connection with my craft. Still I fought on. I had to – this could be life or death, maybe not for me but definitely for Gil.

My skin prickled a path from my lower back, up across my shoulders. Within my safe, dark cocoon I could feel the presence outside the orb. Suffocation slowly crept in.

What do you want?

"Mine." The form hissed with the effort of speech as its words vibrated against the orb, grinding and resonating. "You shall not have what is mine, witch."

A wicked screech echoed around the orb as thunderous wallops ensued, but at the formation of the last word my eyelids flew open in contempt.

Witch?

What?

Was this personal, but how? The concept evaded me. How had I so foolishly offended some supernatural being? *I couldn't have* – I hadn't been a witch long enough.

Outside the orb, the specter was dissipating. Fractured from its ancient battle of fire and wind, a featureless face remained, gracefully floating, slowly dissolving, but so familiar.

"*Witch*," it mouthed.

I stiffened. My skin, now clammy with perspiration,

crawled with every hair standing on end. I couldn't look away – did I know this face?

The fire eddied toward the orb, sucking up the last wisps of lime mist as it went. The face began to shriek again as it was sucked up into the whirling vortex of fire, leaving no trace but the ringing of the word 'witch'. The fiery tornado reached into the sky, retracing its steps back to the camp fire, where it plunged into the earth like water whirlpooling down a bath drain, shaking the ground beneath me.

The world outside the orb returned to the calm night it had been before the unearthly chaos. Hugging Gil closer, I watched as embers glowed from the campfire. Gil seemed so peaceful as I traced the contour of his face gently with my fingertips, a calm smile appeared.

"I'm sorry," he whispered, succumbing to the tide of sleep he so seriously needed. After seconds of internal debate and I hoped no concussion, I cradled Gil's head allowing him to drift off to sleep. His condition was still serious and would be until he could be attended to at Kalispell Emergency.

Gil's cell.

I recalled him stashing it before I had fallen asleep. I patted his pockets before finding the cell, but as I began removing it, I could see it would be no use to me now or Gil in the future. It had been shattered in the craziness at some point. I threw it to the ground, resigned. I couldn't physically get Gil down the mountain by myself in the middle of the night and just hoped that Ruben had received something of Gil's texts, mounting a rescue when we hadn't returned.

I shivered as my mind bolted along on its many tangents. My t-shirt wasn't much help warding off the cold I was now feeling, a small price to pay after having to rip my overshirt into shreds to bandage Gil's bleeding head. Squinting in the darkness, I saw the blanket roll only a few feet away. I retrieved it and stumbled back, half heartily brushing the dust from the roll and lay it over us.

I sat for a while studying our dark surrounds. The orb, still glowing a soft iridescent blue, was beginning to wane. I simply couldn't continue mentally replenishing it to full strength. I was so far past exhausted my mind was beginning to zap, like it was short circuiting. Every now and then the orb would become very faint and disappear. I would freak out and re-enforce it again.

With so much to think about, questions needing viable explanations, and deep frustration hanging over my head, it was no wonder I wanted to snuggle up in my bed and sleep for a week. As the thoughts of my bed, my family and home began filtering into my mind, my pulse eased and the spinning thoughts hushed. My head lightened and the word 'safe' was the last thing I remember before the enveloping blackness.

"Now, it's my turn!" I tugged at the covers, pulling them up to my chin.

Mat and Abi closed in. I'd just finished telling them my mountain rescue tale – how I'd woken at sunrise and freaked out thinking the orb was still visible. How Gil was okay (surprisingly with my basic medical skill), and how Cleaver and Ruben had found us and doubled us down from the range. I left out a few details, it was for the best if the girls were unaware of the Theban letters until I'd spoken with Mom, and I didn't really want to share my joy of waking to the sound of Gil's heart beating. They certainly didn't need to know how he tried to apologize for the 'near kiss' debacle or anything about the events that led up to that car wreck.

By the time we had returned to the Brook's homestead on Foothills Road, to an awaiting ambulance and crowd of rescue volunteers, I had my story straight, testing it out on Ruben on the way down. It was simple and for the best part true. All I had done was omit the supernatural element.

Liberty was there with a serious grin and a quick apology, she had taken responsibility for the entire incident.

I straightened her out with an enormous hug the second Ruben helped me off his horse. In fact there were hugs all round with the Danielses. Ella claimed that I had 'saved' her son. It had worked both ways though and I told her as much.

Standing under the shower for a half hour had almost depleted our household of hot water, normally a sin when the twins were involved, but no one seemed to mind this morning and my body was warm, *finally*. I yawned. I knew it wouldn't be long before the intoxicating familiarity of my duvet had lulled me into a restful slumber and I was more than happy to float along, but first I needed answers.

"Okay Lucy, but what questions can *we* answer for *you*?" Mat gestured to Abi and herself before flopping down on my bed. She gathered up her long legs and tucked them beneath her svelte body. "You've dealt with so much more in two days than we have in two years."

"It's not fair!" Abi paced. Earlier she had let us all know how nothing exciting *ever* happened to her. Her long blonde hair, braided neatly into a pendulum, swung around as she paced.

I glared at her from behind my feather-plump barricade. Here *I* was, desperate to figure a way out of my predicament, and there *she* was trying to scheme a way she could get in on it!

"Abi, *really*?"

As dark images from the last night's chaos resurfaced, the seriousness in my voice stopped her dead in her tracks. "Do you really want to have someone or thing after you for taking whatever the hell is 'rightfully theirs' and you don't even know what you took from them in the first place?"

"Well," she shrugged, twisting her braid in her hand.

"C'mon Abi." Mat patted a spot for Abi to sit beside her, "Lucy needs our support." Mat, who was normally okay with Abi's brash behavior, was straight up. Abi hesitated for a moment.

"I'm sorry," she resigned. She sat, leaning her shoulder against her twin. "It's just so boring around here ... you know, magickally ... and what happened to you was so cool!"

"Wow Abi. I didn't think being pursued by some evil force would be up your alley." The comment earned a hushed chuckle from Mat, who shoved her twin.

"Clearly!" Abi wore an awkward smirk.

"Okay." Mat urged the conversation on. "So, what questions did you have for us?" She tilted her head as she spoke. Of the two, Mat was almost a carbon copy of my mother. The twins' beauty was exceptional, but it had always been Mat's infallible heart, steering her fate with the lightest of touch, that won the masses over, and I was just one of her many fans.

"First, why didn't you guys tell me about the tweak?" Amid the stream of urgent questions bobbing around in my head, I had to know about my physical changes first. I had to learn how to cope with the attention my new 'self' was bound to attract. Being caught off guard several times over the last few days had been gut-wrenching. I needed a fail-safe way to hide or explain my new look. It was borderline that Gil, or Liberty, or Ruben had even bought my 'make-over' excuse, so how would I explain myself at school, when I would be showered and neat.

"The what?" Abi said, twisting her braid around, throwing a frown to Mat.

"I don't know, the changy thing – look at me." I motioned to my face and hair. "I look different, like I've been tweaked. What's the deal?"

"Oh right, *that*." Mat reached out for my hand, turning it this way then that, examining. "Whoa, Abi look." She gasped. "The reflection, it's very strong in your eyes Lucy. I didn't see it before," Mat rambled.

"Reflection?" I asked.

"Yes, I see it!" Abi added, speaking mainly to Mat.

"If we accept the Spirit at our initiation, it reflects in our eyes, but only our kind can recognize it. The Annulus," Mat said and as she spoke a glimmer of light flashed. It passed across the brilliant blue of her irises, encircling the pupils. For a moment I thought I'd seen a willowing shape, a figure of incandescence, brazenly staring back at me. I jerked backward, halted by Abi grabbing my chin and peering deep into my eyes as she turned my head from side to side. Again the same blinding light and shadowy dancing specter flashed across Abi's eyes.

"So strong!" she exclaimed. She snatched her hand away as if she'd stuck it in a wall socket. "Did you see, Mat? Lucy's eyes have the metallic rim. I've never seen that before, I've only heard …"

Mid comment, an image popped up – a large bear. The way in which it had looked at me before its last strike out at poor old Smokey, there had been something there that I had failed to recognize at the time – not knowing what I was looking at. But now, I knew.

I had seen the Annulus before.

One of us!

That Grizzly had been one of *our* kind.

My mouth fell open.

"Ahh, Lucy?" Mat was patting the back of my hand, coaxing me back to our conversation.

I shook my head trying to clear the thought, both twins jumped off my bed.

"The bear, the one that attacked us. It was one of *our* kind."

Mat placed a comforting hand on my shoulder. "Are you sure?" she asked.

I nodded my head. My wet hair now clung to my face in long, loose ropes that I wiped away, tucking behind my ears. "Positive. You said that only another of our kind can see the reflection. Well I saw it in that Grizzly's eyes."

"But Liberty killed it, so what does that mean?" Abi's words made us all gasp. I pulled the covers up to my ears.

"She killed a witch?" Mat breathlessly stole the words from my mouth.

In an instant I propelled from the bed. "Oh crap, oh crap, oh crap!" The twins grabbed me by the shoulders, steering me back to the bed.

"Lucy, calm down." Mat tried to be the voice of reason, but 'hysterical' was beating a solid path to my door; I was ready to answer the knock. "She couldn't have killed one of our kind."

"Why not?" I asked.

"What about the happenings from last night?" Abi returned. "You didn't just imagine the presence up there on the cliff top, did you?"

"No way, something was there alright." I tried to shrug

away from Abi, but her hold was too strong. "So, exactly what are we saying here?"

"I don't know." Mat flung her hands in the air. She paced across the room. "Abi, go get Mom!"

Abi dove down the stairs in a loud clatter, returning with Dana after a silent moment, both carrying mugs.

"Lucy, what is it?" My mother swept across the room. The sudden delicious smell of hot chocolate wafted from the large mugs she held. She pushed one toward me. "Drink this, it'll help you relax."

"What's in it?" I quipped, positive that Mom would be pushing for my rest, whatever the method, but she simply shook her head, tutting at the same time.

"Nothing Lucy. Just an old fashioned hot chocolate. People rarely give it credit anymore – like chicken barley soup."

I took the mug from her hands, happy for another home comfort, taking a quick sip before I continued. "The Grizzly Mom, it wasn't a bear, well it was a bear, but I thought I'd seen something in its eyes. I didn't recognize what it was until now."

"Yes, we were just discussing the physical changes from the initiation when Lucy freaked," Mat threw in as she took a cup from Abi.

"The bear. The one that Liberty shot yesterday. It wasn't a bear Mom. It was one of our kind!" I punctuated the sentence with a few drops of hot chocolate swishing from my cup. The chocolate was soothing, in stark contrast to my physical state. I tried to relax by leaning my body back into the copious amount of pillows scattered around my bed head.

"This is serious." Dana took the mug from my protesting

Mabon

hands, placing it on the bedside table with a faint clink as she wrestled my uncooperative body forward, fluffing the pillows then easing me back into the cozy nest. "Are you sure of what you saw?"

"Positive. When Gil rescued me from the chute, I asked about Liberty and he told me that the Grizzly was dead."

"And if the bear was …" Mat began.

"Mom, could they have killed a witch?" Abi skimmed the question in. She had been waiting for her chance, bouncing up and down on her toes, with a smile like the Cheshire cat.

She received a sharp jab in the ribs from her twin. "Geez you're macabre. How can you be my twin?"

"Girls, please!" Dana raised her voice to the twins. "It's possible, but I honestly doubt it." She paused, placing her mug on my bedside table, untouched. "Lucy, your experience on the mountain indicates that we are still dealing with a *living* threat."

"Okay, but how do you explain the Grizzly?" I asked.

"I'm not sure at the moment, I don't know enough to make a call on that. I know we need to take action." The twins had begun quietly chatting among themselves, Dana cleared her throat. "Okay girls, go down to the cellar and check through the anthology. Look for anything relating to protection and defense. Try the back, fourth shelf down there's a book marked 'Theurgy', bring that one up. And pull out the carpet bag."

There was a spirited silence as the twin's mouths dropped open in unison. They looked at one another. "*The* carpet bag?" Abi shivering with what could only be assumed was excitement, given her usual scholarly pursuits.

Dana nodded. "Let's see if we can find out what we're dealing with here and, more or less, how we can protect ourselves and Lucy, considering this all seems to be aimed at her."

"Okay," Mat replied. She was the only one who could reply as Abi had already disappeared. Mat paused at the door. "Mom, do we need to call the Crones?"

"Not yet Mat." Dana exhaled, reserved in her return as her intuitive twin daughter left the room.

"Mom, there's something else." Ignoring Mat's comment on the 'Crones' – I had an issue that needed discussing while I had my mother alone. "I didn't want to say this in front of the twins because the last time it happened, it just involved you and me … and Mr Vallen."

The name tweaked her interest.

"Christophe?"

"Yes." Opening the top drawer of my bedside table, I extracted a neatly folded square of paper. "On the mountain this morning when I woke I discovered three Theban letters smeared on a rock in ash." Unfolding the square, I glanced up to meet Dana's stare. I passed the paper to her. "Remember these from the kitchen with Mr Vallen. I'm positive they were the same three Theban letters."

"Right … the same you say … 'E.B.D.'" She tapped the paper under each letter in emphasis with a slim finger then turned the square this way then that, as if another answer could be possible.

"Yes. What do you think?"

"Not sure. Do you recall writing them?" As she passed the paper back I could see Dana had comprehended about as much new information as I had – nothing.

"No, but I didn't recall scribbling the last time it happened either." I imitated Dana's paper turning technique, but could see nothing new myself. "Do you think it's related?"

"I would guess so, but as to how … your guess is as good as mine, if not better at the moment." Dana shrugged then went quiet. "Obviously we'll all be on the lookout for anything that represents those three letters. We can tell your sisters, but first …" she hesitated, eyes dropping to the floor.

"What is it Mom?" I asked.

"I truly didn't think I'd have to explain this so soon, or even at all, but it looks as if my hand is being forced." She fluffed about around me, plumping cushions and smoothing down the duvet cover.

"Mom?"

I had waited long enough.

Was it so bad? Maybe I really didn't want to know, maybe it was some scary death curse, or maybe it was something so terrible that I would run wildly, miles and miles into the ranges to jump down another avalanche chute. Could have saved myself a trip!

"This is a long story, are you sure you wouldn't like to rest before we start?" Dana's eyes were kind, almost pleading for more time.

"Mom!"

"Just asking, I am a mother first you know." Her response was playfully defensive.

"How can I rest now? Please?"

I tugged at her hand encouraging her to continue, in turn she settled herself, emphasizing this long tale with a deep breathy sigh. It was the way she reacted whenever the conversation involved my father.

"Okay. So I'll start at the very beginning," she said, crossing one leg over the other and poked at my feet through the duvet. Although she was trying to keep her comments light, there was no Mary Poppins bedtime fable on its way.

I sensed a dark tale, something stormy that I had unwittingly or not, become involved in. I drew a long breath that flagged my readiness.

"I'm not exactly sure but I think this is all about your father's ancestral line." She leaned forward, stretching her hand over mine, took a deep breath and continued. "I'd always hoped your inheritance wouldn't lead to this, but I've just been fooling myself. Like you, I thought, *almost hoped* in a way, it would skip you, but evidently it hasn't."

As she patted my hand replacing it on the bed, she shuffled along toward me. I stiffened.

"Am I in some sort of trouble?"

"Well … yes … and … no!"

My stomach growled. "Not the best of answers Mom."

"The day you were born," she paused, "Your father didn't die in a car accident on the way to the hospital."

"What?" The air was ripped from my lungs.

XI

"*No!*"

A dream?

I turned over in sweat-soaked sheets. I had been with Gil at the oak tree. We had just met. Then mysteriously, I was down the avalanche chute. Only it wasn't Gil who saved me this time. It was my father.

Why had he appeared at the chute to save me in place of Gil?

As I fluffed about in my bed, throwing the covers from my legs, I drew a blank, sighing as I examined the damage. Scratches and scrapes everywhere and intense purple bruises littered my body like ragged-edged polka dots, and I ached all over.

The black swirling scrawl caught my attention.

Lucy,
Put this on. It will help with the soreness.
Don't worry, I don't think it's as bad as it looks.
Love Mom.

I picked up the note, wondering what 'it' was that I had to 'put on'. The note had been leaning against a glass jar lidded with an ornamental gold rose. It looked harmless enough, just a thick white cream with softened lemon peaks. On opening it, my senses were treated to a vibrant citrus aroma, which infused the room. I breathed deeply as I read Dana's note once more.

Don't worry, I don't think it's as bad as it looks
… as bad as it looks …

I limped to my small door-side mirror and gasped at the battered girl peering back at me. Above my left eye sat a crusty graze that followed on from a butterfly stitch bandage plastered on the inside of my hairline. My eye below was swollen in an interesting mix of plum, blue and yellow.

I dipped my fingers into the jar to the cool feel of the cream and layered it onto my face paying special attention to the long unsightly slash in my cheek. As I worked, my thoughts changed track, stepping backward through my dream.

Gil.

Why was he involved?

After our fireside-debacle, I'd decided to follow a different path to love, or not follow one at all. It didn't mean that I loved Gil any less, I felt sorry for any guy that dared step into his shoes, but I was desperate for a clean break. My stomach twisted.

Would I always feel like this?

I knew the answer the second my mind had formed the question. Gil would forever be in my mind and heart, in a way that could control me, if I allowed it. Sleep would provide no cover, no place for rest between flights from his image, that flawless face would haunt me, forever.

Mabon

Great.

I stared hard at my reflection. The bruising on my left cheek seemed to have all but disappeared. The swelling around my left eye had calmed leaving a pretty purple tinge and the graze above it started to crumble and fall away as I brushed my fingertips across it, revealing shiny new skin.

My face wasn't healed completely but at the rate it was moving I wouldn't have anything to show for my mountain ordeal.

"Mom!" I called out, slapping my hands to my mouth. I limped to my bedside table and picked up the clock.

2 pm.

But on what day?

"Lucy," Dana called out. I could tell she was at the bottom of the stairwell. "Is that you up?"

"Yes Mom." I hung my head out of the door and waved. "What day is it?"

"It's Thursday. You've slept on and off since Monday." She started up the stairs at a slow pace, as if I might be frightened away by her approach. "This is the first time you've been coherent though."

"Really? I've been out of it all that time!" I'd slept the best part of a week away.

Dana's hand was cool as she pressed it to my forehead, carefully avoiding the battered and broken but oddly repairing, left side. "How are you feeling?"

"Okay, but something weird just happened." I took her hand and pulled her along until we had rounded the corner into my room, where I could once again peer into my tiny door-side mirror.

"It did." Curiosity oozed, as she looked into the mirror over my shoulder.

Touching my face as I had just moments before, I flicked my eyes back and forth from my reflection to Dana's face. "I put that cream on and was checking my face out, like this, and I could have sworn it healed right before my eyes."

"Oh good, it must be working then." With a swish of her skirt she turned to leave. I lunged for her arm, halting her disappearing act.

I stared her down. "What *exactly* is in that cream?"

"I just threw a few ingredients together and stirred the result into some vitamin E cream." She chuckled. "Eye of newt, Dragonblood, you know, the usual healing remedies."

"Yuck. I have newt eyes on my face?" I didn't even know what it was, but it sounded vomit-worthy. Melange, or herbal mixtures, was just another area of being a witch that I had yet to begin studying. Herb lore, the study of herbs that go into these mixtures, would alone take years to profess any understanding let alone master. My sisters were always at it … a little something here, a little something there … picking wild herbs and flowers whenever they could, it was the basis of their Nitty Gritty Elixir line.

I pondered the grotesque thought of grinding up an eye and nearly puked.

"Oh sweetheart, it was just a little natural remedy to help the healing process. No newts were harmed, you have my word."

"Well, it certainly helped. No one will believe my story now. I've got to have some sort of physical scarring from the ordeal. Some form of proof."

"What about Gil? He was there." She was defiant, making

it clear that my healing was more important to her than my social standing at school.

"Oh come on," I begged. Oddly enough, I actually *longed* to go to school with some hideous facial deformity. Not something that a sixteen year old would ordinarily crave and Dana evidently agreed.

"But it's your face!" she angled.

"Mom!"

"Okay, okay. I see your point," she resigned. "Let's get you showered."

"How's that going to help?" I questioned, missing the blatantly obvious.

"If you wash your face, the water will remove the cream and should put a halt to its healing process. You'll still have plenty of scarring to authenticate your tale." She held my face in her hands turning it for what appeared to be emphasis, but I deduced she was examining her handiwork. "I'm just glad you're okay, Little Soul."

"Thanks Mom," I whispered. I had possibly caused her a few lines over the past week, but at that moment all I saw was the sun in her smile and selfishly basked in the warmth of her compassion. "For everything, I mean."

"Well don't just thank me." She tapped the end of my nose then took my hand leading me into the bathroom. I filled the sink to wash the goop from my face. "Your sisters have kept a bedside vigil – you didn't handle the news about your father well. Especially Abi, my goodness she's been at your side every waking hour around school, and half the nights. When she hasn't been by your side, she's been down in the cellar, poring over books."

I was transported back. The revelation that my father had been a victim of majikal murder, premeditated by his own family, his own flesh and blood, was a brutal slap that left my mind stinging with a desire for instant ignorance.

Wait.

"Abi?" I grabbed a hand towel, wiping soap and shock from my face.

"Yes, surprised me too, considering." Dana started down the stairs, her steps light and even.

Abi didn't have much time (or compassion) to spare. She was highly analytical, put together it made her appear hard, but that was just Abi. She often had an alternate agenda – a slice of mind-swill that instantly made me stop and think.

Abi, just what were you looking for?

"Which books?" I asked, now in the great room, the answer sat before me on the coffee table. Ancient dusty tomes sat stacked, several piles opened at marked pages, others scattered across the floor. I picked up the closest one. There were so many headings: 'Defence', 'House Cleansing', 'Suspicion', and a whole contents full of things you could protect. Individuals, animals, property, any number of items, but the heading that my finger intuitively came to rest on was 'Countering Attacks'. I tapped the page. "What if Abi has been protecting me from something?"

"Well of course she has. We've all been protecting you." I could see the wear, Dana's physical strain. She was tired, more likely than not, they were all exhausted. The last week had been about me. I didn't want this, for me, or anyone. "The house has a constant force field. Every window and door has been sealed with incantation. Every night we plow through these ancient tomes and grimoires looking for something that will help."

"The whole episode seems a bit much for someone whose only flaw is accepting their inheritance." I handed Dana the book for her pile, but she placed it back on the table with a thump.

"Some light reading for later."

I leaned my shoulder against the knotted ebony wood of the bookcase beside me, trailing my finger across the rows and many titles of bound literary volumes.

"I'm scared Mom." It was little more than a whisper.

"Any information you can remember could help, so get thinking Little Soul."

"But how else can I help?" I said throwing my hands in the air. "What do I know about anything related to this – this witchcraft?"

"You may know a lot more than you think Lucy." The voice was similar to my mother's yet solemn.

Abi.

Trying to bounce from my leaning position and somber thoughts, I hobbled toward the twins who stood with arms outstretched.

"Good to see you're up," they quipped in unison as we wobbled a full circle.

"You know Lucy, witchcraft has a lot to do with intuition. How you feel about something from deep, deep inside."

My intuition ... Deep, deep inside ...

During the recent encounters, my chimes had set off like

some kind of magickal alarm. In some queer mystical way, were they possibly an embodiment of something crying out from deep, deep inside me?

And what about that voice that rattled around in my head only surfacing when I was in dire magickal need? I didn't recall hearing it prior to the onset of my chimes, but then again, I couldn't remember a time when I hadn't sensed it, gently guiding, it was so familiar.

So maybe that was it?

Maybe I had always been listening to myself, to my own voice. To that 'something' that was deep down inside. My intuition. Maybe this witchcraft thing was about me, and had been all along?

"And your intuition is strong. It always has been. Don't ever doubt it," Abi said.

"Okay. So I have a strong intuition. It's not exactly helping me out at the moment, is it?" My disillusionment was intense. I was a witch now and solutions had to flow. Didn't they?

"You've practically slept through the last week. Give yourself a break." Mat sounded miffed. It was personal because it was family, we were all treading a fine line when it came to the crux of this matter.

Everything about this situation irked me, but taking it out on my family, not good. "Sorry, I'm frustrated. I just want to know something, anything that will give me an idea of what I'm up against."

"Have a little more faith, Lucy," Mathilda sighed. "We are all in this together. It will never be 'just you' Lucy."

XII

The calendar had flipped pages and although I felt nowhere near ready, I had to return to school. Whatever was after me, was out there somewhere – outside the safe confines of my well protected home. I understood that I couldn't hole up there for the rest of my existence, but after I'd begun helping on the research side and my sisters had stumbled onto my late father's journals, I was completely committed to the cause. Dana had hidden the journals in her old tapestry carpet bag for a time when – with my sixteenth birthday – the four of us could sit down together and be formally clued-in about our father.

A few journal entries provided us with days of magickal speculation. Our father's studies were extensive and well documented. Although a history professor by trade, Ernest Hugh DeBane – Hugh to those who knew him, hadn't left us with much more than a shred of information about his own family tree. We all agreed his doing this was odd, however, according to our mother, Hugh and his family were estranged long before they'd met.

Aside from this, all sorts of information had been noted,

some of which recounted parts of historical public events in utter contrast to the tales that have been passed off as general knowledge. A few stories made me laugh out loud when I thought how my history teacher would react if I suggested a different (and more accurate) account of the Salem Witch trials.

Aside from trying to figure out what was after me, I was finding the whole magickal information dig profoundly interesting, and it was annoying that I had to return to school so soon. This decision had been taken out of my hands, with school work and overdue assignments a winning combination that forced my mother's ruling on the issue.

Arriving at school to much applause and questioning, the support of my sisters was invaluable. "Here she is," they chirped, smiling and waving at those who stared.

"Their interest dies pretty quick," Liberty said. She too had faced this. Heroically shooting the notorious Grizzly and saving me was a cool story in itself.

I sighed, silently hoping I could fly under the radar.

As the first bell rang, the twins who had been chatting sprang into action.

"Okay, we're off."

Turning to walk away Mathilda suddenly spun back in my direction. "Oh hey, I almost forgot." She swung what looked like a pendant roped onto a fine silver chain, just inches from my face. I held my hand out and she dropped it down, closing my fingers around it with intentional force. "Mom wanted you to have this. It was at the bottom of the carpet bag, stuck in the lining." There was a subtle wink that followed her statement. "Don't ask me, she didn't tell me anything else."

Baffled, I opened my hand to examine the trinket.

"Make sure you put it somewhere safe. We're guessing there's a reason for you to have it," Abi shouted back, tossing her hair over her shoulder as the twins linked arms and strode off.

I became acutely aware of a dull pain in my hand, the same one that now held the strange new trinket. I looked down to see Liberty trying to pry open my hand with great gusto. "Oww Lib! What are you doing?"

"What is that?" she grunted, promptly winning the battle, unraveling the chain and swinging the charm before her hungry eyes. "Whoa, way cool. Where is it from?"

"Weren't you listening just then?" I shot her a smoldering look. "It's just something from Mom, probably a forgotten birthday gift after last week's crap," I lied. I had no idea what it was, but clearly coming from the carpet bag meant I had been given it for some reason, highly likely to be magickal, but I couldn't exactly disclose that as a reason. I watched anxiously as Liberty studied the amulet, turning it around between her thumb and forefinger.

"Look at the detail! This part, it looks like an old crest or emblem, yeah?" she deduced.

I shrugged, wondering if Mat had known more than she had let on, it was totally the twin's style to leave me guessing.

"Umm … I'm not sure Lib, looks a bit like that. It may have been Dad's." From a place deep inside me the notion was cast, I simply played along, assuming that the trinket was an heirloom.

I snuck a few 'disinterested' glances while Liberty had been examining it. It exuded something, some kind of drawing force. If it had been in the bag, I wondered why I hadn't felt this pull over the last few days.

"It looks really old and rare. Wonder what it's worth?" she offered, hesitating before eventually handing the amulet back. I turned it upside-down in my palm. It felt warm, retaining the heat from Liberty's hold. The crest-shaped tablet had a worn indent and would have rested perfectly along the chest that it had once adorned. Flipping it upright I noticed crowned in its center, was a stone so dark, I could barely see any color. Tarnished metal workings of a dragon's head and knight's helmet diagonally imprisoned the stone with decorative plumes and flourishes that seemed at odds with the sinister nature of its characters. A tingling sensation tickled my skin as I brushed my index finger across the stone.

"I'm not going to sell it Liberty. It was my Dad's." I frowned, annoyed with her lack of sensitivity.

"I didn't mean it like that. Dad has a great antiques dealer friend that would probably take a look at it for you. He might dig up some history – if it's the real deal."

The idea of handing the amulet over to an appraiser, even for a second, was not worth the worry. Although new to me, I knew this piece held great personal consequence and I would need to keep it safe at all times. I undid the clasp of the chain and fastened the charm around my neck.

Flimsy chain though.

The amulet came to rest precisely in the center of my chest. So perfectly situated, as if designed for me. I fumbled with the tablet, running my fingers across the stone, a habit that would continue for as long as the amulet was in my possession.

"Yeah, maybe. I might take a look through some of Dad's old paperwork first. He might have had it researched already. Mom wouldn't have much of an idea about that sort of stuff."

Liberty and I had homeroom class together. We were a few minutes late which scored us no points when it came to Miss Laforgue, our homeroom supervisor.

"You'd better take off that cap," Liberty warned. I ripped the cap off and stashed it in my bag, raising my head to face a silent audience and a few gasps.

Class settled after a few rounds of questions but Vivienne Channing wasn't having that. She stood up behind her desk, smoothing out her plaid skirt and successfully achieved a double hair flick before continuing. "Lucy, as you would understand, you and Liberty have been the talk of Flathead given your recent adventures and many students here," she paused to wave her open hand around the room, "simply can't believe that you fell down an avalanche chute. It just sounds so far-fetched." Among her many self-sprouted skills Vivienne was also the deputy editor for the Flathead Bulletin, our school newspaper. There was no doubt our story would provide months of fodder, open for all sorts of interpretation, especially if Vivienne had her way.

Yippee!

I wasn't startled by Vivienne's attitude, just annoyed, although it clearly reflected the thoughts of many in the room and a multitude of questions that I would face today.

The gloves were off and we hadn't even started first period.

"Yeah, I guess it does." I took a deep breath. "Sound

far-fetched, that is. I wouldn't believe it either Viv if it hadn't happened to me. All I can do is retell the story as it happened, okay?" Many heads nodded and silence spread across the room as Vivienne took her seat, iPad in hand, and 'unofficially' recorded my story for the paper.

"It's all fact," Liberty shrugged. In fact, none of 'our story' was anyone else's business, especially any of the people who were in this room. I rallied defiantly, the more I thought about it the more annoyed I became, so I was genuinely startled when a faint tinkling of chimes began somewhere inside my head. I tried to ignore them for the sake of my sanity, but with them came magick, and I couldn't ignore that.

"I guess that could have happened," offered Vivienne sullenly.

"It did happen Vivienne," I spattered through gritted teeth. The burning sensation was sudden. I grasped the amulet at my chest, faintly smelling something scorched. I focused on staying upright. I couldn't let this beat me, not now in front of my classmates to whom I was a celebrated freak. Did a supernatural incident need to be added into the Bulletin's next gossip column?

Blistering heat radiated from the tablet. I had to get it off. I clawed at the chain, snapping the clasp and removed the amulet, dropping it into my bag.

What was going on?

Still the chimes pealed on as Liberty fielded a question.

Satis, satis, satis ...

The words formed in my mind as I recalled the Latin chant. I concentrated, attempting to gain mental control, fast, and without making a fool of myself.

Still the chimes pealed on.

Satis, satis, satis ...

The seconds ticked away before I was able to soften their level of distraction. I breathed a quiet sigh of relief, believing that I might be okay. Then. BOOM!

"So are you and Gil Daniels a thing now?" Eddy Geiger's voice bounced around my head, it overlapped and echoed, blending with the chimes. He followed this comment with a second powerful blow. "What does his girlfriend think of that?"

His comments earned mocking laughter from the class.

"Lou, are you alright?" Lib whispered, clearly flustered by my actions. The bell rang but not before everyone in the room had witnessed my bizarre behavior. *Imagine the stories that will come from this episode!*

"No, not OK," I said sickened by the feeling of thirty eyes squinting and rolling for my benefit.

As people scattered off to their next class, Liberty stood square-shouldered and defiant. I cowered behind her, mentally annihilated, shaking my head in disbelief. Of all people I didn't expect Eddy Geiger to be the one with the hand grenade. No pin, of course.

Our lockers were half way to my first class. Liberty was off to English, which was back in the other direction. I needed some time alone to concentrate. The control of my chimes had gone hay-wire, and there was the matter of a little object possibly burning its way through the base of my bag.

Liberty was the first to speak.

"You want to sit out for a while and talk? I don't think

we'll be missed." She was flippant, possibly glad for the allowance of an interruption.

"You haven't done your English assignment, have you?" I chuckled. Liberty's grades weren't fantastic, she just scraped through most subjects, but she was no dummy. Just bored.

"Maybe?" she answered undeterred. "So what do you want to do Lou?"

"We can hang out, but do you mind if I head to the restroom first. I need a sec to get my thoughts in order." I was still unsure of my options for defense.

"Sure." Liberty smiled, which wrinkled up her nose. "Will you be alright?"

I nodded and walked around the corner to the girl's restroom.

I closed the door behind me, and slowly checked the cubicles for any signs of life – or spies, then leaned back on the chilled tiles and closed my eyes.

Satis, satis, satis …

Images of the amulet danced before my eyes, joined by Eddy Geiger's devious face, and Gil head-bound, in a hospital bed.

I feel sick.

Dashing to the faucet, I plunged my head under the cold water, gulping in large amounts then crudely spat them back into the bowl.

I recoiled after catching sight of myself in the mirror above the basin. There I was again, that tweaked version of myself, now only mildly disfigured by the damage received during my ordeal. I realized why most of the students in my homeroom class had gasped after I had removed my baseball cap.

"Okay, okay, you can do this," I fired confidently at my reflection. What I thought had been progress in some kind of control over my incessant chimes, didn't appear to be progress at all.

Then, it dawned on me.

If the chiming in my head was a magickal alarm of sorts, was it warning me about the amulet right now? Why didn't it sound when Mat first gave me the darn thing?

Was my new charm good, or was it bad? As they had previously proven, my chimes didn't exactly distinguish between the two forces. Which left me asking: on the one side was my new trinket a catalyst, perhaps a mechanism to channel my new talents? *Or*, would my association with the amulet plunge me into the deep dark chasms of some evil schematic? And considering the amulet had been given to me without a shred of information, I recognized the enigmatic fact that, again as it had on the cliff top, it would be my intuition that guided my decisions.

I dug into my bag scrounging around the bottom, under books, pencil cases and an apple. The tingle in my fingertips alerted me to the amulet, cold after necessary stashing. Exposed to the light, the stone at its center sparkled like sunlight reflections on water, but the water in this case ... was blood. The dark red was mesmerizing, only the clanging in my head bought me back from its lure.

"Satis, satis, satis," I repeated, absent-mindlessly caressing the stone with my thumb. As I continued, I felt my confidence restoring.

The chiming dissipated.

I was shocked, but felt justified by a niggling feeling that the two had meant something to one another in magickal terms, singing to one another in a pure state of belonging.

What could it all have to do with me, hereditary witchcraft? Was I part of a bigger picture? My mind chased fleeting thoughts of my past week.

I didn't hear the faint scraping.

CRACK!

Petrified, I jumped backward as every mirror along the vanity wall exploded sending shards of glass shooting around me. I cowered against the opposite wall, my bag thrown in front my face. A sea of glittering mirror chips layered the restroom floor. From the corner of my eye I thought I saw a flash of red, like a flame dancing across the shimmering shards.

I blinked hard and it had gone.

I was playing with fire, willfully, with no understanding of its power, and the result – a blazing inferno.

Idiot! What was I thinking?

I couldn't be linked to this mess. Getting through the day relatively unscathed was my goal – not to increase the amount of gossip, but after that explosion, it would only be a matter of time before people came investigating.

Treading carefully over the pieces of mirror, I walked to the door and held my breath as I stuck my head out. There was no one in the hall. I slipped out and whisked back around the corner to where Liberty was waiting for me.

Only she wasn't there. I looked back along the corridor.

No one there either.

Class was in, so actually there shouldn't have been anyone around. But where was Liberty?

Click clack, click clack.

Mabon

I wandered down the hall listening for the idle chatter that usually underlined the school day like a gossipy hum. Maybe the explosion was heard and the school had been evacuated? But how could an entire school empty out without me noticing?

I shivered, sensing something, and turned mechanically. Distracted, I had been unaware of the apparition, slow and vigilant in its approach, following me along the hallway. The first thing that struck me was the volume of red curls. Then the porcelain skin. And then the long dark flowing robes that floated around the entity giving the illusion of swirling black smoke. The only sound I could hear was that of my increasing heartbeat.

Boom, boom, boom-boom-boom

Then, the voice.

"Quisnam audet ciere Atram?"

XIII

"So it's true then," I hissed through clenched teeth. Above my head swayed Dana's mortar, the vessel in which she crushed and mixed her herbs. It was rare, very heavy and had been the first object I'd found that would cause the type of damage I was aiming for. No more pussy-footing around the subject. This time I had firsthand knowledge on my side and my mother cornered, backed up against the glass kitchen cabinet. Beads of perspiration trickled down her forehead. "Aunt Evlynn killed Dad."

"Well that's not the entire story Lucinda," she breathed, a hand outstretched before her, my threat clearly making its mark. "Evlynn always gave an exaggerated or abridged version to everything depending on her own selfish agenda."

"Oh, I would have understood where that evil piece of crap was coming from had I known about her, period. Why didn't you tell me Mom? I have an aunt? Why'd it taken Evlynn to tell me that she killed Dad?" The sentence spattered through my teeth. "What else do I need to know? What else are you keeping from me? From us? Do the twins know?"

"So Evlynn told you that *she* killed your father and now *she's* to be trusted?" Dana stepped toward me, her mouth a puckered line of disregard. "For the last sixteen years I have been trying to save you all the worry and I wouldn't change a thing if I had to do it over, Lucy."

A glimmer of white light flashed, passing across her irises and encircled the pupils. Startled by the brilliance of the display, I stumbled backward, the mortar slipping from my hands. I squeezed my eyes shut awaiting the smash of stone as the mortar hit the floor.

But there was nothing.

I opened one lid.

Dana stood before me with the mortar hanging in the air above us. The unfathomable depths of my mother's powers were obvious. They were an unknown quantity, an aspect of my mother I was just beginning to witness. I bit down hard on my lip feeling something similar to shame. It wasn't lost on my mother as she continued, calmly plucking the mortar from thin air and placing it on the kitchen table. "If you weren't meant to be part of the lineage then it wouldn't have made a single stick of difference. None of you need ever have known of Evlynn."

"So what you're saying is that you weren't going to tell me," I said. My anger heightened, but there was confusion as to why my mother would keep this information from me.

"About Evlynn and her part of your ancestry, no," she defended, "but understand this only comes from wanting to protect you and your sisters, and not from wanting to keep the truth from you."

My shoulders slumped as I felt the gentle waft of air

stirred by my mother striding past me. Dana had pulled the 'protection' card from the 'mother' pack and she knew I had nothing left. My pocket vibrated, no doubt it was Liberty calling considering I had fled school at lightning speed. "I guess you have your reasons. The thing is the story does involve me now, so can we please have this talk? It doesn't matter how bad it gets. We need to know the lot. All about Evlynn. What happened to Dad, and the truth this time, especially regarding how I fit in. It's confusing enough just being me without the added bonus of the whole witchcraft inheritance thing."

Dana's fierce gaze faded into a mellowed look of resignation. "Come with me down to the cellar. I need to grab some of your father's journals and trappings. They will help me explain." She spun on her heels, her demeanor sagging, clearly reflecting the solemn task she was reluctant to undertake. "We'll do this when your sisters get home. I only want to recall this darkness once."

An icy blast of chills scuttled down my back. The last thing I wanted to do was stir the melting pot of emotions Dana held close to her heart, but as a family, we all needed to hear this rapidly unraveling story, and having the true tale off her chest, may even deliver closure to Dana herself.

Another vibration from my phone. Liberty was clearly desperate to track me down. "Hi Libs," I answered, urgently apologetic.

"Gosh, take your time." She sounded less angry than I thought she would have been. I'd left her holding the fort, so to speak, but after a revelation of Evlynn's magnitude, I'd relied on my instincts, which had told me to *run*.

Mabon

Initially, I'd been fooled by the gentle apparition that floated down the hallway. Long flame-red hair fanned across her shoulders, the palest of skin, with the most extraordinary aqua gemstones shining out, the crowning jewels of this beauty, sort of personified. But that gravelly voice was not expected, knocking me backward, flying into a hard wall of clattering metal lockers at full force.

"Quisnam audet ciere Atram?" she'd repeated, somehow I'd known their meaning.

Who dares to evoke The Dark?

"Quisnam negat respondere Atrae?" she'd growled.

Who dares not answer The Dark? The interpretation had come instantly.

She glided closer, and loomed above my crumpled body, wisps of icy air curling around my face.

"I, I don't." Stuttering uncontrollably, I'd forced the words, "sorry, I mean, L … Lucy."

For a moment there was nothing.

I'd awaited the Annulus to flash across her aqua eyes. It had seemed obvious that this apparition had materialized from some magickal realm. Her eyes had rested on the amulet that I had loosely wound around my wrist for safety, and she'd hissed. "Vile trinket."

I'd grasped the amulet with my other hand as the stone began to shine a brilliant aqua, the same hue as the apparition's eyes.

Clearly, I'd gone insane. "What … who are you?" I asked.

Ignoring me she'd continued to glare at the amulet, her hands drifted forward as if to touch it, then had flinched away.

"Metal tomb, I'll be rid of thee yet!" she'd spat. Not only had this odd apparition sounded cross with my amulet, but that anger had hinted on fear.

Her blurred image looked authentic, so I'd reached out to touch the fine veil of flawless skin and flaming hair before me. I'd seen this image before. In the restroom, flowing across the floor – fluidly snaking from mirror shard to shard.

In a flash, she'd pulled away. "Ah. So you are Lucinda DeBane? His prodigy." An ugly demonic grin had broken across her angelic face. "Interesting to say the least." Winding her long fingers into her voluminous locks, she'd pulled a long red strand forward, gazing down its length then had flicked her eyes back to mine, "and the family resemblance is indeed remarkable."

If there comes a day or point in time when you truly don't know what is going on in your life, *that* moment was it for me. There I sat, on the floor in the school hallway, talking to an oddly beautiful ghost who'd professed an intimate connection to me and my family.

Had I been dreaming?

"Who are you?" I'd asked.

"Yes, well I dare say I would be asking that question if I were in your shoes." Her Latin had fallen away as the apparition had spun in a tight circle causing her smoking robes to swirl about her svelte figure. "*I*, Lucinda, am Evlynn Beale-Daray." Her bow had been practiced, a low and slow mechanical dip. "Priestess of the Court of Beale." She'd regained her composure, her eyes penetrating beams. "By the blank look on your face, you clearly have no idea who I am, which makes this situation all that much more compelling."

"You said Beale but … no sorry, I don't know who you are," I'd responded.

"Oh Dana, why blindfold this beautiful creature when her family needs her so?" Evlynn had been dramatic, punctuating her question with sweeping hand gestures.

I'd watched as she swiftly glided around the hallway, returning as quickly as she had set off. "Lucinda I do apologize for your mother's apparent oversight."

"What oversight?" I'd asked.

"You know nothing of this?" she'd questioned, halting her flurry, and had stooped before me. "Do you?"

"No." After a tiresome week of questions, I'd been beyond irritated with her taunting. "Can you please explain who you are and what you want from me?"

A tinkling peal of laughter had rained down around me. "The arrogance of your tone betrays your fear. I would kill for less *if* we had met under different circumstances."

My hands trembled, I'd tried to remain steady.

"But considering you're family," she'd continued.

I was what? Family?

I'd frozen on the spot. 'Beale' had me intrigued. I'd known it was a part of a surname my father had dropped when my parents had married, but I couldn't recall any mention of Evlynn.

"No, you must be mistaken." I'd clambered up to stand in front of the floating apparition. "I told you, I don't know you."

"Oh but Lucinda you do, innately, and once my tale is told, you will know me as you know no other." It had been meant to chill me effectively and had, to the core.

I'd shaken my head in defiance. "What are you talking about?"

"Shall I start with Ernest?" Strategically she had turned away from me, a temptress executing a well practiced maneuver and like an asinine lackey, I'd followed, legs tingling.

"You knew my father?" A tiny piece of my heart had torn away, no one had called my father by his true first name and as Evlynn was clearly not one of the 'good-guys', I'd questioned their connection.

"Exceptionally well Lucinda," Evlynn had paused, again turning away from me, and again I'd followed her alluring circular dance. "So well in fact, that our mothers were one and the same."

"Arvilla?" I'd known my grandmother's name, but not much else. "No, no that would mean that you are … *my aunt?*"

Evlynn had swept several paces toward me and I'd immediately seen it.

The resemblance had been uncanny and I stumbled backward. My father, the face that I'd recalled from photographs positioned around our house. Only it hadn't been my father. My mother had told a story, one of betrayal, involving my father and his family, but her details had been sketchy. There had never been a mention of a sister, a twin. Only Arvilla.

"I'm going to tell you a secret." Evlynn had pursed her lips. "*I killed your father.*"

* * * * *

"Lib … I … I … I," I wasn't sure what part of the lie I had to start with.

"Lucy, what the hell happened to you? I waited and then you disappeared. Where are you?" She sounded genuinely concerned.

"I'm at home," I answered. I had to be smart with my explanation, Liberty was cluey. "I'm so sorry. I can explain, I–"

"Ok! Start explaining," she challenged.

The truth of the matter was that I *had* run.

I ran, and ran and ran, until I couldn't feel the pavement beneath my feet.

After watching Evlynn being sucked back into the amulet, I didn't want to be there, in school, perhaps risking other students' lives when the next magickal happening took place. I was a 'magickal magnet'. I'd been initiated and the door to my magickal world had wedged open, pouring its supernatural contents into my lap.

"I well … I" Excuses evaded me like answers during a major exam, I just couldn't get it together.

"What happened in the restroom? I went in there to find you and …" Liberty softened somewhat.

"I know, I know. I think I can explain the mess." I cut her off.

"What mess?" Liberty questioned.

"The mess in the restroom," my voice echoed, crackling with my cell's reception as I moved down the cellar stairs.

"Lou, what … you talking … out? The … strooms … ere just fine," Liberty spluttered through the broken reception.

I stoppped my descent, silent for a second as the

information sunk in, then turned and jumped up the cellar stairs two at a time, trying to recalibrate my cell's reception.

"No broken mirrors?" I gulped, entering the kitchen and much clearer reception.

"No, why?" she pressed.

Yes, why?

"Look, when you hadn't come out of the restrooms I went in there to find you, but you'd gone." She paused, but I didn't have an explanation to fill the void. "I don't know. It was like you'd just disappeared." She waited, and the silence prickled between us. "What's going on with you?"

"Sorry Lib. This morning wasn't any fun for me." I wanted to answer as honestly as I could without overstepping the line, the witchcraft line. "I didn't feel well with all of the attention. I just wanted to get out of there. Away from everyone."

"But how did you get past me?" Her question threw me, I had only just thought of an excuse, the details briefly evaded me.

"I don't know, I just ran. I ..." Pacing the kitchen floor, my mind searched for 'those' details. "I'm sorry, I didn't mean for you to worry. I just freaked out, that's all."

"Are you sure that's it?"

She didn't sound convinced in the slightest, but I had to stand strong by my excuses from here onward, which delivered an important life lesson: *Witchcraft 101 - The Necessity of Preparedness.*

"Sure Libs." I sang, employing every ounce of charm. "Nothing more to it."

"Okay then." Liberty sighed. "But I'm still coming around after school." I fumbled with my cell as it slipped around in my hand. I wasn't surprised by her visit, I kind of knew she would come, but the idea that I was going to be under examination was nerve-wracking. I could have plonked down and bawled.

"You don't need to, I'm okay." My rebuff was trivial. "I just need some coaching to help with the freak-outs." I attempted nonchalant laughter. It came off with an undertone of 'crazy' that Liberty missed or strategically ignored.

"We can help with that. Ruben's picking me up after school. He wants to come see you as well." Her *'so-there'* delivery kind of bugged me and the mention of Ruben sent my composure into a tailspin. They already thought I was a bit suspect after my 'twins-make-over' suggestion. "Besides, he said he had to deliver something to your Mom, so you can't say no!"

Great!

"I'll see you later then," I mumbled.

"Later," sung Liberty. She might have muscled in using Ruben as an excuse, but I wasn't upset. In fact pressing 'end' on my cell left me feeling empty, shocked maybe, I wasn't sure, and it didn't really matter, the feeling didn't last long, trumped by a sudden tidal wave of apprehension.

What could I come up with to get past Liberty and Ruben's scrutiny?

As I saw it, their call-by was just another hurdle before I could learn the truth about my father. As if a marathon was nearing its closure, I could see it, and was racing toward the thin red finish-line ... *then bam* ... the sudden appearance of a ten-foot brick wall. There was no way around or under it. I was going to have to confront it, and climb over. The thought was debilitating. I began to realize that I had so little control over so many aspects in my life, and the notion scared me.

How could I gain some control?

I needed help and knew who to ask, but from where I leaned against the kitchen bench, the cellar door seemed miles away. Tripping over my feet, I raced back down the cellar stairs to where Dana crouched pulling a large pile of thin books from the bottom shelf of an old rickety wooden bookcase that I hadn't recalled seeing before. I hesitated at the new discovery then shrugged, I knew an explanation would be too time consuming, time I didn't have.

"Mom they're coming here," I panted, pulling at the back of Dana's shirt, as I bent down to help her retrieve a pile of papers.

"Who are coming here?" she smiled, I could see that she had resigned herself to the task she was to face ahead.

"Liberty and Ruben … after school. Ruben's delivering something from Mrs Daniels. What am I going to do?" Panic bubbled and fizzed in the small of my stomach.

My mother pinched my cheek. "It's okay. Calm down. You'll give the game away showing such nerves."

I stared hard at her for a second then pushed her fingers aside, shaking my head. "How can I stay calm? They'll see straight through me." I jumped up and paced, my heart beating like a Hummingbird's wings.

As page after page of handwritten script fell to the floor around my feet, my mother yelled, "Be careful with those!" She roughly seized the books from my hands then scuttled around the floor piecing the pages back into their books.

I looked down at the mess. "Sorry," I began to help her, scooping up some of the pages, but in doing so I caught sight of something familiar. It was a hand drawn sketch that resembled my amulet and the looped scrawls that surrounded it were my father's handwriting. "What's this?"

"Pages from your father's journal," Dana quipped, unperturbed from her task as she flicked through the books replacing pages as she went.

"Ah, not what I meant Mom," I said, tapping her shoulder in reference. "Is this sketch what I think it is?"

Dana glanced up, double taking at the image. "Oh my … Well yes. It does look very similar to your amulet, doesn't it?" She took the page from my hand, squinting to examine the scrawls that surrounded the drawing. "Your father's things have been boxed up. I just skim through them every now and again but your sisters and me, we must have missed this … I'm not familiar with …" her sentence trailed off as her free hand bumped and scooted along the top of the bookcase. Her reading glasses weren't old frames but with repeated heavy use were prone to the odd ill-fitted slip. She tilted her head, sliding her glasses into place. Her lips moved in time with her index finger as it traced across the page, resting here and there with the script's paragraphing. "Good find." Dana looked up briefly. "This is very interesting and I think it's relevant."

"What does it say?" I bounced back and forth on my heels.

"Well, it seems your amulet has quite a history." Completing her translation of my father's scrawls, Dana flipped the page over, in clear search of more information, then looked up at me, her thin-rimmed glasses sliding a short way down her nose. She pushed them back up. "I *really* need new frames."

"Mom," I nervously tapped at the back of the page. "The amulet?"

"Yes, the amulet is fairly new, only a few decades. An interpretation of your father's family coat of arms. See, the dragon and the knight's helmet and the three estoile." Dana placed her arm about my shoulders as she spoke, arranging the page in my clear view then pointed out sections in the text repeating, 'here, here and here.' She looked me in the eye. "But the stone appears centuries old. According to your father's stories, the amulet was made at the same time as the stone's rediscovery. It had negative energy, perhaps being used in a sinister manner, not its actual purpose." She paused looking around the floor. "We need to find the neighboring pages to this one."

I stooped forward picking up the last few pages strewn at my feet.

"The twins and I hadn't combed the entire back catalogue of your father's work, and remember I wasn't clued in on everything about your father either." Dana took the remaining pages from me then placed a free hand on my shoulder. "His past was dark and one that he did not wish to share when he was alive, but now with this information, I'm tempted, and I don't know if that's a good or bad thing." Moving her hand to cup my chin, my mother trembled, but her eyes sparkled with re-ignited energy. "With this information before me, I feel we may be on the verge of opening Pandora's Box. These pages hold the clandestine history of your father's genealogy and delving into his past is something that we all need to prepare for." As her hand left my face, a chill remained, passing through my body to my toes. Dana placed the pile of pages and journals on the rickety bookcase, and pushed the crimson velvet curtain aside, revealing a trunk. It looked positively ancient and was closed with a huge rusted lock, another magickal relic that bore the Tyet of Isis. A few words under her breath clunked the lock open as she passed her hand before it. She paused briefly, tapping her watch, then placed my father's journals inside. "Lucy, this is something that will have to wait."

I stepped backward, knocking into a chair. "Seriously?"

"We don't have a choice. Any minute there will be a knock on the front door." Dana smiled as she closed the trunk, again passing her hand before the lock and muttering some sealing incantation.

"Oh right. Lib and Ruben," I recalled my former panic and the reason I had headed down to see Mom in the first place. A fresh dart of apprehension stabbed into my heart. "I'll ring Lib now. Tell her I'm sick or something." I was pacing again as I pulled my cell from my jacket pocket.

"I agree, their timing could be better, but it's not, so you'll have to get through their visit as best you can," Dana remarked.

My mother was right, the last thing I wanted to do was arouse more suspicion in anyone, let alone my best friend.

"What am I going to say? They already think I'm a bit sus after the initiation and you of all people know how shocking I am when it comes to lying." I was stumped.

"Lucy, this is a lesson you'll have to learn. It's an

unfortunate aspect of our craft, leading a double life, having secrets. Yes we make up tales, but we have excellent memory function!" Dana motioned for help with the trunk and we pushed it back into hiding. "But they are necessary," she continued. "We don't live in times past when our ancestors held positions of respect in communities, even being revered for their talents and I know we're not being hunted anymore, but still our kind are judged and persecuted. I don't want that for my daughters. Our top priority goes to consealment from everyone, even Liberty."

"Great, I have to learn to be a big fat liar," I muttered, slumping my shoulders forward. Dana placed a comforting arm around my shoulders as she guided me toward the heirloom chaise she stashed away in the cellar. It was nothing to look at, a ratty old thing made from durable oak, velvet and leather, fashionable materials of its day. But if you looked closely you could see the detailed work carved into the walnut inlays and even where the fabrics had been originally nailed into the wood.

Sitting on this piece immediately gave way to good thoughts and moods, uplifting on a bad day. My mother often said it had been willed to do so 'forever and a day' by her Dutch ancestor Gleda in the 1700s.

As the story went Gleda was betrothed to Aled. Though a nobleman he was a mortal and a complete grouch. Gleda did as best she could treading the eggshells that shattered around his often wretched moods, but could barely stand to be in the same room as her fiancé. As a last resort she had the chaise built for Aled's birthday and 'willed' it to lift his moods whenever he sat on it. The result was a long and happy marriage.

Mabon

Gleda's 'will' influenced us as well as the many other families this chaise had been bequeathed to. Prior to my sisters' sixteenth birthdays, many a time our mother would find all three of us squashed onto the chaise in fits of laughter. We didn't know about the 'will' until Dana had seen fit to tell us about the chaise's history, and although we all thought 'stupid happy lounge' we would secretly sneak down to the chaise to curl up with a good book on a bad day.

So as I relaxed into its plump cushions, I was aware of the reason my mother had put me there – to even my mood, relax my nerves and try to help her resolve the issue.

"Well let's see how close we can get your tale to the truth, shall we." Dana smiled as she sat, the chaise's effect clearly hitting home with her as well. "OK, so you left Liberty in the hallway at school to visit the restrooms, right?"

Dana had picked me up halfway home that morning. I was hysterical, but after trying to calm me in the car, then the kitchen, my mother had resigned herself to my yelling fit. And I had let go about everything – my cruel 'friends', the amulet, the chimes, the smashing mirror in the restroom, then Evlynn.

"Yes, but I'm sure she thinks I'm crazy, asking her about the mess of broken mirrors in there." Sharing this out loud should have sent me into a state of panic, but it didn't. The chaise was working its magick, and I was more than happy for it to do so.

"OK?" Dana puzzled, sitting forward, she rested her elbows on her knees. "Well that changes things, it puts you in a position that calls for a little magick."

"A little magick?" I asked.

"Why, this could be your very first Melange." Dana was

instantly upbeat and I worried the chaise was clouding her mind.

"Mom, you don't think I should start on something a little less ..." I trailed off trying to think of a good starting point for herbal mixtures.

"Aromatic?" Dana offered.

"No, I was thinking – important, less important," I said getting up from the chaise. I needed a sharp mind if we were going to attempt this. "Shouldn't I try something smaller first? Like, maybe turning a rock into a frog or something?"

"You'll do just fine," Dana chuckled, whispering 'frog' mid chuckle. "Now pass me that large green-bound book on the third shelf down in the bookcase behind you."

"This one?" I pulled the tome from its resting spot and turned back to the chaise.

"Yes that's it," she said as I heaved the book into her hands. Opening to the contents page Dana continued, "Let's see, Infusions ... here we are. Am ... nee ... sik." Dana skimmed the page with her finger. "Situational Erasure Infusion. Page four hundred and thirteen." Placing the book squarely on its spine on the table before us, Dana paused as the book flopped open.

I leaned forward.

Page 413.

Coincidence? I thought not.

My mother skipped her finger down the page as she read aloud. "Skullcap, Chamomile, Passion Flower and Strawberry Leaf. Simple enough. I could have sworn, ah yes, there it is, Jamaican Dogwood, although it comes with a notable caution. To be ingested in the smallest of amounts or foul may befall thee."

"It actually says that?" I asked. In all honesty I didn't want to kill my best friend and her brother with my first Melange. "Mom, is this dangerous?"

"All magick involves a little danger." Dana rose from the chaise, the thick tome tucked under her arm. She headed for one of the many wine cabinets that littered the walls of the cellar. I watched as she pulled five glass bottles from the racks, stacking them on a table.

I loaded up with the bottles and followed Dana as she began for the cellar staircase. "You'll learn that lesson quickly enough. I remember I did. Darn near took my eyebrows right off my face."

I chuckled, imagining Dana eyebrowless.

She caught on and laughed too. "Funny story that. I should tell …"

"Maybe later hey?"

Dana grew solemn and with an incantation sealing the cellar door showed me the significance of the magick I was about to attempt. My confidence plummeted. "Shouldn't you do this infusion?"

"You have to take the first step at some point." We moved to the kitchen bench to prepare for our visitors. "Trust me. Ruben and Liberty will be fine. They just won't remember much of their visit … well … anything much after the tea … but we won't make it strong, so it won't last long." The collection of bottled herbs bumped down onto the counter as Dana continued, "It's a bit temperamental. Jamaican Dogwood can be a little hit and miss. I try not to use it, if a substitute can be found, but we don't have the luxury today."

Am I mad? I thought as much, until I looked at who my teacher was.

"Promise they'll be alright?"

Dana lifted her pestle and mortar, moving it closer to the kitchen sink. "They'll be fine Lucy. Have a little faith in the ole witch."

I did.

XIV

The rap at the kitchen door gave us all a start. Abigail especially, who sent the rest of us scattering around the floor picking up pages like squirrels after nuts.

Having sent Liberty and Ruben home just hours prior, in their collective 'infusion' daze, we were expecting no one. Not even Teddy, who was driving interstate with tea deliveries. It was a good time for family discussions.

"Lucy," Abi's smile was a sly one as she leaned her head on the door. She winked at me. I froze on the spot. "It's Gil."

"But I …"

Too late.

Gil poked his bandaged head around the door.

"Ohhhhhhhhhhhhhhhh!"

I couldn't help but agree with my family. He still looked gorgeous, even with his head three-quarters bound with cream calico.

"Mrs DeBane. Mathilda." Gil dipped his head to each as he spoke their name, his voice strong until it was my turn, "Lucy." Carried with a softened timbre, the word transported me back to that night, and his face again awash with the golden flickering of the campsite fire. "I tried around front but no one answered."

"Hello Gil. How are you feeling?" Dana asked.

"Better everyday, thanks Mrs DeBane," tapping his bandage at the temple as he spoke. Gil motioned toward me, "I just wanted a quick word with Lucy if I may."

"Of course, don't mind us. We needed a break from our family meeting." Dana stood, tucking the collated pages under her arm and gestured toward the empty stools at the opposite end of the kitchen counter as Mat and Abi collected the various books, bowls, objects and herb jars that lay littered across it, scooting them into the kitchen sink out of sight.

"Hi," I mumbled, my eyes hadn't left his. He didn't seem to notice the magickal bits and bobs, proving his visit was premeditated and although I understood it was inevitable, I had hoped to stretch time before having this conversation, perhaps not facing it at all.

"Do you mind if we speak alone?" he asked.

The immediate silence permeated the room as my mother, Abi and Mat bowed their heads, feigning preoccupation. The room had become absurdly hot, an instant sauna. Burning up, I shoved my hands behind my back to conceal their clamminess. Anything to distract Gil from looking at my face as it lit up like Rudloph's nose.

My embarrassment was now plain for all to see. "Sure." I glanced over to Dana for approval, which she gave.

"My room?" I motioned to Gil to follow me. I had no ulterior motive for choosing my bedroom. We couldn't take a walk because it was too cold outside, and if we'd opted for

Mabon

the front room, everyone was sure to hear. I was left with the one option that I was in two minds offering.

Gil quickly, almost apologetically followed, "Only if that's all right with you Mrs DeBane?"

"That's fine. Go on up you two and I'll bring some hot chocolate in a while." Dana flicked the water jug and began clattering around in the kitchen cupboards. The twins giggled. Early on I had tried to keep my feelings for Gil hidden from them. That proved impossible, they were my sisters but they were also witches with uncanny noses for gossip, especially Abi. I think she had worked it out before I had.

"Okay, that'd be great, thank you. It's starting to get real chilly out there. This winter's lookin' to be plain arctic." Gil prattled on a little, and it surprised me, this was a tiny falter in his normally calm behavior; it gave me an odd sense of hope. Hope that maybe Gil wasn't so sure of this situation. As we climbed the stairs in an uncomfortable silence, my anxiety lightened.

That was until I remembered a certain photograph.

The door creaked as I pushed it open due to the weight of the crap I'd hung behind it. The room itself looked like I was having a yard sale. My eyes settled on the photo frame in question of Gil and me that Liberty had taken some time ago.

I prayed that something else would catch his eye.

Luck saw him make a direct bee-line to my work desk and while he was busily amusing himself with the many photo frames that cluttered up the desk shelves, I pelted to my bedside, opened the drawer and knocked the photograph into it then pushed it closed with the back of my knee.

"Boy, you really have changed Lucy," Gil remarked, and as he turned to face me I understood why. He held a picture of Liberty and me taken by him not long after we'd met. A fiery Montana sunset eased down over the western plains behind the Daniels' arena as we playfully lay balanced along the top rails, glowing and smiling at one another after one of my riding lessons. It was a precise moment, not only for Gil to have taken the photograph – I'd fallen off the second after he'd clicked the button – but it seemed to have caught us in our very essence. Two very different people positioned in almost identical poses, gave the photograph a symmetry that I could relate to our relationship.

Oh crap, the tweak!

"Yeah, guess my sisters did quite the number on me?" I forced myself across the room and wrestled the photo frame from Gil's hand replacing it among the many other faces staring out from my disordered shelves.

"Who's that?" Gil questioned.

I didn't have to look in the direction he pointed to know the person he was questioning. I recalled my mother saying that they had traveled to Egypt at the time, hence the moonlit outline of the Sphinx in the distant background. My father was standing alone, his arm outstretched pointing across to the sandhills. The full moon had been unusually strong that night and Dana had relied on its brightness to give a stunning result. My father's face was bathed in silver with hints of his burnished hair and turquoise eyes; no app filter could reproduce the incandescence of this finite moment.

Liberty was enamoured with the photo often urging me to enter it into contests and I agreed, but my mother would just laugh at the suggestion, mumbling 'contest' under her breath.

"My Dad! He ... he died a while back," I answered.

"I remember you telling me. Sorry, he's in a few frames downstairs too, right?" Gil corrected.

I nodded.

Gil picked the frame up with one hand and with the other he reached across and pushed rebellious strands of my hair back from my face, causing my body to tingle. "You look just like him, you know."

"Thanks, I think?" My voice creaked. It didn't go unnoticed.

"That was a compliment Lucy." Gil's brows knitted together. Replacing the photo, he slumped down into my desk chair, legs outstretched, arms folded across his chest and lips pursed. Gil was wearing a black long-sleeve sweater that didn't hide much, and had hung it out over his dark gray Abercrombie jeans, defining his waist and my lustful thoughts.

Visions came flooding back from that night.

Desire, as I watched Gil across the camp fire.

Fear, as I cradled his body against mine after Jackal's fright.

Contentment, as I woke to the sound of his beating heart.

Gil was bewitching. I'd promised myself I'd stay away from that speeding road-train, but he was here, in my room, *in the flesh*, and it was nearly impossible not to think, *what if?*

I must have been staring on account of the heavy tap I received from Gil's boot. Thank goodness he couldn't read minds.

"Okay … *thanks* Gil." I leaned against my desk, taking up the same body position as his.

He chuckled, reaching forward and pushed me at the hip so I lost balance and slid along the edge of the desk, nearly dropping off the end.

Gil lurched forward grasping my arm to stop my fall. Overcome by his stare and the touch of his hands, I turned away, a faint sigh escaped my lips. I eased my arm from his grip, unable to look him in the eye – the sight of those mesmerizing jade green eyes would have pushed me over the edge.

Far, far over it.

"Look, why are you here?" I so wanted this to be a confident stand, but found myself floundering. "We really have nothing to talk about Gil."

"What? So I'm not allowed a casual visit to thank you for saving my life?" Gil asked, that devilish Daniels grin sneaking onto his face.

Not fair.

"Sure." I couldn't prevent the return smile that crept onto my face, but just as quickly berated myself, "… but I know that's not why you're here."

Gil straightened up in the seat. His arms still crossed over his torso gave the impression that there was some internal battle currently in play, almost as if his arms would fly off if he uncrossed them.

"You wouldn't return my calls."

"Maybe you should leave well enough alone?" This would have been easier to do over the phone as I had planned … much, much later.

Stupid *pushy* boys.
Stupid turning up *uninvited*.
Stupid looking so hot *in my room*.
Stupid *me* for suggesting we be alone!

"I wanted to explain to you … what happened … you know." Gil looked me up and down.

I bit my lip hard, hoping to rush blood to my lip instead of my face. Where the heck were those hot chocolates? This would have been the perfect time for Mom to arrive. This conversation wasn't impending *anymore* … it had arrived.

Gil walked to the darkened bay window, his voice carrying over his shoulder. "Look, I know you don't want to talk about this, and I understand you're embarrassed about it 'n all, but I swear Lucy, I didn't know."

"You didn't know what?" I squirmed in my shoes, appropriate really considering I was now acting their size instead of my age.

Idiot!

As fair punishment, I contorted on the receiving end of yet another dazzling smirk as Gil began to wander, appraising his surroundings as he went.

"Awwhhh, come on now. You're not really going to make it this hard for me, are you?" Gil purred, sinking way below the line of fairness into the dangerous and overpowering depths of persuasion. I wasn't sure if he knew what he was doing or if my suspicions were right and we were about to crash headlong into another horrid mistake. "Honestly, I thought we were just really good friends. I didn't know you felt that way about me."

I watched him closely as he stopped before the various

trinkets that cluttered my room into the shambles it was. He poked and proded several objects in a heavy handed manner, until he had returned full circle to my desk and picked up the teddy bear he had once given to me.

Gil glared at me. I knew it was my turn to say something, to start answering his questions or at least give him some semblance I remembered the English language. What appeared before me was the culmination of the last two years of my infatuation with him and as I had decided the best way forward was to push him away, my heart thumped out a resounding 'no' with every venture of that very thought. The butterflies began their rumble, dust-covered wings feathering at my insides, making me want to laugh out loud, *manically*.

"Really cause I … I thought I'd made it pretty clear, you know, the other night." I watched in shock as he plonked down onto my bed. Again I was frozen to the spot, finding it ridiculous to breathe or hear anything over the riot of my heartbeats. My knuckles whitened with the intensity of my grip to the desk.

"Yep, you sure did," he chuckled. I plunged back to that night at the second of our near physical 'connection'. His body, muscles rippling hard against my back as his hand snuggled me closer and his breath tickled across my lips. I felt it all again, to the soundtrack of my favorite guitar acoustic, plucked by the man himself. I recalled the bitter-sharp sting of the aftermath … the humiliation. I inhaled catching my breath. Crossing the floor with a quickened gait, Gil replaced the teddy bear with a soft thud on the desk next to me. Standing far too close again, he pulled my reluctant hand from its strong grasp on the desk.

Mabon

My eyes fell to the floor and remained there until he tilted my face to meet his, eye to eye, there was no escape. "Look at me ... How was I supposed to react? I'm with Lani."

I'm sure my heart stopped the moment her name was mentioned.

Not once during the evening's encounter had I thought of her, and yet her name said aloud, made my current circumstance both real and surreal. Gil was still with Lani, so why was he really here pleading some sort of case?

Could it be?

I was lost again, swimming in my thoughts and those deep pools of yellow-flecked jade, as I followed the curves of his cheek bones to those plum lips, looking as soft as silk and every bit inviting as they ever had. This was so unfair a situation to be in. I just wanted to love him, *simply and unquestionably*, for the rest of my life and he didn't even have to know.

"Are you okay?" Awakened from my absent thoughts by Gil shaking my shoulder, I stiffened in his grip.

"I'm fine," I sighed. "I know you're with ..." I cleared my throat. The rugged scent of Gil mixed subtly with the sweet cologne he wore, like diesel and jasmine. I shook my head. "I didn't mean to put you, or myself, into such an awkward position."

"Yeah, well, you really have put us into a situation Lucy." His eyes shone with hunger and lust and desire ... all of the things I'd dreamed of seeing in Gil's eyes, but believed I never would.

I stumbled backward, bumping into my bedroom wall, my eyes never leaving his. I wasn't scared of Gil or this moment, I was however going completely out of my mind, scared of what *I might do* giving into my desires.

Gil pinned me against the wall without so much as a touch, his arms fencing me in. I swallowed hard forcing myself to look into his eyes, sure that they would tell me the truth. He was staring straight through me, the usual brilliance of his eyes, gone. He ran the back of his fingers across my cheek.

"Gil, please," I pleaded, placing my hands at his chest. His muscles hardened beneath my fingertips.

He eased back, dropping one hand from the wall, but the other remained on my face, my chin fitting perfectly into his palm.

"I was happy before. Now you've made me question myself. Question what I'm doing – why I'm with Lani," he exhaled. "I had no idea …" His thumb passed feather soft beneath my eye. "… no idea that there was anyone else except for Lani for such a long time."

The statement hit me like a slamming door.

"I don't understand!" I pushed at Gil's chest, but as I did he passed his thumb every-so-softly across my eyelid. It was a tender action that halted me dead in my tracks. I breathed slowly. It was all I could do to stop myself from brushing my lips against his palm.

"Neither do I … after that night, I feel alive again. Like you woke me from a dream, one that just kept going around in circles in my mind."

Confusion had led to frustration. All aspects of our conversation attracted my every fiber – his words, his touch, his smell, the heat that radiated from his *way too close* body. I was wholly intoxicated, and for a second I thought I wasn't alone in my feelings as he trembled slightly, still cradling my chin in his palm.

"Gil, are you talking about Lani?" I whispered.

"Yeah, I think so," he hesitated. "I love Lani, but I just can't be that sure anymore."

"What?" I couldn't believe what I was hearing and certainly couldn't continue on living this moment. It stung too much the first time and I wasn't willing to make the same mistake twice, *or was I?* I didn't know the answer, but I did know what was bound to happen if Gil kept on the path that he was traveling.

"I just want to know …" Gil breathed, as he very slowly leaned his face closer to mine, knotting his fingers roughly through the back of my hair with one hand and traced a line down the ridge of my nose with the fingers of his other.

I clenched my fingers together, bundling my hands into fists. It was all I could do to prevent myself from responding in the manner I had wanted to for so long.

What was stopping me?

Gil was leading the way here. So what was stopping me from melting into his arms and indulging in that long-mused-about first kiss?

Elania Wordsworth.

That's what was stopping me – her name, her face and the fact that I was seconds away from luxuriating in a kiss, my first, from her boyfriend.

Gil had blatantly remarked that he loved Lani and yet here he was perpetrating some crafty maneuver that he knew would be almost impossible for me to resist. He had prior knowledge and the upper hand. It was all too clear that he fully intended on using it as he slowly eased his lips down onto my skin, allowing them to brush along my cheek.

The musky sweetness of his breath dissolved my resolution. I couldn't stop him, I was physically weak from trying to defend Lani's honor. It was obvious that Gil had come here on a mission, one that he had meant to succeed in achieving.

"… want … to … know …" he whispered, but the words were lost to me now. My body had surrendered, giving itself over to him, limp putty in his strong muscular arms as I sensed the heat exploding from his lips, merely a fingertip from my own.

XV

Liberty's shoulder thudded softly against mine as the clapped-out charter bus lurched its way over the many potholes on the 93 just before the loop southbound into Missoula. The seats in front of us were occupied by Eddy Geiger and Ash Dresden. They had laughed and joked the whole way, clearly as excited as Liberty and I were about the Euterpe gig and the possibilities of a parent-less excursion.

Part of me had wanted to stay home to continue on the research track I had been following with Mom and the twins. Besides, it was Mabon – the Autumn Equinox, and my first sabbat as an initiated witch. Plus a full moon was due … I didn't want to miss a thing.

We hadn't missed out on our traditional Mabon meal, just had it early. A table laden with a late harvest feast; grains and buttered corn, baked squash stuffed with nuts, thirteen bean soup, and poached pears in a red wine my mother made herself – organically of course.

We hadn't missed out on Fall either, decorating in the orange, browns and gold of the season. Mat had woven a fragrant garland of grapevine and ivy with highlights of dried Huckleberries and Rabbitbrush. With the recent troubling events at the forefront of our minds, Abi and I had threaded Hazelnuts on red yarn as protection charms and had strung them around the house.

We hadn't missed out on Mabon's message of equilibrium. Each person reflected, giving thanks for their individual triumphs, and asked for guidance with delicate affairs that had occurred throughout the year. As with the harmonious arrangement of light and dark, we each lit one white and one black candle to signify the balance of our requests. Although I had many questions relating to this new witchcraft world, I'd secretly petitioned for strength of character for those times when I lacked confidence. Feeling as useless as I had in the past was not an option I would be happy with in future.

I was 'okay' with missing out on the concert, but as my family had 'gently' reminded me I needed a break, we all did, and this night out would hopefully be the perfect distraction.

Since my mountain top incident, it had been quiet on the 'magick-front'. We discussed the probability of something happening at the concert, and although we all agreed it was possible, the likelihood was low. The twins and I were willing to take that bet to see Euterpe.

After much fuss, I had finally been able to talk Liberty round, convincing her that she should offer Eddy the two 'spare' tickets she had, making up some lame excuse about 'her crappy math-mind' and how 'he could help her with said 'mind' as payment for the concert tickets'. Eddy had readily agreed to the tickets and tutoring.

Mabon

I was right, he really liked Liberty but hadn't had the opportunity or the guts to ask her out, and the Euterpe concert provided a perfect platform for them to get to know one another in a group of friends. Even with the added ominous cloud of Liberty's four brothers also attending, Eddy had appeared comfortable with their jovial threats, returning fire when he could.

I did question Liberty's motives – only weeks before Eddy had blasted me with a mind-blowing question about Gil. I'd wondered if she had revenge in mind, but we'd found out through Erika Blabbermouth that Ash was the core of the question – he'd wanted to know what or 'who' was going on, with me.

Ash had been a completely different matter. At first he'd told Eddy and Liberty that he couldn't make it as the concert was scheduled on the same night as the try-outs. He was bummed but the try-outs were for the Missoula Maulers, the 'Junior A's' that played out of Glacier Ice Rink, the very same rink that Ash's family drove him, two hours, three nights a week, to practice meets.

I wasn't much for ice hockey, but I knew Ash had natural talent and with his family's tireless support, he was developing into something lethal, something that the industry scouts were watching bloom. I knew this because Daniel Kelly and Ash sat together in my English class. Their easy banter often revolved around Ash's practice or Sunday games, keeping me entertained and on top of happenings in the ice rink.

By some stroke of insane luck, Ash had gotten the date wrong and bounded into the cafeteria the following day announcing that if the offer was still there, he could make it to the gig. It put my mind at rest, for two reasons. Firstly, Eddy wouldn't change his mind and chicken out, and secondly, I kind of liked Ash, I always had. He was a really nice guy, a little traditional maybe, but that gave him a descent head on his shoulders.

Ash and Eddy were inseparable, kind of like the boy-versions of Liberty and me. Eddy stood slightly taller than Liberty and he was almost as rail thin as she, but in that lean, swimmer way. Both boys had blonde hair – Eddy's was longer, and flopped forward, highlighting his hazel eyes.

Ash was of similar height to Eddy. His was a more solid build, the result of the many hours of training on the ice. With a more classic cut, Ash's hair was darker, sandier and groomed into a short back and sides, the top however stuck out in every which way. It was messy, at odds with his clean cut personality.

Although I hadn't paid much attention to boys, other than Gil, I had always had a feeling about Ash. I also shared Biology and English with him. Our seats were close by each other and when he would ask me easy or irrelevant questions, the hair would prickle on my arms.

As I sat share-listening to Euterpe on Liberty's phone, absent-mindedly thumbing the crested amulet strung around my neck while our bus ambled along, I realized I could really like Ash. If only I could let Ash in, but that would be a difficult task as long as I held onto Gil.

From the seat directly behind us came the incessant high-pitched chatter of three cheerleaders. Ethan and Aiden, the two brothers that completed the Daniels' family, sat in awe listening to my sisters and Elania Wordsworth's prattling on about their current cheerleading exploits which, given their opposing schools, appeared no different.

Well, there was one difference and it was on our bus…

… every now and again I felt the cold creep across my shoulder making the tiny hairs on my neck rise. With every peripheral glance I stole, I flushed with discomfort. *'His'* death-stare drilled through my skin into my heart, melting my soul. I was relieved when Liberty had told me we were almost there, at The Palace. I could get off this bus of personal torment and get as far away from Gil and those hypnotic searching eyes.

Gil was pissed.

Why?

I had no idea, considering he had left me in the lurch … again!

I'd been sitting on the floor when Dana had entered my bedroom, hot chocolate in hand. I'd been staring up at the ceiling and wondering what was going on in my life.

"Everything all right in here, Little Soul?" Mom had asked. At the sound of her mellow tone I'd burst into flooding tears. "I thought something was wrong. Gil practically took the kitchen door with him as he ran out of the house."

"Mom, I don't know what's happening." I'd hiccupped and blurted out in between loud sobs, plunging my face into my hands. My mother was at my side kneeling on the floor in a flash to comfort me. "H … he tried … tried to kiss me."

"Oh sweet girl, I didn't think that would be such a terrible thing for you." She'd cradled my body, stroking the hair back from my face.

"B … but then h … he didn't. He … he just ran out," I'd blubbered out of control. "I … I don't understand."

It had been the oddest thing.

One second Gil had me cornered, and in the next, I'd been plonked on the floor with only my vivid recollection for company. What had happened in those few seconds to make Gil change his mind so quickly and definitively?

"He made you cry?" Mat had appeared from behind my mother, her eyes sad.

"Yes, it's quite unlike Gil, isn't it?" Dana tried blanketing me in her saving graces, but I was so hurt and confused.

I'd muffled a sob.

"That's it, he's dead. I don't care how fast he can ride," Abi shouted from behind Mat.

"Can you just shut up for once! I'm sure she doesn't want Gil dead." Mat wasn't having any of Abi's nonsense.

"It … it's okay." The more I thought about it, the more upset I became. For the life of me I couldn't understand what had just happened. "It just doesn't make sense."

"Some men rarely do," Dana cooed.

I just had to get Gil out of my mind, but this night, with its endless possibilities, just kept circling around, bringing me back to him.

Still, I was trying to have a good time.

Trying … very hard …

… but it wasn't working.

The speakers barked and the floor pounded. The mosh of a hundred bodies flinging sweat, crashed blindly around me.

Mabon

I just couldn't get into it, couldn't let go no matter how desperate I was to get lost in the thumping beat.

Eddy and Liberty, and Ash and me, were all getting along famously, jumping around, moshing with the best of them. I had put up a front, a smiling, energetic version of me to hide behind. Liberty must have figured out my heart wasn't in it, five minutes into Euterpe's first song – and Ash in the next five.

But I was *trying*.

The band was ripping it.

In his element as the guitar sliced out the first few bars of their current hit, Flex Rheinholt had astonished the crowd with his blatant sexual nature on stage: hip thrusting, tongue poking, gyrating swagger. Flex epitomized the modern-day metalist, with long blonde ringlets clinging to his face as it poured with sweat. He was attractive in that odd-rocker way – far too thin, far too much partying and far, far too little sleep, with a lethal *'f**k you'* attitude, living out an ideal that most dreamed about. His shredded black t-shirt did little to hide the lean rippling body beneath, glistening with perspiration, and although he was twice my age, I had to admit my heart fluttered whenever he directed those mischievous coal eyes in our general direction. Something kept catching his eye – no two guesses as to the identity of the gorgeous blonde twins that had Flex on the move and out doing himself – twice over.

Only once did I find a smile creeping across my face when Abi had called out, "Flex! What's your vintage?" At his request, the band had stopped. Flex had thrown his head back in laughter, jumped from the stage and sauntered directly to the twins. Grabbing them both around the waist, he bellowed, "A very fine year, my lovelies."

Cackling aloud, Ash and Eddy slapped each other's backs, later admitting their surprise at my sister's boldness. "It's a shame Dion didn't see that!" Eddy said, with their boyfriend's amiss, the twins harmlessly flirted at full-throttle.

Apart from that tiny moment of comic relief, I couldn't relax with Gil there. He'd shadowed me from the moment we'd disembarked the bus, dragging Lani along to keep me within sight; even earning a few odd glances from Ash, and a positively miffed look from Liberty.

"What's his issue tonight?" Liberty challenged. "He's really not himself. I don't even know why he came, he hates this band. Lani must have done some number on him."

Liberty probably perceived my flinch was caused by the mention of her name.

But it wasn't that.

I flinched with the tinkling of bells, distant and faint, but perceived by all of my human senses, loud and crystal clear. I scanned the room a full 360 in seconds flat.

Nothing!

Abi and Mat.

I had to find them.

"You okay Lou?" Liberty frowned and squinted as she spoke. I could see Ash trying to inconspicuously lean toward us.

"Yep … it's me – I seem to be Gil's issue tonight."

I had to get out, get into the chilled night air. My heart beat increased to rapid fire and the room swam around me.

"Seriously? What's happened now?" Liberty had returned

to the step-jump-step jiggy-thing she called dancing, it looked kind of unconventional for someone so lanky, but she pulled it off. Eddy didn't seem to care either, surrendering to his own version of Liberty's signature moves. Every now and again she leaned toward me to carry on our conversation.

Clang, clang, clang!

A jarring din of chimes amplified and I struggled to keep my hands away from my head. "I don't know and I don't want to talk about it," I blurted, clamping my hand to the amulet as it stung my chest with a blistering heat. "Ahh … actually I'm going to head out for some air – back in a sec."

From the moment I'd entered the Palace, I'd received unwanted attention. I was accustomed to my sisters receiving the lust-fuelled stares, but didn't have the confidence to handle them myself. And besides that, I was positive that Gil would tail me all night, to all but the one place he couldn't.

Pushing through the mosh, I headed for the restrooms. A chill rode the back of my neck like an animal sinking its teeth in. I spun around on my heels and fell, landing at the feet of some random loser who promptly announced it was *'his lucky night'* before setting me on my feet and asking me for my cell number. I'd thanked him and retreated, stammering out something about *'not having a cell'* all the while waving mine around dismissively.

A hand grasped my shoulder.

"Hey Lucy." As I turned around, the look on Ash's face summed up his view, "It's okay, it's just me. I thought you might want some company or a pro-tec-tor out here in the wild," he gestured around at odd groups of people.

I heard Ash, only barely. "Umm … thanks Ash. That

was really nice of you, but I gotta go," I gestured toward the restroom door trying not to make this moment any more awkward than it was.

"Oh, OK," he said. He leaned in, his hand partially covering his mouth and continued, "I could wait for you here, if you like?"

I shrugged.

He was so sweet and I would have responded if I wasn't trying to wrestle a brain full of bells who thought my head was a tower.

There was no queue at the restroom so I headed into a cubicle, I didn't need to go, just needed privacy to evaluate the situation. My amulet stung. It was so hot, it should have burnt a mark into my chest, but it didn't. I wasn't surprised – *witchcraft and all!*

I was, however, desperate to calm my brain-bashing bells. I needed to figure out my next move. *Actually* next several moves. As I'd worked out, my chimes were magickally related, but I still wasn't sure if the volume was related to the severity. I leaned back against the tiles which sent me back to the last time I was 'chiming' and in a restroom. I needed back-up, and now. As my hand fell on the lock, I heard her voice.

"No, are you kidding? He hates it when I say that. He is a guy remember."

Unmistakeable in its lyrical timbre, Elania Wordsworth's voice carried into the room and she wasn't alone.

"Wow. You know, I would never have known."

"Not many people do. It's not a secret or anything, just something that I don't feel the need to share. You know?"

"Well Lani, it's a great job. Can I ask just who this mystery hairdresser is?"

"Yes Em, you can ask all you like."

The girls giggled.

Should I walk out now? I thought, then reneged. Lani was hiding something. Perhaps I wanted to know this secret.

"It's red you know."

My mouth dropped open.

"No way – red, red or like red, auburn red?"

I could distinguish handbags zipping, compacts slapping shut and the sounds of various lip glosses plinking from their color tubes.

"Em, are you drunk? That was like the dumbest thing to say, ever."

"Sorry, I just can't believe it."

"I know, right. Thank God Je – *my hairdresser* can fix it every three weeks or I'd look like … like Lucy DeBane."

My hand shot up to my mouth before the whimper could escape. It wouldn't have made a difference if the sound had come out, the girls wouldn't have heard me over their hysterical laughter.

"Let's go. I've got to find out what's going on with Gil, he's being a real buzz-kill tonight. It's so totally draining."

I was sad for a moment. Although I had a lot to answer for, almost kissing her boyfriend twice, I had never intentionally thought badly of Lani, just not liked her very much – for the quite acceptable reason that she was dating the love of my life.

Another sting of penetrating heat seared my chest. The smell of burning skin flared my nostrils. I doubled over with the onset of deafening chimes, rendering my legs useless. I crumpled to a heap on the floor.

"Lucy, are you in here?"

Mat.

"Here," I whimpered. I couldn't reach the cubicle door latch. The lock began to remotely undo itself, revealing Abi waggling two fingers in instruction. The chimes were peaking beyond my control. I didn't have the focus to dispel them, grappling with the clasp of the amulet had zapped my energy. I couldn't remove it.

'Calm yourself Lucinda.' As the voice sounded in my head, I sighed with instant relief. I would be ever thankful to the owner of this voice – that was if I ever found who or what was attached to it.

"*Satis, satis, satis,*" I chanted. I knew my sisters were by my side so physically I would be protected. From some far reaching corner of my mind I could hear them in tempered discussion, but it didn't concern me now.

"*Satis, satis, satis,*" I continued, slowing the rhythm.

Though there had been a marked difference in their volume, my chimes still clanged, refusing to be ignored, but now at a level I felt I could cope with. I wasn't sure how long I had stayed in my trance state but as the fog lifted I could see that my ordeal had drawn a small crowd.

"She'll be okay … just give her a minute." Mat knelt at my side, hand clasping mine.

"… and some space. Move, my sister needs some air." Abi stood, flapping her arms and basically scaring the rest of the crowd away. I felt distant, as though it didn't really concern me.

One thing that did concern me was the amulet. My

fingers had wrapped themselves so tightly around it that my hand was numb. Mat placed her hand over mine again. "Relax Lucy, or you'll draw blood soon."

"I can't relax. The chimes, the amulet … this is what happened last time." I was covering the amulet, hiding it from view. Curious eyes were again gathering outside the cubicle.

The twins looked at each other.

"OK get out. Nothing to see here." Abi whipped into action trying to evacuate the new crowd that had drawn around our little party, but they just stared at her. "What part of get out don't you understand?"

"This is a public restroom, you can't tell us to get out," a tall brunette challenged as she began for the nearest stall.

"Oh and you are the restroom police? I said *get out*!" Abi, a foot shorter than this intimidating girl, stepped in front of her. She never was one to mess with, and after a nervous glance at the girls behind her, the brunette tutted as she turned and walked out, leaving the room clear. Abi locked the door to stop any future interruptions.

"Lucy what's going on?" Mat asked.

"I don't know." I leaned forward bracing my weight. "I was dancing, and the next thing I know I'm hearing bells. I looked around the room for you guys but then the amulet started burning and the chimes got louder … I couldn't get out of the crowd fast enough." My hands flapped like descriptive birds telling their own story. "Oh and then Ash …"

"We know. He got really worried about you and came and found us." Abi put her hand out, pulling my arm over her shoulder so that I wouldn't fall.

"He did?" Ash was definitely winning some serious

brownie points with his sensitivity, warming me to him that little bit more.

"Lucy. Concentrate, what's happening?" Abi asked, walking me to the basin. Mat splashed some cold water on my face. It felt good and I leaned heavily on the basin with both hands.

"I don't know Abi. It's just the last time this happened …"

Crack!

The bathroom mirrors shattered, glass flying at all angles. I covered my eyes and screamed.

"Evlynn!"

The shadow that snaked across the shards was fleeting and inky black, trailed by fire.

"Lucy."

I had been left here and told to 'stay and wait' while Abigail and Mathilda searched the concert hall for Ruben. The metal side of the bus was cold on my back, I shivered with the thought of being here alone. Abi had wanted to stay with me, guard me from a possible Evlynn attack now we knew she was out of the amulet. The last bathroom illusion had translated into Evlynn's escape route. We'd raced out, Mat dialling Dana and relaying the situation on path to our bus.

"I'm already halfway there," Dana had said.

"You knew?" asked Mat.

"Just had a feeling," Dana replied. "Be watchful, protect Lucy with everything you've got, and please, get away from the crowds."

For their safety and to retain our 'cover', we had to run from the concert, so I'd been hidden behind the bus, hoping no one had seen our escape, let alone followed us.

I was wrong.

"Shoot!"

"Sorry Lucy. I didn't mean to surprise you," he whispered from somewhere in the shadows.

"Why are you hiding?" I squinted in search of his familiar outline.

"I wanted to talk with you. No scratch that! There's something you should know." It sounded urgent.

"Come to explain about the other night?" The comment was flippant, designed to get under his skin.

"The other night?" he questioned.

He didn't remember?

"You're kidding right?" I decided to go with straight-forward. I was getting a little tired of this game Gil was playing. "You tried to kiss me … but you didn't! Any of this ringing a bell?" I winced at my own 'chiming' reference, in my head they sounded steady at a level I could cope with – for the moment.

Silence.

"Oh, so now you're quiet. You started this conversation Gil Daniels – you wanted to talk to me and now you can't even face me." My blood was boiling. "Show yourself."

Again nothing.

"Why am I even bothering?" I sighed, throwing my hands into the air.

"Lucy, I wanted to get you alone, without those other two," his voice struck out, not sounding like the Gil I knew.

"What?" Without who Gil?" The clacking of rapid footsteps approaching from the opposite direction drew my attention. I leaned back against the bus, eyes focused on the ground, trying to look the picture of *sanity*. Dark gray Abercrombies and black motorcycle boots entered my peripheral.

"Gil?"

But how could that be? I'd been talking to him just seconds ago.

I switched back, looking into the shadows again, and there in the darkness I saw movement, like the night itself had begun to swarm. Inky swirling smoke wafted from the shadows like fingers, curling and spreading. From within, silver slits glinted with turquoise blue. And as she drifted into the light, her flaming red hair unveiled a sight I'd prayed not to see.

Not tonight.

She smiled her smile, which I imagined was an expression that had never been sweet on Evlynn. It was all angles and chicanery, just the way she preferred it.

"But, I thought you were …" I glanced from Evlynn to Gil as the penny dropped. What did Evlynn have in store for me, and now that he was here in body, Gil too?

Abi, Mat? Where are you?

"Wow." A lyrical voice interjected. "That's like way cool."

I jumped, looking to Gil for some sort of explanantion, but his face was a blank, as if his features had been smoothed over. It was with an eerie, sallow look that he stared back … right through me.

Lani stepped from behind Gil, allowing her hand to untangle from his. "I have to have one," she mused.

That's funny. I would have thought she of all people would run petrified from a floating apparition.

"Gil?" I beckoned, waving a hand before his face, but there was no sign of mental activity at all. It was clear there was something wrong with this picture.

Lani completely released his hand, stepping toward Evlynn who stood invitingly, hand outstretched in dark welcome.

"Lani don't," I warned, noticing that the second Lani's finger tips had left Gil's hand, he had crumpled to the ground, deanimated like a floppy puppet.

"Gil!" I shrieked, diving to the ground next to him. I lifted his head, tracing my fingers across his forehead and down the side of his face, frozen from emotion.

"Oh don't be such a big baby Lucy. He might be okay … it depends."

What?

Although aware of Lani's presence, I hadn't really taken anything she had been doing or saying seriously.

"Wait, what did you say?" I demanded, drilling her with my stare.

Lani circled around Evlynn waving her hand back and forth through the apparition, causing billows of black smoke to stir like ink through water. "This is too surreal," she announced, ignoring my question. I wondered how long it would be before Evlynn got annoyed with Lani and what the repercussions would be. To be honest, I didn't care.

Gil murmured. It was then I noticed tiny traces of lime green froth that littered the corners of his mouth.

"What have you done to him?" I spat in Evlynn's general direction, remembering the warning words Dana had spoken about Jamaican Dogwood and wondered how many other killer herbs were out there.

Gil had begun panting shallow breaths and his face had a

purple tinge to it. I placed my hand to his forehead, he was burning up, but his body was trembling as if he was cold. I hugged him tight, trying to stop his shivering.

"For once I have done nothing and yet proceed to receive the acclaim. How disappointing," Evlynn answered in a huff as I fumbled around in my pockets desperate to find my cell and call for reinforcement, but it wasn't there.

Damn! The twins must have it after the bathroom incident.

Glancing up at Evlynn and Lani, I noticed they now appeared at some sort of Mexican stand off, staring at one another. They had been quietly conversing but I hadn't caught what they had said to one another. This was a bad situation for any of us to be in, but I had no time to explain the ins and outs of witchcraft to Lani, especially considering the jury was still out on my personal point of view with the whole business.

I had to get Gil to safety.

Gil's cell!

I was certain he would have his new cell on him, and as the trembling subsided, I patted down his pockets in search of it. I was in luck. He had stashed it in his back pocket, so I eased his body over slightly to retrieve the cell.

As I rolled him back, I noticed it.

Gil had on the same silver chain that he always wore, the gift from Lani. Hung on the thick chain was a flat name plate that peeked out from under his black crew neck, only it had flipped over and was face down on his skin. This I hadn't seen before. I glanced up scanning the situation between Evlynn and Lani. They seemed consumed in their personal repartee, which I figured made Lani safe for another second or so. I turned the name plate over. There was a small inscription of plain English letters:

E.B.D.

I read the letters, repeating them, staring into the darkness that surrounded us.

E.B.D.

Where had I … ?

A string of lightning images hit me like a freight train. Theban scrawls on note paper, and on granite in charcoal. Christophe Vallen, his eye sockets glowing green, a dead sheep's head extended before him. The slashing claws of a Grizzly. Swirling debris. Blood, so much blood and the faceless lime morph, "You shall not have what is mine, Witch!" And all the while a voice repeating over and over, "It's red you know, it's red you know, it's red you know."

I looked back down at the name plate.

Lani!

It was a cold night in Missoula.

Despite the chill that made me shake, my body pulsated with blood that boiled and rushed through every vein. My anger bubbled like a lidded cauldron, snapping and hissing the hotter it got.

After the trembling calmed down, I took my jacket off and slipped it under Gil's head before commencing my tirade. Fortunately, my sisters had arrived not long after the slinging match had begun, only to find that I was the cause of the commotion – Evlynn had simply refrained from speaking at all.

The sound of an approaching stampede alerted me to the twins rounding the bus with trouble in tow – Ruben, Liberty, Ash and Eddy, Ethan and Aiden all stood with mouths flapping open. They were bound to turn up at some stage, but as Evlynn cackled hysterically, finally receiving the type of ovation she yearned for, I realized just how convoluted this witchcraft mess was becoming. Somewhere in the back of my mind I had to believe we'd be unharmed and that there was some magickal way to remedy the harsh memories this episode would leave behind.

I wasn't in the right mind to deal with questions nor would I be when the four finally found their vocal chords. My sights were set, and all else would have to be dealt with later.

"You were meant to get the keys, that's all," I muttered at the twins from the side of my mouth.

"We know, but Ruben got sus. Said he wanted to make sure you were okay, you know, being that he's in charge 'n all," Mat started.

"They all followed. We wanted to get back to you," Abi finished, eyes flitting across the bizarre scene before us.

A second passed before I heard Liberty scream Gil's name, followed by Ruben's gruff, "What the hell's happening here?" I knew Ruben would want answers, but I couldn't avert my eyes from *her*.

I had to be prepared and that meant total concentration on one figure alone.

"Aunt Evlynn?" Abi was unforgiving as she settled by my side.

"Wow. She really does look like Dad." Mathilda fronted on my other side, her arm rested against mine, a slight quiver shuttling between us. This was the first time the twins had seen Evlynn, who was stunning in her own nefarious way, but hardly a picture of lollipops and pink ponies. "Can she … can she hurt us?"

I hesitated, thinking back through our last encounter.

I recalled flying back into the lockers at one stage in the empty school hallway, but put that down to a case of nervous clumsiness and shock at the mysterious arrival of Evlynn and her supernatural appearance.

"I don't think so, but I wouldn't underestimate her. So far she may have just chosen not to hurt anyone," I answered, tilting my head toward Mat.

Evlynn drifted closer, the twins stealing her attention from Lani who now stood quiet, her eyes flashing back and forth between Evlynn and myself.

"Ahh, the fabled twins," Evlynn sighed, finally breaking her silence with a sweeping gesture aimed at Abi and Mat. They inched a little closer to me. "At your birth we all thought great things were to become of you. Twins, born under an intuitive Pisces blue moon but alas, it seems your powers are so less grand than Lucinda's," she mocked, twirling her near transparent hands about as she spoke. "Doesn't it make you mad?"

"Don't listen to her," I snapped back, shoving my hands onto my hips. "She likes to get under your skin. It's her thing."

"Well she's doing a good job at it." Abi pushed past my elbow, winding up for a strike. "Listen up, you vapor vamp ..."

"Abi, don't." Mat glanced at her sister then back to Evlynn. "You need your head in the right place."

"Who ... er ... what is that?" the voice sliced my concentration.

I was watching, waiting for her next move, adrenaline pumping. Every sinew of muscle stretched tight ready for action. I'd almost forgotten about the onlookers when Ruben stepped up next to Mathilda, shaking his hands loosely at his side, like a gun fighter. "What happened to Gil, Lucy?"

"I can't answer you Ruben because I don't know." I spoke more evenly than I thought possible. I was reluctant to take my eyes from Lani, although she hadn't moved much since my reinforcements had arrived.

"I'm ringing an ambulance!" Ruben declared, pushing past me.

Mathilda grabbed his arm. "I've called. Help is on the way." It wasn't really a lie. Help was on its way, just not the type of help that Ruben would have phoned for. How would we be able to explain Gil's condition to paramedics when it was magickal? We didn't know what was happening to him ourselves.

"Is it a ghost?" Liberty asked in little more than a whisper. She had joined her brother. Her eyes were white rimmed, peeking out from under her bangs.

"Sort of." Knowing they were all looking to me for an explanation made me want to tell the truth, but I didn't know how to. I still held out hope my mother would know how to fix this.

Mathilda glanced sideways at me. "Look, you wouldn't believe us even if it was the truth." She took Ruben and Liberty by the arms and tried leading them back to where Ash and Eddy were attending to Gil on the ground.

"I need to protect you," Ruben stuck his ground, pausing before muttering through clenched teeth "… from that thing – whatever it is. Look what it's done to Gil."

"Ruben, please trust me." Mathilda coaxed, master of persuasion was one of her many talents. "Let us handle this."

"Okay," he said as he walked away, leading Liberty back to Gil, an arm over her shoulder. "Tell me if there's something I can do."

Lurking quietly like a viper watching prey, Lani had crossed behind Evlynn who positioned her body, almost protectively. "Not much you could do for him. It's beyond even your like, substantial capabilities Ruben." She capped the sentence off with a wicked giggle.

"What?" Ruben spat. "Did you have something to do with this?"

I sensed the movement before he made it. "Please Ruben, Gil needs you." I continued watching her, waiting for my sisters to catch on.

It didn't take long.

"You're kidding right?" Abi riled.

"Lani, you know this ghoul?" Mat's eyebrows jumped, "Are you like us?"

"Are you messing with Lucy?" Abi cut across Mathilda's sentence eager to get to the core of the issue.

Evlynn swept a hand in a long glowing arc before her. "Her actions have been minimal in comparision to the damage I would have caused you, you stupid girls. Your deaths would be considered an act of kindness."

Silently, I repeated the sentence.

… *the damage I would have caused you* …

Evlynn had admitted that, in her current form, she couldn't hurt a fly let alone any of us, but she wasn't the one I had eyes on.

"I have been a little soft on them haven't I?" Lani smirked, her eyes dancing. "Aunt Evlynn!"

"What? Look, whatever she is … Evlynn is our aunt," Abi was curt, almost breathless with shock.

"She was our father's twin," Mat continued. "What exactly are you implying Lani?"

"Just wait you guys," I said, my eyes still locked on Lani. "… there's more."

"Clever little Lucy! You figured it out, but you're not going to ruin my surprise now, are you?" Lani asked.

"Abi, Mat. This is not Elania Wordsworth," I spat back at her.

"Well, it is my name," Lani whimpered like a spoilt child. "Oh now that's just not fair Lucy."

"Lucy, where is she going with this?" Mat asked, her eyes darted from Evlynn to Lani.

"Think back Mat. The Theban letters I scrawled … E.B.D. They don't stand for *Evlynn* Beale-Daray as I had originally figured." I stood my ground.

"Why didn't you tell us straight up?" Abi muttered.

"It was too obvious, but now I know for certain that Evlynn can't actually harm any of us in her present form." I glanced over to see Evlynn's apparition stiffen in retort, or was it denial? "I've only realized myself that it couldn't have been her actions causing all the trouble."

"Then you're saying it was Lani?" Mat deduced.

Lani giggled, "Crazy huh? A little Grizzly bear here, a few hundred dead sheep there, and a little wind storm up on that mountain there. Don't you remember Lucy?"

The familiarity of the fog face!

Lani tossed her hair back. Raking her fingers through, it changed color from her bronzed chocolate mane to an undeniable familial connection of flaming red. She then passed her hands before her eyes unveiling the turquoise blue that would further this link, and cement a change from the cheerleader who had danced around to Euterpe beats only an hour ago. A glimmer of light flashed, encircling her pupils.

It was indisputable.

"That Grizzly." I heard Abi mutter under her breath, it was a whisper meant exclusively for me. The words reached into the furthest corners of my mind, recalling images of snapping teeth and steel rimmed eyes and blood. My poor Smokey had fallen prey to the torment of this horrible creature surfacing before our eyes.

Lani was bad, pure Black Majik. She had played us, plagued the entire valley for the past two years, spreading her malice without care. I glanced across at Gil, crumpled and shivering on the ground and wondered how Lani could have been so deceitful. I gasped with the thought of the years she'd strung him along. Had she loved him at all? Was she capable?

"Aunt Evlynn, would you do the honors?" Lani's voice ripped through my thoughts, and left my mind reeling with sudden clarity – the depths some witches would go to get what they wanted!

"Certainly, my dear," Evlynn rounded, her black-smoke robes swirled in the night air. She dipped into a low curtsey, her head bowed. "May I present to you Elania Beale-Daray. Stygian Princess to the Court of Beale and … your first cousin."

Lani stepped forward as if receiving an award, clapping and bowing as she did, her newly hued eyes locked onto mine, allowing herself a triumphant grin. "I know right. Cousins … first cousins. Bet you didn't know you had another aunt? She's dead. Oooh, was that another first?"

"What!" I said. Finally my synapses seemed to have overloaded. I waited for return of my chimes, in fact, I longed for their return – anything to pull me away from the terror that was becoming my normal.

"Dad had another sister?" Abi stepped forward, defiant of my warnings. She was angry.

"Yes, a truly miserable creature," said Evlynn. "I never could understand why mother had allowed her to live after Wynona disowned her craft."

"I would have hated her. How could she turn away from all of this?" A bright ball of flame erupted in Lani's hands. She threw it at the charter. As it shattered into tiny sparks, she let out a rasping cackle.

"What are you saying?" If it was true, it meant that we had another tale to extract from Dana. How many other relatives were 'floating' around? I glanced sideways at the twins, my confusion clearly reflected on their faces.

"I'm saying that you three stupid little witches over there, and I, Elania Beale-Daray, are family y'all." Revelling in the moment Lani cackled again. She crossed behind Evlynn, stopping at her side.

"Someone better start explaining." Abi's hands were now balled up, ready for action.

"Yeah." Ruben had returned. He pushed Abi aside and stood face-to-face with Lani. "Start explaining Lani. Witches? Stygian Princess? Friggin' illusions?" He fanned his hand up and down at Evlynn. "Have I just walked into some freaking fairytale?"

"I don't have to explain anything to you," Lani exclaimed.

I realized that with Dana on the way, I had to buy us time,

and although it was certain to be existentially revealing, Lani's explanation would be as complex a rubik cube the real story had turned itself into.

"You don't have to explain anything to any of us." I tried to pass as flippant. "And so I guess I'll never know what I have that is so *rightfully yours*!" I hoped to stoke the fires of ego, guide Lani to feel the need for lengthy explanation, but Evlynn's shrill tone cut through my strategy.

"Proof that gift should never have been given to someone so unworthy." Evlynn, pointing at me, outstretched the other transparent hand toward Lani. "Enough with this pointless banter. Elania, please take the amulet from Lucy, it will make what's necessary a great deal easier." She waved her hand in the general direction of our group of friends, "… and then we can be rid of this rubbish."

The last thing I remembered was intense heat.

XVIII

The ground was unyielding, but it wasn't the hardness beneath me that caused pain. I was being squashed. Heavy masses weighed down on either side of my body and I kicked out, but it didn't help.

All around there was shouting and screaming.

"Lucy, stop struggling."

My sister's voice calmed my retaliation.

"What's going on?" I whispered.

"Abi's holding off Elania's attack, but she's real strong," she said. "More practiced than we are."

What had happened? Had I been knocked out? For how long?

Gil?

His distressed image came back into mind. I struggled to sit up, assess the situation, only to find myself being bundled in behind Mat.

"No Lucy!" Mat shouted. She scooted backward, ramming hard against my folded knees, providing a barrier as best she could. "We have to protect you."

"Mat, she's ... she's too strong!" Abi cried out.

"I can help," I snapped.

How though? Casting a circle and calling the elements didn't seem the right choice. We needed more than defence, we needed an army. We needed Mom.

My surroundings were frightening.

As Lani and Abi battled, their eyes ablaze with brilliant flashing light that strengthened and weakened with each other's counter blows, incantating and pelting energy forces at one another. Gil lay on the ground motionless, with Liberty and Ruben hovering over him. Ash, Eddy, Ethan and Aiden watched on, faces white, their eyes darting between Gil and the supernatural battlefield.

Becoming a witch had taught me one thing – I knew nothing.

A sparkle caught my attention. It was the amulet. I was surprised that it was still hanging from my neck and was not with Lani, as Evlynn had commanded. I caressed the center stone, but quickly stopped, remembering the last time I'd touched the stone. Had I again inadvertently evoked Evlynn with my touch? Was there a way I could use the amulet's powers to save us from this downward spiral?

I tried to move forward, away from Mat.

"No Lucy, it's too dangerous." Mat's gaze skittered from side to side. She took a deep breath and pushed forward thrusting her arms out front, and closed her eyes. Her lips moved rapidly, incantating over and over until the sound that came from her mouth danced and twisted with the same sound that Abi was making in battle with Lani. Stronger together, the way the twins worked best.

Lani faltered, the light flashing across her eyes weakened with her softening incantation.

I pushed myself onto my knees, trying to listen to the

words of her chant, but all I could hear was my sisters' entwined spell, alluring and undeniably effective.

"Elania concentrate," Evlynn's command was venomous as she drifted in an agitated circular motion. "Your practice should make you stronger than they, even combined."

Lani's head began to drop forward, her eyes may have lost their radiant glow but she fought on, slumping to her knees.

"Aunt Evlynn … I … I can't hold," she gasped for breath between energy blows. Evlynn swirled on a non-existent breeze, red mane fanning around her face and spilling down her shoulders. It was the closest to pretty I had seen Evlynn.

"Then let me Elania," Evlynn enticed, her eyes twinkling. She shifted direction, her face floating close to Lani. "I can help you defeat these miscreants, but not without your specific permission." It was soft, I could only just make out what she had said.

"Yes," Lani whispered, accepting Evlynn's proposal and acknowledging defeat either way. "Yes, Aunt Evlynn … I allow your guidance. I will you my …"

"As you should, Stygian Princess. The Court of Beale will be greatly in your debt," said Evlynn, smirking. She rose into the air, her inky robes billowing and puffing about her. The result was mesmerizing in the cool air swirling and gusting around us.

"*Corporis et animae tuae natura semper fiet mihi.*"

I watched on helpless.

Evlynn's heavy Latin had been lost on the stupefied group that surrounded us, but the translation crashed in my head, clouding all sanity.

Mabon

"*The essence of your body and soul combined are mine, forever.*"

"No Lani. No!" I heard my voice scream out. Too late.

Evlynn's calculated laughter pierced the night air casting echoes off the surrounding mountains.

XIX

It was surreal.

Lani's mouth moved, but Evlynn's voice projected from it – it was like watching some demented ventriloquist show. "And now, it is you that I need." Cocking her head to the side, Evlynn waltzed a step closer, pointing an index finger in my direction. "Only you, Lucy."

I was at 'brain-overload'. Evlynn had just murdered her 'niece' in front of us, because she needed a pliable empty shell to transplant into. What was she going to do to us – her other nieces? The twins and I sat huddled together, arms stretched around each other's shoulders, trying to create a barrier between our numbness and the eerie figure that taunted us.

"Are you going to possess me? Kill me off too?" I asked, still trying to buy time before Evlynn's inevitable end game came into play.

"Well, that makes no sense. You're a much larger part of the puzzle Lucy." She paused, pointing to herself. "She was too big for her boots, may have even fought for my place." Evlynn paced. "I couldn't have that now, could I?"

"Well, what then?" Abi spat. I could see the muscles in her shoulders, taut with a slight vibration – ready to fight.

"How about we don't wait," Mat uttered under her breath.

There was a weighty pause before the twins kicked into action, like a nanosecond of twin-telepathy had passed between them. Mat jumped to her feet, glancing at Abi. Vivid light flashed across their eyes encircling their pupils as both girls extended their arms before them, four hands perpendicular as if holding a shield. Their lips moved, synchronized in their intention. The haunting notes carried forth, entwining and lifting into the night's sky.

Evlynn returned with her own incantations, blasting along the steps between herself and the twins, daring them to equal her power.

Ruben dove across Gil and Liberty as the windows of the bus exploded, firing splinters of glass in every direction. What would happen to my friends if we couldn't defend ourselves? They were innocent bystanders, but that didn't matter to Evlynn.

"Lucy, run." Mat's scream prompted my legs into action before I knew what I was doing. There was a loud hissing as something missiled over my head, detonating a tree to the side of the escape path I was heading toward. I skidded to a halt, narrowly missing the obstruction, pivoted, then raced off again, darting around and behind Evlynn.

Like a shot, heat bit into the small of my back bringing me to a dead stop. My body collided with the tar, shoulder first. It should have hurt – but it didn't. I tried moving my arms, but there was nothing. I called out – nothing, I couldn't get any parts of my mouth or vocal chords to work.

I was … paralyzed.

"Someone get to Lucy," Mat stuttered, clearly strained with the effort of battle. Ash jumped to his feet from Gil's side and scuttled toward me, his back never turned to Evlynn.

"Lucy … Lucy … are you okay?" he whispered, clicking his fingers in front of my face. I could barely blink, but it had to suffice as answer. "She blinked!" he shouted, then propped me onto my side.

With the distraction, Mat and Abi caught Evlynn off guard and the group crumpled to the ground, the twins having the advantage. They struggled for a moment, hissing and slapping, before Evlynn reclaimed her position, bringing the twins to their knees before her.

"Stupid girls. Do you think this is not easy for me?" Evlynn lunged forward with a whallop that knocked Abi yards back – her body still. Evlynn grabbed Mat's arm, her eyes dancing fire. I couldn't see Mat's face, she knelt with her back to me, I could, however, see the ferocious insanity that contorted Lani's features.

My fingers involuntarily twitched. Ash must have seen, I felt his hand slowly move to mine. Squeezing it, he smiled.

"Do you?" Evlynn screamed, shaking Mat into the air from her knees, her body hanging limply from Evlynn's grip.

Evlynn stopped.

Her face a blank. Squinting, she drew Mat in closer, searching.

"Well, well." Evlynn's eyes sparked, her tone was lyrical, comical even as she threw Mat back down to the spot she had lifted her from. I could see Mat cower in pain, holding her arm. Evlynn paced across to Abi and back, then a full circle around Mat. Lani's boots clicked on the tar, the only sound other than the distant twangs of a rock guitar, a reminder of how normal everything had been just a short time ago. "A welcome turn of events I must say." Evlynn paused before continuing in Latin. "Tu sequere."

Puzzled, I mentally translated – 'you will follow.'

Follow?

Evlynn drew my focus back, as she paced another circle around Mat. She stopped and crouched in front of her, placing her hand under Mat's chin, lifting her face. "And for that … you shall live," she said.

Then, just as abruptly as she had morphed from nasty to nice, Evlynn tossed Mat backward like a rag doll, her body slamming into Abi.

"Lucy," Mat whispered. She faltered, trying to right herself, but Ruben had rushed to her side. Effortlessly he lifted both girls dragging them back to where the others cowered distraught – disbelief on every face.

Even with Evlynn striding toward my paralyzed body, I only had eyes for the twins. Abi lay still, cradled in her sister's arms and Mat stared at me forlorn – possibly our last link. I watched as Ruben held Mat, caressed her, brushing a muddy blonde strand back from her face, his features contrasting, so light in such darkened circumstance. I cast my eyes across to where Gil lay motionless. Would this be the last time I saw him?

A tear made its way across my nose, holding its position on the tip, tickling sensitive skin in its path, as sensation returned.

Ash jerked backward pointing to my face.

"It's black!"

What?

Evlynn's paces had brought her to her mark. One blow and Ash's body buckled to the ground by my side.

"Lucy, don't you see?" Evlynn crouched low beside my face, her shoulder to the ground and cold breath wafting around my face. "This is a sign … a sign of your destined fate." I flinched as she wiped the tear from my face swirling it around and around in her palm, finally stopping very still, then throwing her head back in loud unhinged laughter.

"You are one of us!" she shouted to the night sky. "You shall not … you cannot dispute this. Our history courses through your veins." She looked back to her palm and whispered, "Our line, it will go on."

"No." It was croaky and barely audible but I managed to speak, "No, I'm not like you."

"No. Not yet in any case." She was standing again, pacing back and forth as if enlightened notions were coming to her thick and fast. Her arms exclamation points for emphasis, shot out in staccato. "But my tutelage will see you become a powerful witch indeed, possibly the most powerful of witchcraft history to date."

I spluttered.

Pins and needles ran the length of my arms as feeling returned, but I was reluctant to move them. I was scared of the sinister soul that boasted before me. I glanced across at Gil, afraid that I may lose him and a single thread, a knot of burning heat swelled in the pit of my stomach making my toes curl. Breath came faster spreading a sensation of loathing, yet even with biting hatred invading every atom I still wouldn't move.

"Lucy, our kind will always exist, as with the balance of good and evil, for as long as the seasons turn. Death and birth and death again," Evlynn declared, her erratic to-ing and fro-ing venturing close to the petrified group watching over Gil. "Why, even on this Autumnal Equinox the balance is present, day and night are even and the moon is once more full."

"No," I muttered through clenched teeth, keeping her focus on me.

She faltered for a second then smirked as she continued, "It is your personal history that I speak of Lucy, your true blood line that extends back time immemorial." Evlynn stormed back toward me.

"I don't care." I could hold back no longer, I pushed my torso from the ground and knelt. "I am not like you," I said.

"You'll come to your senses once we've arrived." Her eyes blistered with the intense heat of the anger she spewed forth, turning her attention back to the group beside our bus.

"Evlynn," I said firmly, regaining her focus, "arrived where?"

I shuffled one foot forward testing my strength to stand. Evlynn cautiously approached. I swayed, a tall tree in an unstable wind.

"I am taking you away from here and all of this inappropriate influence." She stretched a hand before her, gesturing at the group. "We are headed for hearth and home." She smiled that angled smirk, still recognizable as her own even though it now tainted Lani's features beyond recognition. "England." She sang.

"I'm not going anywhere with you Evlynn." I slapped her hand away.

"But you must." She paused, looking at me in shock. "Once the Supreme High Priestess has the amulet and The Interceptor, her plans will once again commence and we shall welcome the return of those souls damned to forever haunt our hallowed Soul Bank – your relatives – the Dark Souls."

Evlynn smiled a faint and distant smile, almost gentle. She folded Lani's hands inwards across her chest and walked a pensive circle, stopping to gaze up at the brilliant full moon. I watched her – her changing moods were volatile, I was desperate to stay atop the game for everyone's sake.

The little group was quiet, but not calm. In my heightened state, I could feel the tension humming, zapping from person to person. Mat and Ruben nursing Abi had been joined by Aiden, awkwardly kneeling alongside his brother. Mat sat cross-legged with Abi's head in her lap, brushing her fingers through Abi's hair and sobbing. Ethan, Liberty and Eddy monitored Gil who sporadically coughed, each time filling me with new hope that he would live. I was responsible for the actions that had brought this group here, captives answering only to Evlynn the Dark.

"You see Lucy, as The Interceptor you must be present." She briefly looked back at me from her moonlit enchantment. Her face calm as if she had delivered the winning argument. "The counterparts have come to align, and if we don't act, we will again battle time for our existence, a preposterous notion."

I stared at her with the same hate-filled eyes. Churning heat from the pit of my stomach rose, prickling at my throat.

"You want me to go to England with you *willingly*?" The

tears fell. Drawn back to where Gil lay injured, I was so angry. I wanted to rip Evlynn's soul from her chest, throw it to the ground and stomp it into the earth beneath my feet. That would be too good for her. "You're one twisted witch."

"Be that as I am, but simply put … yes, you will come with me to England." She spoke as if there was no doubt in her logic. "You are The Interceptor."

"The Interceptor? Look, I don't care if I'm made of freakin gold Evlynn, I am not going anywhere with you. No England. No Court of Beale." I shook with the effort, my legs weakening but I was not going to ground again, not in front of this monster.

"I see." Her tone was even and gentle. "My powers of coercion fail me. You are upset with me, though soon it will be clear that my actions are necessary. I thought you may see the situation in a different light, in line with that of the Court of Beale."

"No." Searing anger surged through me. "I WILL NEVER JOIN YOU!" It came from the depths and Evlynn flinched in the wake of my outburst.

Was that fear in her eyes?

Even if it was, I was in no condition to start throwing around barely learned incantations that wouldn't make a dent in her armour, irritating her to the point of vengeance. There was too much at stake, too many valuable lives would be lost.

"I wished for you to come to agreement. Alas, you leave me no other choice." As Evlynn came toward me I felt like I had on the mountain precipice moments before I'd heard Gil's voice – hopeless. She flew at me like the wretched winds had that night. I wanted to close my eyes, narrow the field of my imminent pain.

I couldn't, I wouldn't be able to see Gil.

I heard the familiar hissing as a brilliant globe of light burst above her wildly flaming hair. Directed at me, it missiled toward its target in unexpected slow-motion. I dropped to my knees, finally closing my eyes to await the obliterating impact.

I felt nothing …

but heard the impact …

and an unearthly scream.

My eyes sprung open to a glorious scene. Evlynn, limp and face down on the cold ground, Lani's body scorched and smoking.

Standing above her in majestic carriage, hands still sparking, was a vision that smiled gently at me before joining Myrtle and Violet at Abi's side.

Finally my mother had arrived.

And for us, not a moment too soon.

I was positive there was a reason for Gil's condition, some Black Majik control that held him in painful contortion, but what was it? A detrimental herbal concoction? Maybe an incantation direct from Hades himself?

Possibly, but my heart told me otherwise. The hold over Gil must have been one of Lani's early exploits, not something that Evlynn had recently fabricated – that would have killed him by now. But it puzzled me that Lani was still reaching Gil from beyond the grave. I'd assumed that when a witch died, any remaining magick cast would fade out.

Liberty leaned forward grasping my shoulder then whispered, "Could it have something to do with Gil's chain, you know, the one that Lani gave him?" I eyed Liberty. "You asked," she added.

"I did?" I been talking aloud, idiot! The light bulb sparked above my head – *of course it was the stupid chain.*

My hands snapped down around the chain, pulling hard, but there was no movement. I breathed slowly, refining my actions. Threading the chain through my fingers, I moved it around Gil's neck, and found the clasp. Next to it was the flat nameplate. The letters E.B.D flew at me, reminding me of Gil's strange behavior in my bedroom that night a week ago. The cunning fox in his discovery of my feelings for him, his deliberate lingering touches, and that last explosive mishap – the 'almost kiss'. He had wanted knowledge, but of what I didn't understand at the time. Now it was beginning to make sense.

"It was like he'd been under a spell," I muttered to myself. Gil was under some enchantment that had connected to his body via the silver chain Lani had so 'lovingly' gifted him. "Surely a spell, any spell, can be broken, can't it?"

"What?" It was Liberty.

"Sorry just thinking aloud again." I shook my head. Even if this was one of Lani's spells I wouldn't be able to break the chain without extra help – extra magickal help. Luckily, we had help. It had arrived in the forms of my mother and the Crones – Violet and Myrtle. News to me – the pair were powerful witches in their own rights, and healers. A bonus for Abi who had been assessed as only having a broken nose and slight concussion. I'm sure they could assist me with something as simple as breaking Gil's chain spell.

My mother and the Crones had Evlynn backed up against the bus. She seemed contained, but the ear-splitting wail she produced made focus impossible. I fumbled back the spring. Still nothing.

"The clasp, I can't move it." Twisting the chain around, I looked for other variations in the links or a random inscription, but there was nothing. "I have to get this off. There must be another way."

"Let me try," Ash said leaning forward. The air between

Mabon

us had changed the second Ash had rounded the bus into this witchy mess. I think he knew. On the path to fooling myself, I clearly hadn't fooled Ash.

"Can't you just break it?" Aiden added, he'd sneaked in next to Ash, and the pair pushed and pulled at the chain.

"Forget the chain. Where are the paramedics?" Ruben asked, though it was little more a question than it was a frightened demand. "He's choking."

"They won't be able to help Ruben," I began. "I know this is not going to make any sense to you …"

"Try us," Eddy interrupted. "Has anything else made sense tonight?"

"I know I have some explaining to do, but can you please let me think?" I begged raking my fingers through Gil's sweat-soaked hair.

"What can we do?" Liberty murmured.

"I don't know. This is all new to me too." I looked up at Mat. She and Abi were my only hope while my mother and the Crones had Evlynn incapacitated. "Mat, do you know anything about a chain spell?"

"A few talisman spells come to mind but they're not Dark spells," Mat offered.

Abi mumbled something prompting Mat, "What about something in Latin? Spells incantated in the old language are usually more powerful."

"I don't know any."

The tinge to Gil's face had now changed to a bruised purple and as his heartbeat slowed I could feel his life force slipping. Liberty sobbed quietly on my shoulder.

"Abi says she doesn't know if it will work, but try this. In your head visualize Gil better again, looking and acting as he normally would. Not under Lani's spell," Mat said.

Closing my eyes, I tried to remember back to a time when Gil wasn't wearing the silver chain, but I couldn't remember when it had appeared, so I settled on a time when Lani hadn't been in the picture at all. It was difficult as they had been dating almost the entire time that I had known Gil.

Almost.

I took my mind back. A warm, sunny afternoon just days prior to our Summer holiday break and my first visit to the Daniels' farm. Gil had held my hand as he led me toward his then foal Jackal and encouraged me to pat the spirited quivery thing. I remembered the laugh Liberty had belted out when the foal had rounded on me, nipping at my hand. In a flash Gil winked as he raised my hand to his lips, softly brushing them over my fingers, his jade eyes sparkling. "Not even a scratch," he murmured, "I'll have to sharpen his teeth."

I remembered the heat I had felt, the tingling sensation that had traveled up my arm leaving me flushed. It had been a delicious moment in time that I'd hung onto, for not long after Gil had met Lani and fallen under her spell, literally, and my 'Gil' moments had all but disappeared.

Gil had remained Gil. Even though his behavior around me had changed from flirt to familiar, Lani's spell had been seamless, clearly as she had wanted – her plans to drift under everybody's radar accomplished.

But why Gil?

Lani must have read the picture way back, had all corners covered, dating Gil allowed Lani to know my movements without appearing to pry. Clever.

Mabon

In that thought I found my happy memory. It hadn't mattered what Lani had done to Gil – how she had tangled herself in his every movement, he had always been nice to me, we had always had fun together, so it didn't matter what spell Lani had cast over him. Trying to keep us apart hadn't worked, although Gil had often seemed restrained when the boundaries of his spell had been pushed.

"OK Lucy. You in a good spot?" she asked.

Gil's image before my closed eyes drew toward me, his eyes alight, peering deep into my soul as that gorgeous crooked Daniels' smile illuminated my memory. I wanted to remember him always this way. "Go ahead."

"*Spell created in evil,*
Spell broken for good."

Abi chanted slowly, allowing me time for the words to set and sink in. Then the Latin came easily, as if I had known the language my entire life.

"*Cantio facta in malo,*
Cantio confracta pro bono."

I felt a certain sense of empowerment from these oddly familiar words. Something stirred deep within me and from the pit of my stomach there began a heat, a burning sensation, something dark. It wasn't painful, but it pushed my adrenaline into overdrive.

"Lucy!" Liberty screamed.

I felt certain that Gil was slipping away beneath my hands. His eyes rolled back into his head. I repeated the Latin over and over in quick succession.

"Say it again Mat, I'm getting it wrong," I spat, angry with myself. With Gil's life in my hands there was no room for stupid error.

"It's enhanced!" Violet screamed from her defensive position near us, on the supernatural battlefield. "You can't break the spell like that. It … will … kill him."

"Violet, what can I do?" I was sobbing. I couldn't help it and didn't bother hiding it, possibly being just moments away from losing Gil altogether. "Please, please I can't lose him." It was the first time that I had publically admitted some form of impassioned feeling for Gil.

"It's a possession talisman," my mother said. "Lucy!"

Evlynn was on the move.

She had pulled away from her pinned position against the bus, looking every bit as dangerous as she was. A thunderclap erupted, a sound so fierce that I threw myself across Gil's body.

"No!" I heard Mat gasp.

Through the littering of bodies across the carpark, Evlynn strode toward me. Dana, Violet and Myrtle rebounded to their feet and raced to block her path. The four witches now stood in gridlock, their eyes blazed at one another, no side giving way to the other.

Evlynn finally spoke. "A suggestion I have for your consideration," she said, pausing to digest that Abigail and Mathilda had dragged themselves from the ground and joined the stronghold my mother and the Crones formed before her. Evlynn relaxed and sauntered several steps sideways until she came into view from behind the witchwall my allies had formed. "A trade. Lucy, you come with me to England and I will spare them all." She gestured toward Gil, "including the boy."

"You did this?" She knew what I was referring to.

Mabon

"I am waiting," she whispered.

It was a bargain. Who in their right mind would trust the vicious dark witch that stood before us? But still, it was a bargain, and I was the prize. To spare the lives of all the people I loved I had no other choice than to surrender to her wishes.

All eyes fell on me to answer. It was my mother's voice that rang out in clear denial. "No Evlynn, Lucy will never be part of your world," she spat as she raised her hands before her, "Never!"

Evlynn ignored my mother's rebuttle. I could feel her eyes boring into me as I looked down at Gil. "I can save him, Lucy," Evlynn said in little more than a taunting whisper. "I know what he needs to live."

My answer was quick – her request was nothing I needed to think about.

"I'll go with you."

Evlynn's victorious smile burned into my mind.

His heartbeat quickened like a jack-hammer in his chest.

I'd agreed to go with her ... and now this?

"Evlynn!" I shouted.

Gil's breathing labored, it came wheezing from his deflating lungs. Death waited close by in the shadows, ready to snatch his precious life away.

"No!" I screamed.

His body became limp beneath my hands, out of sheer panic I grabbed at the chain, the death sentence noosed around Gil's neck.

"No Lucy," Violet snapped. "You mustn't break it."

Evlynn's hysterical cackle repeated into the night.

"If he dies witch, the deal is off," I warned her, snuffling through my tears. The words stopped her dead. She was hovering, wanting to approach, but the witch-wall pitched in front of her barricading the way and I was hesitant to ask them to let her through. Evlynn couldn't be trusted – I knew that, but who else knew how to save Gil?

"Lucy, there is no deal," my mother refuted, answering as if she had been listening to my thoughts.

"I won't let him die because of me!" My lips curled around the words as if they were poison.

"Lucy," she began but was interrupted. In the confusion, from the back of the pack, came a voice. Quietly at first, then working into a roar as I linked into her train of thought and began the Latin translation.

"Evil woman, evil eye, evil mouth, evil tongue, evil spell, evil deed, evil thought. Get out of this man now!"

"*Mala mulier, male ocule, malum os, mala lingua, mala cantio, malum factum, male animae, hunc Viro nunc relinquite,*" I repeated.

"No!" Evlynn growled. The incantation must have been heading in the right track if it was ruffling Evlynn's feathers.

"Again and again and again Lucy," Mat shouted over the commotion.

The other witches turned to stare in disbelief.

I trusted Mat. There was something new in the way she spoke, something commanding, unlike her usual flowery self.

Her simple commands filled my being, pouring in light and a feeling of hope that I hadn't felt all night. I nodded, my attention not leaving the task.

"*Mala mulier, male ocule, malum os, mala lingua, mala cantio, malum factum, male animae, hunc Viro nunc relinquite,*" I repeated.

"Believe what you're saying Lucy," Abi added, the 'twin-thing' had kicked in, which bolstered my confidence. If the ever-studious Abi was backing Mat – we were definitely on the right path.

I closed my eyes and grasped Gil's hand, the other I had

locked around the silver chain. My thumb caressed the name plate in a firm circular motion, keeping me engaged.

Meanwhile, about me, all hell had broken loose.

Evlynn had not received Mat's 'spell-break' well; she'd flown into a rage, which the five witches barely contained. As if she'd summoned the full force of nature, forks of lightning cracked across the night's sky and the wind whistled sour as it whipped at my face, stirring up debris that stung on contact.

I tried not to allow the physical to affect my mental state. I was repeating the spell-break so quickly it had formed a haunting tune in my head, a tune that accompanied the quiet tinkling that had been playing unnoticed.

Oh no, please no!

There was no time for a sudden appearance of my mind obliterating chimes, and with no time came no patience, I had to ignore them and hope they would stay just as they were – a quiet accompaniment to my insanity.

Had I been too hasty saying yes to hereditary witchcraft without enough knowledge on my behalf? As I weighed up all that witchcraft had bestowed on me, all the pain, the suffering, and mental anguish – my friends and family included, I began to realize that accepting this apparent grand gift was questionable. Dark thoughts picked up where they had left off, diminishing the feeling of hope that Mat's instruction had instilled.

I smiled trying to push the darkness away. Abi's words echoed around my mind, *"Believe in what you're saying."*

What am I saying? I squeezed Gil's cold hand tighter. It wasn't so much the words I repeated that would free Gil from Lani's spell. I had to have faith. I had to believe that I could prevent Gil's death through no other resource than my own 'green' mind. It was a big ask.

As the words tumbled out of my mouth I pieced them together, understanding each one and its place within the spell. I had to force out whatever evil sat within Gil, irrelevant of who had placed it there. I felt my internal balance go, as if I would faint. A prickling burn traveled across my fingers and toes then shot into my torso, crunching the breath from my lungs. I doubled forward, catching myself on Gil's chest. I started to sweat, and wiped black tears from my eyes.

He's dying right here, right under my hands.

I sucked in air, my lungs were paralyzed.

'Calm yourself Lucinda.' The voice drifted in, even and calm. 'You are a DeBane and you are a Beale.'

It clicked.

I knew this voice. I inhaled a great balloon of air, expanding my lungs almost too quickly, but relief flooded my body.

'This is who you are.'

I looked up at Evlynn barricading herself against the witches with the strength of her mind alone, making it look as easy as if she was containing a mouse. Whatever coursed through Evlynn's veins, was in mine. I was a DeBane but also a Beale, from the same family – only it was different paths that we chose to follow. And being from that same genealogy meant there was no fighting my inheritance, it was an intergral part of the person I was destined to become.

I clapped my hands to my head as the chimes amped up, wailing at an ear-splitting volume. I was hit by a blast of light and fell forward onto Gil's chest, my mind numb. It was here, in this place of utter torment that I found a solution.

This is who I am.

After watching Evlynn's devastating displays and finally understanding our connection, I knew I had power. I just had to believe in myself the way that I believed in my family, my friends, and my world.

My new world.

I can save Gil. The thought pinged around inside my brain. I steadied myself into a kneeling position, grounded at Gil's side. My hands jolted from their braced position over his chest and a brilliant blue light erupted. I was knocked backward, shaking with the effect, but returned to my position and again suspended my hands over Gil's chest.

This time, I sensed the Annulus encircle my pupils, eclipsing them with brilliant light, and I felt it ignite through my palms jerking Gil's chest upward twice in swift succession.

He gasped.

My hands defibrillated, again launching Gil's chest, yet this time filling him with light that ran the length of his body, sparking until it reached his boots.

With a loud pling the metal gave way and Gil's death sentence fell to the ground. A low moan sounded as Gil's lungs inflated. His face softened, and the color returned.

Both Liberty and Ruben scrambled to my side. Ruben took over and began repeating Gil's name over and over. I was not needed there anymore. Magickally I had done what was necessary.

I lifted my aching body to stand and stared directly at

Mabon

Evlynn. She was at peak performance with my mother, sisters and the Crones all fighting back against her powerful will, but there had been a turn to the balance of who dominated whom.

They needed my help.

I moved fast toward Evlynn. I was the only chance we had, she would never harm me. I was far too valuable to destroy.

"Evlynn," I shouted.

"A moment Lucy." Her eyes flickered across to mine. "I will finish here, with these cretins and we shall leave."

I felt the Annulus encircle my pupils. "These cretins are my family and my friends. I will not let you harm them."

Evlynn faltered, "But there must be no witnesses."

"You will not harm them. Do you hear me?"

"You're confused." Evlynn turned toward me, her tone softening, "You will come to England. It's your destiny. You are The Interceptor and someday you will stand as the High Priestess of the Court of Beale."

Evlynn seemed so sure of what she was saying I almost questioned my own logic. "I'm not going to England," I refuted, going back on my former promise.

"It has been scryed."

"What?" I was astonished by the revelation. Scrying or Divination was big in my family. My sisters used it all the time, a kind of cheat-sheet in many ways – Abi being hands-down gifted at it. A vision scryed was a vision true. I looked across at my mother for an explanation. "It's been scryed? For when?"

"It won't be happening." Dana looked away. "Circumstances can change."

I felt betrayed, my mother again hiding something from me. My eyes moved from one familiar witch to the next with the same result, each one of them looked away. It struck me.

They all knew.

"Well, you can tell the powers that be, I'm not going anywhere," I shouted at Evlynn – at them all.

The burning swelled in the pit of my stomach, startling me. I twisted my hips as the heat intensified.

Gil.

He lay on his side with his eyes wide open, clearly projecting the pain he felt. I hated Lani for doing this to him. I hated Evlynn even more. The anguish she was inflicting on my family, the witches, I could understand. But she had involved innocent people – my friends, in a night that would scar them for the remainder of their days, *if* they survived.

The more I allowed the thoughts to ruminate, the more the fire grew, until all that fitted into my mind were four short words that revolved incessantly.

I will kill you.

I will kill you.

I will kill you.

The fire within had compacted into a tight flaming ball. It shot from my belly, up my spine and into the base of my skull.

I wanted …

… I craved … *revenge*.

I wanted Evlynn dead. Again I was on the move before I had processed the thought, the blue Annulus eclipsing my pupils.

"Where my father failed, I will succeed."

Mabon

I had Evlynn on her knees before she had time to put up any defense. I stepped forward, squaring off and grounded my feet solidly, muscles pulled tight and at the ready. My hands clapped tight to the sides of her head, thumbs to her temples in one swift movement. At some stage I had switched over to automatic and now watched myself from a secondary vantage – a spectator with a front row seat. I choked back on the knot forming in my throat as I pictured my father smiling and buoyed by the onset of my own righteousness, I began to recite in Latin the same archaic incantation that Evlynn had used on Lani, its dark words volunteering themselves.

Flat against my chest, the heat grew, burning my skin. I flinched and the pain gave way to an intense glow. I heard Mat scream. Lani's eyes were listless and rolled from side to side.

I gasped, my hands were strung with blue light that flowed back and forth, finger tips to fingers tips through her head. I almost pulled my hands away before remembering that inside the vessel on its knees before me, was a soul so black, so sinister that it somehow made the most appalling crimes blush with humility. How many people had Evlynn tortured or killed, or both, for the sake of her beloved Court? How many more would it take until she'd had her fill of death? My hands reanimated, pushing forward on the pressure points.

"No Lucy!" Dana approached from behind Evlynn, cleverly aligning herself so that I had no other choice than to see only her. "You mustn't kill her."

Closing my eyes helped. I was able to elbow her radiant

features from my mind yet the shadow of her stare remained. "Why?" The sound growled from the back of my throat. "You heard her. I will go to England or she'll die trying to get me there." It really was a concern of life and death – our lives for Evlynn's death. After all that she had put us through, there seemed no other action to take. I opened my eyes, a sinister ache pulsed through my fingers. "Well this is her dying."

"It's not for you to end Evlynn," Dana said. She sighed, raising her palms in plea. "Lucy, your powers, they mustn't be used in this way."

A murmur of agreement lifted in unison from the witches who stood behind her.

"It will consume you Lucy," Violet put forward.

Myrtle stepped around Violet placing her hand on her friends arm as she did in the manner of support, the physical ravages of their recent battle beginning to show. "It's true, and it's the quickest way for you to become exactly like her," she said, dropping a bomb with her last three words.

"No, that can't be true!" I shouted. Although my hands were still in position, they were shaking. I was confused, I thought my actions would have been applauded. Evlynn needed to go where she could no longer hurt us. "I'm doing this because of what she has tried to do to us, all of us."

"You're right, but it's the intention that your power is coming from." Dana gestured toward the amulet. Did it really matter what my intentions were? Wouldn't it be good to know that we could move forward without having to watch over our shoulders, forever on the lookout for Evlynn The Dark?

Mabon

Again Dana spoke as if in answer to my thoughts. "Think of your reasons Lucy," she pleaded. "If they come from anywhere other than love they are not good and therefore neither will your power be."

But I was almost there.

My amulet throbbed, my chimes sounded out like a typhoon warning. I could feel Evlynn slipping away. The heart beat of her 'borrowed' body had slowed, the blood sustaining it moved sluggishly, and the steel rim to her irises had begun to fade.

Was it true?

Could killing Evlynn be a negative thing?

Is that where the awesome power that now flushed through my body had originated – from unabashed hatred of this Black Majik witch before me?

I stood for a moment, my hands barely touching Evlynn's head yet the blue current continued to flare, flickering back and forth across my finger tips. I looked up at my mother and sisters – their faces pained in empathy.

It would have been so easy to keep going, force Evlynn's twisted soul from Lani's dying body, sending it to a place that she deserved, but the look on Mat's face held me back. She was again staring forward at nothing in particular with the same expression she had worn the night of my initiation.

There was doubt and there were questions.

It's Beale Majik!

The blackest kind.

I faltered, yanking my hands from Evlynn's head. There was a thunderous crack as a red flare erupted from Lani's eyes and soared into the night's sky like a firecracker. It shot straight up and froze for a moment well above our heads before returning to the amulet hissing as it went. The impact knocked me backward.

Had I killed Evlynn?

Lani's body flopped to the ground.

The amulet cooled and darkened against my chest, taking with it my resolve and any hint of chimes that had so heavily made their presence felt. I fell to my knees lifting my hands before me. The current passed to the tips of my fingers then flared into the air beyond.

XXII

The picture painted was a somber one. Rain whipped bunches of flowers tagged with heart-strewn notes, the camera focus pulled back to show the horrific scene close behind.

The Missoulian News crew was the first to arrive on the scene:

"A mechanical fault has been blamed for a freak accident that occurred last night just outside St. Ignatius about 50 minutes north of Missoula, resulting in the death of a teenager and the critical condition of another.

A southbound pickup towing a float crossed into the northbound lane of Highway 93. The vehicle jack-knifed sending the flatbed float into the rear side of a chartered minibus, which tipped into a spin and flipped several times before coming to rest at this point." The reporter lowers to one knee, touching the flowers in ceremony.

"The bus was carrying a group of friends who had attended a rock concert at Missoula University. Montana Highway Patrol trooper Chaz Brown said it appears that the driver of the truck attemped to swerve around on-coming cars.

Firefighters from Polson Rural fire department helped treat several victims before two were taken by ambulance to Missoula. The accident occurred shortly before midnight and closed northbound lanes on the 93 for an hour while the wreckage was cleared. The driver of the truck received superficial injuries and quoted mechanical fault as the reason for the initial swerve. Forensics will analyze the truck in an attempt to solve this mystery.

Jamie Burgert, a witness to the accident had this to say: There was no way of knowing where that float was headin' …"

Abi hit the remote and the screen instantly blackened. "Wow huh!" She wheeled around to face the small group of witches squashed together on Gleda's chaise.

Dana had taped up Abi's nose after applying one of the many herbal remedies in her stash. It caused her speech to make a comical nasal twang, "Whin da DeBane's gowout … dey *weally* gowout!"

Although sorry for the loss, we all understood the enormity of the situation we had somehow managed to escape, relatively unharmed.

Lani was dead.

Gil was badly hurt, but stable and in hospital … again.

Ruben, Liberty, Ethan, Aiden, Ash and Eddy were all cruising their respective homes like mindless zombies, memories wiped of last night's extra-curricula activity. The treating doctors in Kalispell had suspected head trauma, which wasn't far from the truth, but the reality was a nasty after effect that my mother had sworn would wear off in a day or two, leaving the group baffled over their riotous concert experience.

The physical damages – bumps, cuts and scrapes, littering

the bodies of our wayward group, had been conveniently sustained during the witchcraft clash. A blessing really as Myrtle alluded to the idea of what would have to have happened if the group were in any way 'injury-free'.

Mat, who hemmed me in on one side, rose. "More tea anyone?"

Myrtle held her cup out, sliding it into Mat's hand as she passed. "That would be lovely dear." Her eyes caught mine attempting to skip back to the motionless TV screen. "You must have a few questions Lucy?"

My empty tea cup felt heavy with the weight of the unknown. For some time I'd held the floodgates together, bulging with questions, for the sake of my own sanity. I sighed, shuffling to the end of the chaise, gates finally bursting as hundreds of queries came bubbling to the surface in a race to see who could get answered first. "I mean, I have questions about … well, everything that's happened." I dipped my hand, placing my tea cup on the naked floorboards with a soft clatter. "I'm not so sure where to start."

"How about with these two?" Mat said, gesturing as she passed a tea cup to Myrtle.

I nodded.

"Violet and Myrtle are sisters." Dana drew an invisible line between the two. After the fact had been stated, Myrtle and Violet, all of a sudden, looked very similar.

Violet yawned, evidence of the chaise's effects. "Originally there were five of us."

"Time and occasion have changed that number," Myrtle sighed, shifting off the chaise. "Bless their souls, the Crones of Usat. Together we were a powerful force."

"Once," Violet whispered, she switched to the sofa

following Myrtle, an action of dependency I hadn't noticed before.

"Usat?" Mat asked.

"The Goddess Usat. It's her title derived from the ancient Egyptian language. She is our family deity," Myrtle answered, her eyes flicking across to Dana who smiled stiffly. "You would know her as Isis."

"Isis is our family deity," Abi stated, her eyes wild.

"As I said, *our* family deity," Myrtle was firm, unbending.

Mathilda faltered, her eyelashes were a flutter, as if she'd missed the point. It was nothing I couldn't relate to.

"Whad are you dalking about?" Abi interjected.

I exhaled loudly, glad I wasn't the only one who seemed to have been left in a maze, blindfolded.

Dana paused and looked over at Myrtle and Violet, a silent exchange passing between them. She gathered Myrtle and Violet's hands in her own. "The Crones of Usat were the blessed five sisters born of Tilley and Albert Martins."

Our mother's lineage was no secret.

Abi's hand flew up to her mouth, "Our creat, creat cranparents!"

Dana's smile twitched at the corners. Her hands shook as she tightened her grip, eyeing each of the Crones as they winked encouragement. "So that makes Violet and Myrtle …"

I slapped my hand down on Mat's shoulder. "Our great aunts?" she blurted out.

Silence.

Then, three mouths inhaled at the remarkable disclosure and three exhaled clearly from relief.

"Er, no, there was no mention of family." Mat refuted the

revelation. She pushed herself up from the floor. "You told me and Abi that they were of our kind, yes. That you were happy for us to practice together, but no coven would be formed."

"Now you're delling us they're family?" Abi didn't allow an answer before her second attack. "You carn'd be serious."

"Why weren't we told?" Mat followed Abi, the connection it signaled between the two once more left me out of the picture.

"Welcome to my world," I snapped. I figured I'd been left out of this loop having not reached my magickal maturity at the time.

We stood divided across the coffee table. Age and wisdom on one side, youth and volatility on the other and one side was seconds away from exploding. Abi fumed, Mat moped and I questioned.

"Girls, we apologize for the illusion," Myrtle began.

Following on, Violet stood, "Really we do but we had no other choice." Her kind eyes blinked out from behind the mess of white hair that curled around her temples.

Abi, intent on pursuing the guilt angle, shot Violet down. "No other jhoice than to keep da fact that you're family from us." She stepped backward, including Mat and myself in her range, reading our faces. "*We* don't understand."

Dana had been quiet. "Implication," she offered. "It's the only reason. We didn't know what was coming."

"But you're witches, surely you could have scryed," Mat refuted.

"We tried, many times," Dana said.

"Violet is exceptional in the area," Myrtle quipped.

"I found nothing relative," her sister offered. "Besides that, we didn't know what relative was."

There was a pause that I couldn't fill. In that moment I didn't know what to say to anyone standing in the room. Dana left the Crones and came to rest by my side. The twins exchanged glances. Too exhausted to have showered, I looked down scuffing my boots together and spied a large patch of blood that had dried high on my left thigh. I brushed my hand across it slowly. It was Gil's, the result from when he had first fallen last night re-opening the wound he had received the night of my mountain rescue. I imagined the weight of his head as it rested on my legs and found myself wondering if witchcraft was always going to be like this for me – blood and battles and questions, so many freakin' questions.

"None of us really understood what we had to look for," said Dana. She had placed an arm in the gentlest motion around my shoulders. It felt comforting yet spiked the hair on the back of my neck. Did I want to be comforted?

"Hang on, this is off point," Abi remarked. During the last strands of conversation we hadn't uncovered the reason for our great aunt's identity cover-up.

"You lied to us." As gently as it had been placed, I shrugged out of my mother's protective barricade and paced to the front window. "You *all* keep lying to me."

"It's not like that." Dana followed me to the window. She stood apart from me, staring out into the bleak Montana morning as the sun began to stir from its resting place under the canopy of low gray cloud. "Until last night, none of us knew what we were truly dealing with." She paused, emphasizing the weight of her disclosure. "Look, your father and I, we didn't foresee what was going to happen here, but he did foresee you Lucy. He told me of the bells, to listen out for the bells." She held back.

A moment passed, and Mat, feeling much more than we all had, offered Dana a supportive arm. Passing Mat a faded square of paper she had been holding, she continued, "It's the note a nurse gave me that night after Hugh had died, she had been concerned with his ramblings. All those years ago, I must have interpreted it incorrectly. Luckily Violet pulled up the possible mistake after we'd found it in an old diary last night." She trailed the words of the note with her finger as Mat read, stopping at two particular spots.

Listen for the bells they come for my soul mother.

"We now think it's missing a few periods. It should read 'Listen for the bells. Stop. They come for my soul. Stop. Mother. Stop'."

"Wait, what?" I snapped. "Evlynn confessed, it was her, she killed Dad."

"After her appearance at school, I thought so too, but I … we have reason to believe it was actually your grandmother Arvilla who killed your father."

"How could she?" Mat whispered.

"It's that Black Majik line. Nothing good will ever come of it," Myrtle said moving toward Dana in a show of solidarity.

"Please. Let me finish," Dana pleaded, gently dismissing Myrtle's offer of support. "As much as I know, now you will all know." A group at odds, Dana herded us back to the sitting area. Abi and Mat piled on the closest sofa, both sitting upright on the edge. I however, had forced myself back to the chaise, my mind buzzing with activity. I needed to stay positive and at present the chaise was my only medication.

"After your father died," she began, standing before us.

"You mean was murdered," Abi interjected, eyes blazing. I shuddered at the thought of what Abi might try to do if she ever met her paternal grandmother.

"Fine," Dana sighed. "After your father's murder, Lucy had to be kept out of harm's way, out of sight and sound from the Beale-Daray family. With your father's prediction came the realization that you might play a large part in a future incident orchestrated by our Black Majik relatives; when you told me you heard bells the afternoon of your birthday, things fell into place. I had been able to hide you for so long, moving from town to town, but as soon as you were initiated, I assumed the Court of Beale knew how to locate you. Even though your father had foretold of your inheritance, I wasn't one hundred per cent sure if you would be favored or not." She paused, pushing her glasses back up the bridge of her nose. "Perhaps I was naïve, I hoped that we wouldn't, and we have never, forced our craft on you. You see, I'd been protected from this situation almost as much as you girls have been and perhaps for the same reason. I guess your father had meant to include me, but died before he had finished his investigation. If it wasn't for Myrtle and Violet helping me last night …"

Myrtle took over, "Prior to Dana's 'feeling' about Lucy last night, we had stumbled onto some major information regarding your amulet."

"It led to other snippets and we began to see exactly what

your father had been digging up," Dana said. She moved forward and cleared a spot on the coffee table that sat before the chaise, the only space that was left unclaimed by books and paper work.

"I began to see connections – the journals, the repeat trips to Egypt, and the complete avoidance of all things Court of Beale – it made sense. He was trying *and succeeding* to uncover what your grandmother was seeking." Dana stood up and headed to the fireplace. "Lucy, don't be alarmed by this." She reached into the parting flames, removing a dark wooden box, no bigger than a shoe box. Its lock clinked softly as she returned.

"Random," I quipped. This level of magick would take a little getting used to.

"He didn't uncover everything before his death." Myrtle ignored me. "But there are answers to some questions."

"Questions that I previously had no answers to." Dana sat in the empty space on the coffee table and placed the box at her side.

"And now?" I was intrigued by the box. The smoothed grainy wood was hand carved with an Isis Tyet on the top surface, like the one on our cellar door. Sunken into the corners were four gleaming carnelians, surrounded by a fine metal edge. I leaned forward, running my fingers across the top of the box.

"Hugh escaped his family too early to know of this saga himself, as we discovered trawling through his journals. All he had was the amulet. He left England under a shroud of secrecy with the amulet in hand and had been working toward uncovering the truth behind it ever since, without any real knowledge of what he had in his possession, only that it had been vitally important to his family for some dark reason. His research took years," Violet said.

"Those journals have been the key. The ones I hadn't had the nerve to open," Dana sighed. "After his death, I just couldn't re-live the pain over and over. I had three young children and I loved your father so much, so I left them alone." She leaned toward me, gesturing at the amulet. "I'm so sorry Little Soul. Hugh had left a paper trail. We could have known so much more, perhaps even been prepared for all this."

We all understood the depth of the river that ran between my mother and father. It was a connection I hoped to find during my own lifetime and for that reason alone Dana couldn't be held responsible.

"Maybe," I said, my eyes flicking to the twins, wanting reassurance at a time when none could be given. I traced the amulet. It lay cold against my skin. There had been no movement from it since Evlynn had been sucked back into it, but that didn't stop the weight of its presence bearing down on me.

I couldn't breathe.

I wanted to erupt, I should have been angry, but the chaise had muddled my feelings, softened them. I stood and walked to the great room window. As first light slipped along the Swan Range, it seemed a good idea to inhale a huge breath, as though sucking in the sharp gold that vibrated along the mountain peaks would clear my fog.

So I did.

And it did work, for a minute, but the questions merely

swirled in the inky ether, they didn't go away. I needed to face this head on. Face the questions and finally have my answers and hopefully some peace inside my much afflicted gray matter. It was a better idea than exploding, even if I'd been left in the dark at almost every corner of my short but traumatic journey, we'd taken the first steps toward illumination. I turned back to the waiting faces.

"What's that?" I nodded toward the coffee table shrugging away the questions.

Dana had opened the wooden box and laid out a yellowed envelope and a small royal blue pouch – the same pouch that Violet and Myrtle had surprised me with on my birthday weeks back. It tinkled at the beckoning of its owner with twig and silver leaf charm inside.

"A kind of safety deposit box, if you like. But it's what's inside that'll most interest to you," Dana said offering the envelope.

Almost unreadable, the looping scrawl dominating its front had an ingrained familiarity. "It's for me?" I said extracting the letter.

Dear Lucy,
This story has been passed down through the ancestors of Djeserit, the Third Oracle, the last of three sisters of the Bakit Hills, Nile Delta, Ancient Egypt, circa 2400BC.

It is fabled that Djeserit brought King Biti to his knees with a defeat over Kamenwati, a man of ways, who had cast a plume of death over Biti's kingdom. Djeserit was then respected almost beyond the King himself and so was cast out by the same hand she had saved. Bitter, Djeserit and her son settled in the hills, a hermitic existence their only solace.

But this story is not of The Third Oracle, it is of a young temple servant by the name of Rhama. It is a tale of love, ancient magick and death.

When Rhama was young she came into the service of Odji by way of gold, as many girls did when tragedy befell their families. She was sold to the temple priest for a fair price, fair – as almost no one knew what Rhama actually was. It never occurred to Rhama that Odji knew she was different, he'd never treated her with anything other than cruelty and contempt, but as an Interceptor she was different. Through her pulsed a power that was undeniable, it was the aspect of her being that she could never quite place.

Her tale begins with love.

Rhama, as the priest's slave, was kept confused and berated often over Odji's actions. Odji was not a good priest, nor a smart priest, but he was a cunning one. His savior and leader was Irisi, the High Priestess of their temple, the Temple of Usir, and as his sister, she often overlooked his many dark shortcomings.

With the coming of the Blood Moon, the two had been working together on the upcoming ritual more closely than usual, which allowed Rhama time away from her temple duties. Time she spent with her true love ... Nomti.

In direct contrast to Odji, Nomti was good. Good of heart, soul and mind. As the son of a wealthy gold merchant, Nomti was highly desired by many, which left Rhama often wondering why he had chosen her ... he had, and together their love was envied by the pyramids themselves.

It was during a stolen moment with Nomti in the darkened halls of the temple, that Rhama first became aware of an ulterior motive, a ritual that differed from what she had been preparing at Odji's command. From the little she had overheard it seemed that Irisi and Odji had procured an object of immense power. With the mention of the Goddess Usat, Rhama's understanding of this exchange took on a grave significance. Rhama had spent much of her younger life in the company of The Third Oracle. She was eager and had learned much from the masterful seer before being moved on to the temple for her service.

This new information paired with her extensive knowledge set Rhama's mind into motion. She knew the object in question could only be the Usat stone, but its last place of rest was in the Temple of Usat in Sebennytos, many hundred iteru (river-unit) away. It held many powers, but was renowned for resurrection and if successful, Irisi would plague her people with certain death. Finally with her beloved in the Underworld, Usat would take unkindly to being ripped from the peace of his arms.

Rhama needed to work quickly, and preferably without Nomti. His life was too valuable and her love for him would dull her insights.

Among the hills of Bakit, Rhama would find salvation.

The Third Oracle.

The Oracle was now old and the day of Rhama's visit, seemed ill at ease with herself. More demanding than usual, she pushed Rhama away while keeping a firm hold on her. It worried Rhama to see her old friend like this and so she skirted around the reason for her visit, but Djeserit knew her better than that, telling her to look inward – she would find her answers there …

… But Rhama was left empty by the Oracle's parting words. "The city may appear to be made of gold, but is it not sand?"

On her return, she interpreted the Third Oracle's warning so that by the night of the ritual's commencement there lay the beginnings of a plan.

A plan that began with deception!

Rhama betrayed Nomti.

A necessary evil on two accounts, for he was captured (kept from danger) and so her loyalty proven to the High Priestess Irisi, and her inclusion to the Blood Moon ritual secured.

With her mind set on halting a resurrection ritual, a passing comment from the poison lips of Odji remained Rhama's point of inner conflict. Entrusted with a mysterious muslin wrapped package, Rhama had stumbled clattering the package's contents onto the temple altar.

"Rhama if you ruin this for me by Sutah's hand I will take your life girl," Odji had spat out. The use of Sutah's name was not common among temple people.

As the evil brother of Usat and Usir, he had caused the death of the beloved Usir, dismembering his corpse and spreading the pieces far and wide across Ancient Egypt. Sutah was an odd reference for a divine priest to use.

The comment nibbled at the edges of Rhama's plan, pushing her to revisit Djeserit's warning. All was not what it seemed, and as Rhama watched Odji re-wrap the package, what she saw then confirmed her fears.

Two turquoise tablets glowed from beneath the muslin wrap – Sutah Creed. It was the only known ritual directive to be etched onto plates of pure turquoise. Etched by his golden scribe, Sutah had left the listed directions to a long fabled ritual said to open a bank of souls, a place for the resting evils of the Upperworld.

The Soul Bank had been brought into existence when Usat had managed to resurrect Usir twice after his death at the hands of Sutah's cunning plan. Sutah was a jealous God, he could not bear sight nor sound of his brother and so created the Soul Bank to access the power it was enchanted to hold in order to rule over the boundaries of the Upperworld, knowing that his brother Usir would be forever bound to the Underworld. At the death of a dark one, the soul would transition to Sutah's Soul Bank instead of continuing on to the Underworld, and so the fable came to be.

Whomever opens the portal of the Soul Bank gains its unholy powers within.

According to Djeserit none had ever been successful

as the four necessary counterparts to perform the breech had been 'lost'. Until now.

The High Priestess's arrival on the temple platform wearing the Usat stone in a cuff cupped about her neck, sent Rhama into a spin. Irisi then produced a large scroll which she proclaimed as the incantation that would aid her work, the powerful Immemorial.

The Usat Stone, Sutah Creed, The Immemorial.

As the elements came together, Rhama realized that she would soon be dead and by the hand of the High Priestess who wanted her blood. For it was not a resurrection ritual the people would witness, but the almighty 'Breech' – access to the Soul Bank and the twisted souls within. Irisi needed to acquire one last element, an Interceptor – Rhama.

Rhama had failed. Looking out into the crowd she saw Djeserit. The Oracle had managed the trip and Rhama was glad to look upon her shining face. She stared at Rhama with such intensity, it drew forth tears, causing Rhama to wipe at her eyes. Her tears were black. Rhama cried blood for the lives of the people who were lost. She closed her eyes listening to the thundering screams of revelation around her. They rapidly faded, replaced by a spark, a notion and as the fourth element – an Interceptor – Rhama finally saw her path.

The smile she harbored for Djeserit was knowing as she shook free of Irisi's grip. She snatched a turquoise plate from the altar and flung herself into the fire pit below.

Mabon

Sacrificial lives had been saved and a ritual that could have spelled the end of humanity had been destroyed, but Djeserit knew a true protector of Rhama's kind would never die.

… And so the story goes, Rhama saved humanity from the opening of the Soul Bank, but broke a heart whom still wanders the plains – Nomti. Irisi and Odji met with a quick death at the hands of their followers. The Usat Stone, the Immemorial and the tablets of the Sutah Creed were said to have been destroyed in the fire pits that night.

Sixty years ago at the Bakit Hills dig in Egypt, something was found.

My family thought it was theirs. I knew it belonged elsewhere, and when your mother told me she was pregnant, I knew it belonged to you Lucy.

I love you,
Dad.

I stared blankly at the pages wanting so much more than my father's words had given me. Dana placed her hand over mine. "We figured that letter separated from your amulet in the mess of the carpet bag. It explains so much, in a strange way. What we're dealing with, what we're looking for, and even you Lucy – an Interceptor."

Mat tapped at a page on the journals littering the floor beside her. "Is that your amulet?" she ventured, pointing to a rough sketch, the same sketch I had found weeks before after returning from my first encounter with Evlynn.

"It sure is!" Myrtle bent, picking up the sketch and the few pages around it. She began to read:

The Usat Stone or Stone of Isis, fabled to have been destroyed by fire, has been found by Professor Richard Beale-Daray, on his last archeological dig in Egypt. He has returned to England, where he lectures at Oxford, to further his studies of the stone.

"Richard was your grandfather, married to Arvilla, I think. Haven't heard much about him at all," Violet offered.

I fumbled for the amulet, resting my fingers on the stone that lay at its center, and felt an ancient pull from deep within its core. The confusion was beginning to lift, but some questions still remained, the most ominous being what my Black Majik relatives had in store for me.

"So that's it then. Arvilla is aiming to open the Soul Bank and I'm her main ingredient. Guess I will end up in England."

XXIII

October brought a fine dusting of early snow and with it a peaceful vibration that filtered through our house, giving a quality of light after such darkness. Following the letter and many nights of 'Q & A', I was as up-to-date as any other witch in my home, and it felt good, having answers, well some at least.

I was an Interceptor – a 'pure' witch of pedigree, born during the Path of Totality and designed for some ultimate task – although what, we had yet to discover. None of us believed that I was destined to open the Soul Bank and release havoc on humankind.

From our father's notes we now understood that combined with an Interceptor, the amulet would supply a line of power sourced from its center – the Isis stone. This union, plus an omnipotent ancient spell, opened a metaphysical storage tank, the Soul Bank, devised as legend had it, to contain evil souls dating from the time of the ancient Egyptian God Osiris and his ruling over the Underworld.

Hugh had learned little regarding the Isis Stone, only that the Goddess Isis had imbued into it the mother-load of all supernaturalism, hiding it from her wayward evil brother Set in the Nile River delta. It had been discovered in an archeological dig by my grandfather more than half a century before I'd been born. My father found there had been questions of its apparent power riddling the records his family had kept. Time and time again, the mention of the other counter parts to the Breech came into play and we wondered if the Court of Beale had possession of any. A fact which Hugh's research neither confirmed nor denied.

And that was it, as far as our father had recorded. These discoveries appeared far-fetched, but when reminded of Evlynn and Lani and the supernatural damage they had thrust upon a certain set of unprepared witches, they were merely a tall tale. This perceived fantasy realm was a thundering reality in which I had two options:

Stay in Creston, embrace my new craft, study and continue with my father's research?

Or, embrace my new craft, study and continue with my father's research (there really was no way around that part) and move, again?

Much to my relief, the six of us decided that our current existence in Creston was worth fighting for – too much invested here and no sense in continuing to run. Any doubt I had regarding my own destiny had disappeared, whether liked or not, my fate would play out as some divine tarot reading. If we ran, Arvilla would have found us anyway, being an Interceptor made sure of that.

The idea had originally come to Mat. She put forward questions we'd all thought at one time or another after Evlynn disappeared, and the answer seemed easy enough. Gaining access to the Soul Bank was clearly paramount to Arvilla. She had killed her son for it. She would stage another attack, but when and where? How many more Beale-Daray's did Arvilla have on hand to commit her atrocities? Contained in Mat's idea, were several tenacious pushes to go on the offensive. Search Arvilla out and vaporize the hag in her tracks, but Dana wouldn't have it.

"We need more time," she'd responded over and over after Mat had turned Abi to the cause.

As a necessary part of the plan, I was nowhere near ready and the commencement of my witchcraft study was daunting enough. Most of my available time, meaning time spent lounging with Liberty or daydreaming about Gil, would now be filled with reciting incantations, Melange and all matter of things *bubbling caldron*. My question bubble remained, though it was somewhat more transparent than the darkening mass it had been weeks ago.

On the pages of reality, there were other factors scripted that I wanted answers to. Gil had been ringing my cell non-stop, his message the same, he wanted to 'talk' and finding myself in a truth-challenging situation for a second time, it was the last thing I wanted to do. Apart from the torrent of sweat drenched nightmares I endured every night since Lani and Evlynn's departures, there had been a niggling mental bite, a reminder that at some stage soon I would have to face Gil. Although I hadn't wished them on him in the first place, Gil's injuries had forced his absence from school for several weeks. A lucky break for me, and time to gather my thoughts.

After the concert night, I had been left with no doubt

that I wanted Gil in my life – I was in love with him and no traumatic witchy event had swayed my heart from this feeling. I assumed this was common knowledge and I'd taken some time to ready myself for the ridicule that comes with such disclosure. To my advantage, the 'Erasure Elixir' used on our concert group after the 'crash' that night had managed to wipe any memories of my announcing my feelings, along with all the bothersome supernatural hoo-hah.

So I was back to square one with Gil, and that suited me fine.

I tugged at my scarf, pushing it well into the neck of my puffa jacket. The cool wind lifted my hair and fluttered the last of the leaves holding fast to the oak. As I leaned back on the trunk, I felt every point of contact my body made with the tree. Where it pressed into the back of my head, where it lay clean and smooth down my spine, and where a blue-chalk-smudged leaf lay in my palm, spiking into my fingers.

I gazed down half smiling to myself and shelved, if only briefly, the gorgeous image of Gil my mind had conjured. This is where it had all begun, with this leaf that danced on air through my art class window, heralding a thorny period of time to come. *If only I'd have known the events that you would bring.* I crumbled the dried leaf and scattered the pieces around my feet. *Time for you to return to your own.*

In my mind, it restored the balance between the oak and me.

"Hey Lou." Although I was waiting for her, Liberty's voice startled me.

"Oh hey Lib," I squeaked, fingers still tingling. I brushed away the chalky blue residue that had transferred to my hand from the crushed leaf.

Mabon

Liberty eyed me over and smiled, "Up for a ride this weekend?"

"Nah, probably not." It wasn't like I would never ride again, that was a definite, but the loss of Smokey had cut deep, making it hard to move onto another horse. "You don't mind, do you?"

"No, I get it," Liberty said off-handedly. She stomped her army boots loosening the light crunchy snow that had bunched across the laces.

The witchcraft stuff had come between us only by way of it being a secret I had to keep from her, that was hard enough. I wouldn't allow there to be anything more.

I smiled politely as we were interrupted by a small parade of nods and waves from students who had never noticed us before. It was becoming the norm. Briefly glancing at one another Liberty and I chuckled. Going from obscurity to celebrity in this small town, along with other supernatural gained aspects, had yanked me from my shell. There was no mistake, I still blushed like a red traffic light, but at least now I owned it.

"Don't think that's gonna settle down any time soon," Liberty quipped.

I grunted in agreement.

Hard as it was to keep the real events of that night from Liberty, the fact that it kept playing like a movie reel through my dreams every night since, had kept me on track. No one could know the truth. We couldn't stay in Creston, the Valley or Montana for that fact, perhaps we'd have to flee the country.

"Hey, how are your brothers going?" I switched gears.

"Okay, I suppose," she said in an off-handed manner.

Although my concern for all her brothers was genuine, Liberty knew my question was incognito, directed at one person in particular. She shrugged, "Why don't you ask him yourself?"

Caught out, my face flushed and I began in a high whiny tone. "Cause Lib, you know it'd be easier for everyone if you … er …" I skipped, my gaze narrowing.

Liberty's eye-line had risen slightly above my shoulder and her mouth curved up in the corners. "Behind me?" I muttered, heart jumping.

"Hmmm," she chuckled. "I'll be over at the car Gil." She headed off in the direction of Gil's Chevy. "Call you later Lou?" She winked in a provocative manner.

I shook my head, resigned that once more my hand would be forced.

"Lucy."

"Hey," I breathed, preparing myself before I turned to face Gil.

"Ah, I'm so sorry Gil, you know, about Lani." I said her name in a much softer tone than I thought possible. The fact that she had tried to kill us all had a lot to do with that, but that was something Gil would never recall.

He leaned his shoulder against the oak. "Can I be honest?" he asked.

"Sure," I replied, although I wasn't exactly being honest myself. Lani wasn't a subject I had ever felt comfortable discussing, more so now in her death, but it would have been senseless to think our conversation would be void of her.

"It's sad. And I'm sad … but a bit … I don't know … hollow? Like I don't remember a whole lot from our time together," Gil muffled a cough with a closed hand. "That's weird right?"

"I don't think so," I said. "You've been through a lot."

It wasn't actually the powerful potion my mother and the Crones had mixed that had caused this particular section of Gil's memory loss. Myrtle had recognized the stamp of the spell by it remnants; the chain and flat disc Gil had worn around his neck intertwined with long strands of red human hair. "Compelling necklace," she had muttered over our kitchen table one evening we had convened for research and discussion.

Violet had sniffed at the chain. "It's faint, but I'd say Sweet Flag and Licorice, perhaps a little Bergamot and Vertiver for potency. Much of that relationship will seem a faded dream to Gil now. At least Lani had been considerate enough to leave him with that."

Gil leaned in closer, making my pulse soar. "I guess. I've been pretty banged up over the last couple of months, but even from the concert night, I hardly remember a thing," he said, lowering his head. "I sound like an idiot."

"You don't," I offered. "Suffering so much in such a short period of time. What were you expecting?"

He was silent, answer enough, scuffing his boot at the snow and fallen oak leaves, a crease furling across his brow. "Do you remember much from that night?" He switched, drilling me with those hypnotic eyes once again.

"A bit."

"Everything's fuzzy, like a distant memory. I can't seem to fill in the blanks," he said rapping his knuckles on the oak's trunk.

"I'm a bit like that myself," I lied. "The doctors said it was shock."

"Yeah, I don't know if I believe that," Gil said, quickly following up. "It just seems so weird that we all remember exactly the same stuff. Not one of us can put a different spin on any part of the night."

I could have.

"It seems a bit strange. Guess that's just how it works, blocking out the stuff that we perhaps shouldn't remember. Too painful, you know." I looked into his eyes and saw the struggle and sorrow he felt. I wanted to reach out to him, just a touch could help his present state of mind, but I stopped myself. It was too close to his loss and I didn't want to push Gil, so I had to bide my time and allow the natural healing.

He huffed, seeming content with that conclusion, then looked off down the street and I watched him carefully, trying to listen-in on his mood. Hearing his name called he fluttered a quick salute to a friend and returned his focus on me in a way I instantly wished he had not.

I gulped, steadying myself against the oak.

"I heard it was you," Gil smiled, his eyes alight, peering out from a face that still held heavy remnants of a battle. Still every bit as intoxicating as he had ever been.

"What was me?" I asked. I pulled my sleeves down over my thumbs, a sudden chill, in contrast to the heat eminating from my stimulated core.

"You saved my life ... guess you're one up now!" he said, fingers tracing over the ridges and hollows in the oak's exterior.

"Actually, if we're keeping score, I think that's even," I corrected.

"So you have a legit way out?" he asked. I didn't understand his inference so he continued, "You know, of mucking out Jack's stall."

I winked at him.

It was easy being with Gil, like breathing or daydreaming. Although it could have been different, he'd made me feel comfortable from the very beginning and now, given the past events and future certainties pertaining to my witchcraft heritage, all I wanted to do was to make Gil feel comfortable. His memory loss had no effect on what we had endured together over the last few months, although he didn't recall everything, I did – I was there. I had seen his actions and the innate protective instinct he held for me. Inside I knew this was more than 'just friends'. We had a connection, deep and binding. Witchcraft had punished our bond, but I hoped it would also make it stronger, and in this lay my uncertainty. Gil was an unknowing victim of my craft, of a power I still had no real knowledge of. His involvement with me had already physically harmed him. Was this something I wished for him? Although I couldn't bear to be without him, maybe his life would be more stable and fulfilling if we went our separate ways?

I paused my whirling thoughts and studied his face for an answer. As if reading my mind he simply smiled that smile – that lopsided handsome Daniels' smile – the one that I liked to think he reserved for me and me alone.

He muffled a chuckle. "You've grown up Lucy. Not that same little girl with the purple streak in her hair," he said, referring to a trend I had followed sometime ago. He reached out taking my hand in his and stroked at the last bit of chalky blue residue from the crumbled oak leaf, until it disappeared. My pulse quickened once more with his admission – Gil no longer looked at me as too young, perhaps now I was on equal footing and perhaps this was his way of letting me know.

He leaned in, but he lingered here only a moment before his lips grazed my forehead. It was the action I'd expected and couldn't have hoped for more. Gil was still fragile and I respected his distance, although delighted in his physical nearness.

"See you soon?" he whispered, releasing my hand, leaving me with phantom yearning.

I nodded and headed off in the opposite direction.

Mom, Teddy and Abi stared intently at me from the Mustang. I hurried forward, but looked back, smiling in spite of my embarrassment.

Gil had been watching me.

My obsession was offically re-instated.

I crunched the snow and fallen oak leaves beneath my boots, tripping at the sound of the faint chiming of bells.

Did you like Mabon?

Leaving your thoughts about my story helps build reviews, which mean a lot to a debut author like me.

If you would like to, Amazon and Goodreads are top places to start.

You can also jump over to my website to say 'Hi'.

Thanks
Kellie

Coming Soon

Yule

THE CLANDESTINE CHRONICLES

Book 2

I leaned forward to look out the plane window, hesitating at the greasy smudge a passenger had left on the plexiglass. Beyond the glistening metal wing, the outside world was in miniature – tiny hills, tiny square fields, tiny houses. It all shined an iridescent emerald in the bright foreign sun.

How was I ever going to find her down there in that tiny world?

Mathilda was gone, without a word. It was an organized manoeuvre, too precise for someone as vague as my sister – more at home picking daisies and gazing at stars than dealing with the mundane of plotting some clandestine plan.

Abigail instantly withdrew. From dynamic, she'd become a shell, so Abi was packed up, on a plane and in England – on the hunt for her twin. She'd been given 3 days. If Abi had no leads on Mat by the third, back up would be sent – me.

The in-house witch feud over my volunteering had caused a gaseous purple vortex in the cellar that gained momentum every time a voice was raised. But I was mentally in England before the Mustang's tyres had screeched to a halt at the airport curb.

Mabon

I folded down the page corner and laid my latest knowledge conquest on my lap; a plain cover grimoire of advanced mixtures – Melange. The window once again beckoned.

Mat, where are you?

A low hum answered and beat dull, like an ancient drum sounding its verse against my chest – my amulet was calling. I pressed a finger to its polished center, then traced the casing; dragon to knight and floral plumes in between, snatching my hand away before the call was heard.

Evlynn – would the vapor vamp appear here? On the plane?

The last time she'd shown her face, Evlynn had remorselessly murdered her niece Elania, tortured my Gil – almost beyond repair, and wildly suggested I join her in England. I was fulfilling her divination, she'd be amused by that, at least.

The plane's descent pushed my patience. I huffed hot, wet air to fog up the window then drew a small sigil for protection under the greasy smudge. To say my witchcraft skills had 'arrived' was like saying 'look at the light snow' during a blizzard, they had consumed me from the second I had begun my training. And controlling these inherited gifts … ha!

I picked up the grimoire, and flipped back to the marked page. The title 'Controlling your Desires' shouted out exactly what I was thinking. I needed control – just long enough to find a witch, kill another and return to love.

ACKNOWLEDGEMENTS

Sure, this story flowed from my head, but to get it to your hands and devices has taken magic ... that and a small army that warrants mention. Please forgive me if I've missed anyone, I'll probably have that 'midnight moment' of recognition ...

To the publishing and production team of Aurora House. So much appreciation for your talents and handling of this writer and her raw manuscript – Linda Lycett, that letter way back in late 2017 seems so long ago; I cried and shouted and danced in my kitchen. Josepha Dietrich, you were able to break through and show me what the original script needed. Your kindness and generosity of spirit buoyed me through this challenge. You were just what Mabon and I needed. Simon Critchell, you turned my cover on its head and made it striking and relevant and just wow! A massive thanks to Sarah Vogler – every conversation added to the learning curve of what we are doing here. Your support has been amazing. Debbie Watson, your proofreading finess truly finalized this process, thanks for your patience.

To the industry mentors and friends. Invisible arrows that silently direct, business-coach ninjas – stealthy and articulate. Each person here has advised me or gently guided my journey – I am deeply thankful. Fiona Horne – the trailblazing, flying, spinning, singing, flaming beauty that answered my request, bless your heart you beautiful soul and incredible woman. Cathie Tasker, editor, publisher, judge, teacher, mentor – without Cathie's constructive criticism of Mabon as a result of her assessing the manuscript – way way back – I wouldn't have thought I had something to expand on; I've looked back on her conclusions often to reinforce that. Ron Armstrong, author and brother-in-law, our chats were as insightful as they were necessary for me. Penny Webb, editor and friend, strength and inspiration and laughter, you amazing being. Gary Honan, your guidance has been a blessing. Katrina McElvey, children's book author and mentor; and Kirrili Lonergan, children's book illustrator – the lunch we had together re-ignited my love for this project when I'd disappeared on a mental holiday. Katrina, your kind words and advice have been invaluable. John Coombs, Latin lecturer – your willingness to help with my translations made the process easy, thank you. Amanda Hayward, the insight you shared with me challenged my concepts of publishing, thank you.

To the support circle of readers and cheerleaders. These people – so much love for them. Sharon McFarland, you have been here from inception, you have never let me put this down, you have always listened to my prattling – can't thank you enough. Early readers: Nicole Baldwin, Robyn Rees, Alana Callus, Sonja Callus, thanks for your honesty and support. Tracy Callus: equine-related queries. Late readers: Leanne O'Brien and Kathryn McEvoy. Lee your enthusiasm kept me going. Whitney Wales, your notes were spot-on, you scared me the most but from that, incredible things came. Mary Quinn, you were always excited to hear the progress and champion the pathway. Courtney Comisso, Debra Oram, and Janette Beedle, ladies you don't know how close I was to throwing it all in, then you.

To my family, whose patience, guidance and support has been second to none. My husband Shane and daughters, Miller and Asha – you have my heart, my thanks and my love. My parents Margaret and Gregory – a lifetime of support and love and faith. My brother, sister-in-law, niece and nephew – a mountain of thanks and love in return.

To my extended family, many thanks for your belief in this project and acceptance of this slightly crazy lady.

Lastly, a big thank you to everyone who has been involved, continue to be, and always will be involved in Lucy and Gil's story.

ABOUT THE AUTHOR

I live in Sydney with my husband and two children.
In researching this book I discovered two things:
True witchcraft leads to insightful and respectful people –
of others and nature.
Montana is genuinely magnificent.

Mabon is the first book of The Clandestine Chronicles,
with *Yule, Ostara* and *Litha* to come.

Please follow me:
www.kelliemdavies.com
Instagram, Twitter

Milton Keynes UK
Ingram Content Group UK Ltd.
UKHW051101250324
439991UK00007B/722